Gripping the wheel, Thad kept his eyes on the road. *Women!* They were nothing but trouble. He didn't know why he continued to bother with them, especially this one. Forget the script! Forget everything! He had made every possible attempt to be civil to Darnell over the past few days, and what had he gotten for his kindness? Slapped in the face every time. If he hadn't been raised to be a gentleman, he would drop Darnell Cameron off on the side of the road and let her cute little butt hitchhike home.

He glanced at her with this thought in mind. She was looking at the speedometer.

"You're going a little fast in these mountains, aren't you?" Darnell looked up through the front windshield at the blackness ahead of them as they climbed the winding mountain highway leading to Santa Cruz. It was a dangerous trek in broad daylight, and at night it could be treacherous.

Thad grunted unappreciatively. On top of everything else, she was a back seat driver! Annoyed, but not wanting to frighten her or harm them both, he heeded her warning and slowed the car down a little.

At that very instant, there was a pop, and the car swerved left.

SINGING A SONG . . .

CRYSTAL RHODES

Genesis Press, Inc.

INDIGO

An imprint of Genesis Press, Inc.
Publishing Company

Genesis Press, Inc.
P.O. Box 101
Columbus, MS 39703

All characters in this book have no existence outside the imagination of the author and have no relation whatsoever to anyone bearing the same name or names. They are not even distantly inspired by any individual known or unknown to the author and all incidents are pure invention

Copyright © 2009 by Crystal Rhodes

ISBN: 13 DIGIT : 978-158571-283-0
ISBN: 10 DIGIT : 1-58571-283-3
Manufactured in the United States of America

First Edition 2009

Visit us at www.genesis-press.com
or call at 1-888-Indigo-1

DEDICATION

This book is dedicated to the memory of my beloved
Aunt Flora, who will always be my she-ro.

ACKNOWLEDGMENT

Thank you Eunice and Joni for helping me get this one out there. As always, your support was as steadfast as ever. I'm grateful.

PROLOGUE

A week had passed since the pearl gray limousine pulled up to the sprawling estate located in the quaint oceanfront Mecca of Carmel-by-the-Sea. There was no gated entry leading to the exclusive property, but strategically placed surveillance cameras monitored the movements of any visitors.

A Middle-Eastern businessman owned the estate. He rented it out when he was away. The latest tenant—the one in the limousine—was a slim, well-dressed black man of medium height who spoke in crisp, precise tones. The staff had been instructed to refer to him as Mr. Waters. Those who thought they knew him called him Moody Lake.

The staff liked him. Unlike many of the estate's previous tenants, he wasn't rude or demanding. His manner was reserved and refined, but he gave directions with the confidence of a man used to being in control. The staff couldn't help noticing that during his short stay he was on his cell phone often, and that he spent most of his time upstairs in the sitting room connected to one of the smaller bedrooms. It was there that he chose to sleep. None of them could imagine why. The master suite, with its sweeping view of the Pacific Ocean, was much more comfortable. The only view from the rooms that he chose to occupy was that of the street below and the homes of the neighbors beyond.

He had inquired about the neighbors who lived in the other four houses on the secluded cul-de-sac. The staff had been discrete in providing information. This neighborhood was a wealthy enclave of people with power and influence. It wasn't wise to reveal too much to a stranger passing through. He didn't seem disturbed by their discretion.

As the days passed, they noticed that he had settled into a harmonious routine. At the same time each morning, he would leave the house and head toward the beach, where they assumed he ran or walked. Later, he would return home, where he would dine in the sitting room and very often remain there the rest of the day. Other times, after his return from the beach, he would leave the house in his rental car and return at varying times during the day. He rarely went out in the evenings.

No one on the household staff questioned his movements. It wasn't their place to do so. They were to serve his every need, nothing more. So no one noticed that the daily movements of Mr. Waters mirrored those of the neighbor who lived in the house directly across the street—Darnell Cameron, musical superstar.

CHAPTER 1

"Listen, you shiftless, insufferable egomaniac!" Darnell Cameron fumed as her hands twisted the front of Thad Stewart's sweater into a tight ball. "If you ever bring your conceited behind on my property again, I swear I'll sue you!"

Thad Stewart glared down into the huge brown eyes, dark with anger, and stated coolly, "If you don't get your hands off me now, Ms. Cameron, I will sue *you*! I'll sue you for harassment, assault . . ."

"Assault?" Darnell's grip tightened.

"With intent to do bodily harm," Thad continued unperturbed, "and . . ."

"And what?" Darnell's eyes narrowed. "And you'd better get off my property." Releasing him, she took a step backward, her nostrils flaring. Placing both hands on her shapely hips, she watched him with disgust as he calmly attempted to smooth the wrinkles out of his sweater. The attempt was unsuccessful. Thad stared down at the misshapen fabric.

"I don't believe it! This is a five-hundred-dollar sweater." He looked at her incredulously. "You ruined it!"

Darnell gave him a smug smile. "Oh, really? All right, wait just one minute, then you can be on your way."

Marching inside the house, she reappeared a few seconds later, writing a check as she approached him.

Signing it with a flourish, she tore it from the leather-bound checkbook, crumpled it into a ball, and tossed it into the front seat of his bright red Ferrari convertible.

"Money well spent," she huffed. "Now, get that gaudy piece of junk out of my driveway before I have it towed. And don't let me see your face around here again!"

With an abrupt turn, she headed back toward her house.

"You don't ever have to worry about that!" Jumping into his car, Thad slammed the door with all the force he could muster. Snatching the check from the passenger seat, he tossed it onto the circular driveway that led to her spectacular cedar and glass estate. "And I don't want or need your money."

Darnell whirled around in time to see the check hit the pavement. "Oh, no you don't, Mr. *Movie Star*." She stomped over to where the paper wad lay and snatched it up, waving it at him angrily. "For three solid months, all I've heard about is how I promised to fix that stupid car of yours. I'm not about to go through the same thing with that sweater."

With that, she threw the check back into the car. "And you better not toss it out again." He did.

"I don't want one single thing from you, lady." Thad's voice was granite as he pointed an accusing finger at her. "As for my car, it was *you* who drove the wrong way up a one-way street and hit *me*!"

Darnell was so angry she was trembling. Her head was pounding, and did she feel her eye twitch? Oh, God! How she hated this man.

"Listen, you idiot. I'm not going through that again. We've settled that matter. You were the one going the wrong way down that street. Even your own lawyer said so!"

Thad fought for calm. This woman was not going to make him have a heart attack. "Correction. My lawyer said, and I quote, 'There was not a posted sign on the street in question; *however*, the direction in which the street was intended to go is not in dispute.'"

Darnell's chest heaved in indignation as she threw the check at his head and hit him in the middle of his forehead. "Then he's an idiot, too!"

With that, she stormed back toward her house, refusing to look back as Thad gunned the motor of his sports car. With tires squealing, he sped out of the gate to Darnell's property, barely avoiding a collision with a car turning into the driveway of the house across the street.

This time Thad kept the money. It was small payment for the weeks of hell he had endured. He had to put distance between himself and Darnell Cameron. She had to be the most annoying woman that God had ever put on this earth.

Everything in his life had been great until three months ago. After all, he was Thad Stewart, superstar. He was among a select group of African-American comedians whose transition into acting had been successful. As one of the most highly paid actors in the world, things couldn't get any better. Until that day in San Francisco, driving along in his brand new Ferrari, as happy as a lark, when *BAM*, out of the blue that despicable woman ran right into him.

He recognized her as soon as she leaped from her car—Darnell Cameron, the hottest singing sensation in the country. He had all of her CDs and, until she hit his car, he would have called himself a fan. She was talented, there was no denying that, and she was beautiful, too. A man could drown in those huge, doe-like eyes. Her heart-shaped face was a rich mahogany brown, framed by thick corn-rowed braids that tumbled past her shoulders. And that body! She certainly wasn't one of Hollywood's anorexic bags of bones. Her bosom was ample, and those curvaceous hips emphasized her small waist. Yes, he had recognized everything about her that day except her attitude. It turned out that she wasn't as sweet as she looked.

It was only natural that he got a little upset and maybe yelled a little. After all, his custom-designed Ferrari with the special paint job had a visible scratch, and her little Mercedes barely had a dent. But did she have to rant and rave at him like a lunatic? *He* had been the wronged party, not her. He should have called the police immediately, but she'd batted those big brown eyes at him and, in a moment of weakness, he'd let her talk him out of making that call. What a sucker he had been!

Darnell claimed that since they were both celebrities she didn't want the publicity over "some little fender-bender." She made the suggestion that they settle the accident quietly, without their insurance companies becoming involved. That sounded reasonable. Little did he know that going along with that suggestion would be the biggest mistake of his life. He could have walked on coals barefoot through the fires of hell with less pain. Never in his life had he met a woman more troublesome.

Everything had started amicably enough. The accident was her fault, and she'd agreed to pay for his repairs. It couldn't have been simpler, yet Darnell Cameron had a way of making simplicity quite complicated.

He had called her with the estimate of repair on his car. The amount was a mere pittance for somebody with her wealth. At least that's what he'd thought. She felt differently and had challenged the estimate, demanding that he get additional ones.

Calmly, he had asked, "Do you think, Ms. Cameron, that I have nothing better to do with my time than run all over the San Francisco Bay area and get estimates for repairs?"

Oh, she had really gotten nasty then. "Well, Mr. Stewart, if you want your car repaired, I suggest you comply with my request. I showed my mechanic a picture of the scratch on your car, and he assures me that he could repair it for much less." She gave him an impossibly low figure. "Bring it here to Carmel to my mechanic, and I'll pay for it. If not, I guess your car will continue to have a *scratch*."

From that moment on, it was war. Letters of demands passed between their attorneys. There were threats to sue for breach of verbal contract. The fight went on for weeks, until both attorneys—battle scarred and war weary—demanded a meeting and a compromise between the two opponents.

At the meeting, he had been played quicker than the lottery. Some compromise! His attorney and best friend, Ray Wilson—otherwise known as Benedict Arnold— took one look into Darnell's eyes and sold him down the river. He ended up having to drive his luxury automobile to Carmel to some no-name garage for repairs, and even that deal fell apart. The result was the fight they'd just had.

Thad pressed the accelerator to the floor. The quicker he got out of this hellhole, the better! He'd pay for the repairs on his car himself. The money wasn't worth the aggravation. Right now, all he wanted was to forget that he'd ever met Darnell Cameron.

Propping her back against a multitude of pillows, Darnell tried to relax on the chaise lounge in her bed-room. Closing her eyes, she counted to ten.

Oh, Lord! What had she ever done to deserve this? Her time at home in Carmel was supposed to be one of quiet reflection. She had been on tour for a year, and it had been hectic. She had looked forward to the serenity of being home, but so far that had turned out to be a joke.

Darnell threw her arm across her eyes, blocking out all light. If only she could block out all thoughts of Thad Stewart as easily. The man was impossible!

After he had barreled down the street like a maniac, with the obvious intention of doing bodily harm to someone, she'd tried to be magnanimous and come up with a fair solution to the little accident they had. Out of the goodness of her heart, she had offered to fix his car. The solution was so simple, but did he appreciate it? No, he had rejected her kind offer, with no logic at all. What a fool!

The press described Thad as the "consummate playboy." He would flash that dimple-cheeked smile on the silver screen and women would go wild. Men liked him because he was macho. Little did the public know that behind that façade lay a ton of trouble, but she didn't have to worry about that again.

Punching the pillow, Darnell burrowed deeper into its cushioned comfort. There would be no more threatening letters from his shyster lawyer, and no more smart-aleck telephone calls from Mr. Stewart. Her business with him was over. The coming months would be much more peaceful. Thank God and hallelujah!

CHAPTER 2

"No! No! No! No! No! No!" Thad's response vibrated across the room like the rat-a-tat-tat of a machine gun. "I will not ask that woman for a thing!" Angrily, Thad flopped down into the leather swivel chair behind the walnut desk in his office. Opposite him sat his manager, attorney and friend, Ray Wilson, who looked less than pleased. Thad didn't care. Turning toward the open French doors leading to the patio, he took a deep breath, inhaling the sea air. He was home in Tiburon—home in his redwood showplace perched high above the San Francisco Bay. Here, he could look out onto a magnificent view of both the San Francisco skyline and the Golden Gate Bridge and feel peace. Now Ray wanted to disrupt that peace.

"I'm telling you, Thad, if we can get Darnell Cameron to make her acting debut with you in this movie, I assure you that you will be one step closer to your dream." Leaning forward, Ray looked at him steadily. "Do you want your own movie studio or not?"

The room was quiet. Both men knew the answer to that question. There was nothing that Thad wanted more.

At thirty-five years old, he was at the top of his game—a movie star in every sense of the word. Yet, he wanted to be more than a handsome face on the silver screen. He wanted to be a power in the industry, someone who could initiate change and offer opportunities to others. He wanted to make a difference.

His career in the entertainment industry began as a fluke. His fraternity brothers dared him to go on stage on open mic night at a comedy club. He took that dare and was a hit. After college, he toured the club circuit, and from there he landed a television sitcom. In a short while he became a major movie star earning millions. It had all happened quickly, and it had been overwhelming. Young and immature, Thad hadn't known how to handle the fame or fortune. That was when Ray had stepped in and helped him take control of his career and of his life.

At age forty, Ray was five years older than Thad, and the two of them were like brothers. Thad trusted him completely. Together, they had carefully laid the foundation for a career with longevity. Over the years, Thad had moved from comedic to dramatic roles, and his acting range earned accolades. He was respected in the industry and ready to take the next step as a producer.

Since his early youth, he had enjoyed writing—short stories, poetry—anything that expressed his creativity. He had never shared them with anyone. It became his little secret, and he always used a pen name, his own name spelled backward. But recently he had tackled his first screenplay, *Sensuous*. He felt good about the work and was determined to take the script to film as the producer. Yet, the process was not a simple one. There were financial investors to please and compromises that had to be made. Some of them he had expected, but this—

"Darnell Cameron would be perfect for the female lead in *Sensuous*," Ray reiterated. "It's as if you wrote the part for her."

"Oh, please," Thad groaned.

Ray was amused at the look of disgust on his face. "Well, your backers think that she would be perfect, and they won't budge on the monetary issue unless you make an attempt to get her. Rumor is that she's looking for her first movie role. Put the two of you together, and we're talking about a hit film. This first movie needs to be a hit, my friend. There are plenty of people in this business who see you as nothing more than a spoiled ladies' man, and they would love to see you fail."

Thad knew that was true. It needed to be successful. A flop would not only cost him financially, but it could also be a blot on his professional reputation that could affect his career. Still, even with all of this at stake, he couldn't fathom working with Darnell Cameron.

"I'd rather go broke and stop acting than have to deal with her again."

Ray shrugged. "I say ask her anyway. If she reads the script and turns you down, at least we can tell the investors that you tried."

Thad leaned across the desk and looked his friend in the eye. "Read my lips, Ray. I don't want to work with Darnell Cameron. I don't like her, and never want to talk to her again. Understand? Anyway, we don't even know if she can act!"

Ray nodded absently. "You're right, but she looks good, so who cares?"

"Very professional." Thad rolled his eyes.

Ray chuckled. "All I know is that if she can't act, she sure puts on a good show when she's mad at you."

"Ha, ha." Thad shuddered, remembering the last verbal sparring he'd had with the woman. "If you think so much of her, why don't *you* ask her to do the movie?"

"Because you're the writer and producer," Ray reasoned. "It's your film. The offer should come from you. It's only right. The woman is a music superstar. Besides, I think she hates me more than she does you." It was Ray's turn to shudder as he remembered the contempt she had openly displayed toward him when the car wars were at their height.

"You're probably right about that, but I'm still not asking her a thing." Thad folded his arms across his chest to emphasize his determination. "I'm telling you, man, the woman is mean. She's spiteful, spoiled, stubborn . . ." Thad sputtered, looking for more words to describe Darnell.

Ray grinned. He had the perfect word. "She's *Sensuous.*"

"There are four crates coming inbound from South America in a week, and Wochev is sending in more product via the Ukraine."

Moody gave a satisfied smile. "It sounds good, Russ. Thank you, and keep up the good work."

Disconnecting, he pocketed his cell phone. He had gambled and won, and he felt great. Everyone in his drug cartel had been skeptical about this partnership with the Russian mob, but it had proved profitable beyond anyone's expectations. The success of the decision had solidified his position as the leader of the most organized business machine on the East Coast, and it all appeared legal. Who would have thought that the son of an illiterate barmaid and a truck driver whom she barely knew could have risen to such heights? He had never had any doubt. Confidence was his forte. He was a self-made man. Everything he knew he had learned on his own—the cultured speech, the foreign languages he spoke, the social graces that opened the doors to membership in the highest of circles. It had taken time and patience, but he had moved steadily through the ranks of the underworld, destroying those who opposed him and rewarding those who had proved their loyalty. He was a determined man, and it was that determination that had brought him to this house on the cul-de-sac.

With a sigh of satisfaction, Moody looked out of the curtained window to the house beyond. It felt good to be away from the demands of his position. Only Russ Ingram, his most loyal employee, knew where he was residing. He felt safe here in Carmel-by-the-Sea and had forgone bodyguards despite the objection of his security staff. He knew that it would be difficult to explain their presence if they had accompanied him. It would have been equally as difficult to conceal why he was here. In the end, he had gotten what he wanted: a chance to travel alone to the West Coast on an extended vacation, of sorts. Of course, he always got what he wanted—several homes, a fleet of cars, more money than he could count, and the respect of his peers. There was only one thing more that he needed to make his life complete.

Reaching into the pocket of his tailored sports jacket, he withdrew a leather wallet and opened it to reveal a small snapshot. Tenderly, his fingers caressed the sharp cheekbones, traced the voluptuous lips and the feline eyes of the woman staring back at him—Darnell Cameron. He had come to the Monterey Peninsula to claim the biggest prize of all.

He had found out from sources within the entertainment industry that when her tour was over, she would be resting at her home in Carmel, *alone*. That so-called boyfriend of hers was preoccupied in South America. He would present no problem. The time to get to know her was perfect. There was no one to get in his way. He had set the stage for the possibility when she was on tour. Anonymously, he had sent her flowers and gifts in every city in which she appeared. He hadn't wanted to be too pushy. A woman like her had to be approached with finesse. But she had sent the gifts back to the post office box that he had used as a return address. He had suspected that she would. The lady had class.

He had known that the first time he saw her perform on stage years ago and had determined that he would meet her. He had followed her career from the first time she stepped into the spotlight. He had read everything about her and eventually laid the foundation for the plan that would take him to her. There was no denying it— she was his obsession.

Gently, he pushed aside the lace curtains to get a better view of the expansive structure beyond. A light appeared in what he reasoned might be her bedroom. He wondered what she was doing. Soon he would know. He planned to make Darnell Cameron a major part of his life.

As Darnell turned on the lamp next to the lounge on which she had been sleeping, she was surprised to see the time reflected on the face of the digital clock. Her short nap had turned into a long one. The sun was setting. The day was nearly gone. A rumbling in her stomach reminded her that she hadn't eaten. Slipping from the lounge, she grabbed her robe and headed downstairs to the kitchen.

Her nerves were still on edge, no doubt because of the altercation with that idiot earlier today. If she were a drinking woman she would have a stiff one now. Instead, she settled for a glass of orange juice and a view of Mother Nature.

She headed out the door to walk the grounds. Her home was a contemporary showplace, nestled among pine, fir, and windswept cypress trees high above the Pacific Ocean. From nearly every direction she could look out onto sweeping vistas of majestic beauty. The view brought her peace. It was something that she very much needed in her life.

Fame had come relatively easily for her. Talent and luck had both prevailed. Music and business had been her double-majors in college and she had put both to work when she embarked on her career. Her voice rivaled that of Aretha Franklin; her business acumen that of Bill Gates. Few knew the extent of her wealth or that she had complete control over her musical empire. She owned it all—her music, her labels, even the production facility in which she and others recorded. With the help of her family, Darnell had orchestrated her success, leaving little to chance. Doing so had not been easy in the misogynistic male-dominated music industry. She had made enemies, but she had prevailed. The constant effort to stay on top had taken its toll, however, and it was here where she sought relief.

Whispering a prayer of thanks for the blessings bestowed on her, she turned and headed back to the house. As she tried to throw something together for dinner, the ring of the telephone in the kitchen interrupted her efforts. Darnell frowned. This was the only telephone in the house without caller I.D. She made a note to remedy that as she reluctantly picked up the receiver.

"Hello!"

"My, my, aren't we grumpy?" The voice on the other end was that of her cousin, Nedra Davis-Reasoner. She and her family lived nearby.

"I'm sorry." Darnell relaxed. "I didn't mean to be rude, but it's been a tough day."

An intuitive Nedra translated her words. "Oh, you thought this call might be the hunk, didn't you?" She was referring to her nickname for Thad. "I thought your business with him was over."

"As of today, it is." She related her latest incident with the beast. Nedra had been her confidant throughout her long ordeal with the man. "It's all water under the bridge now, thank goodness!"

"I still say he's your ticket into the movie business. Maybe he can help you come a step closer to your dream." Nedra was a fan of Thad's and could not conceive of him being the ogre that her cousin painted him.

Darnell guffawed. "Thad Stewart? Help me? That man can't help himself across the street."

Nedra was one of the few people in Darnell's life who knew of her goal to own a film studio. She wanted to be more than a singer with good vocal chords. She planned on becoming a power in both the music and movie industries. However, she would do so without the help of Thad Stewart. "Please, Nedra, don't ruin the rest of my day."

Her cousin complied, and they turned to making arrangements for Nedra's oldest son to spend the next day with Darnell. Then they disconnected. It wasn't until later as she climbed the stairs, prepared to turn in early, that Darnell gave her cousin's words regarding Thad any thought. Over the next few weeks, she planned to wade through a stack of scripts that her manager had sent her to read. It looked as though it might be an arduous task. She wasn't sure what she was looking for in the role that she would choose for her film debut, but hell would freeze over and elephants would fly before she would need Thad Stewart's expertise in that area, or anything else. *That* was a certainty!

After a quick shower, Darnell turned off the light in her bedroom and retired for the evening. Nearly simultaneously, the light in the bedroom in the house across the street went off as well.

CHAPTER 3

Thad couldn't believe what he was doing. Were there no limits to how far he would go to make this movie? Here he was back in Carmel-by-the-Sea, where he had sworn never to come again. He could only pray that he wouldn't live to regret it.

It was all Ray's fault. After trying verbally to persuade Thad to ask Darnell to join him on his film project, he had put facts and figures together on paper to illustrate the financial difference between a hit and a flop. The numbers spoke for themselves. While her addition to the cast might not insure a hit, it would certainly add to the possibility. As a prudent businessman, it was a reality check that he couldn't deny.

He planned to use the repair of his car to explain his return. Knowing Darnell, she wouldn't make it easy, but hopefully he could at least get her to read his script.

The whole idea of humbling himself before that woman galled him, but Ray had added fuel to the fire. Miraculously, he'd produced a tape of a screen test that Darnell had made some time ago for one of the major studios. She was phenomenal. If Thad had harbored any doubts about her ability to handle the lead role in his film, they had been dispelled. Ray's sources had informed him that the only reason that she had not made her acting debut before was failed contract negotiations. Thad wasn't surprised. She had probably asked for the moon. Ray felt that it would be worth providing her with a lunar eclipse if they could also strike a deal with her to score the film. She had been nominated for an Oscar in that category last year. Her involvement in his film could prove to be a coup on many levels. So, here he was, ready to sacrifice both his car and his pride to achieve a dream. It had better be worth it.

After arriving at Darnell's house, Thad rang the buzzer at her entrance gate, and was greeted by a boy's voice through the intercom. He informed Thad that Darnell was unavailable. Despite Thad's best efforts to find out where she might be, the kid was mum on the subject. In desperation, Thad decided to trudge down to the beach, wait there, and go back to her house later to see if she had returned.

It was still early morning. The ocean fog was gradually lifting. Waves lapped gently against the shore while, further out, angry breakers crashed against the rugged rocks. Seagulls perched on the rocky crevices, enjoying the misty spray. Their cries echoed in the morning stillness. Thad began to slow his purposeful stride to enjoy the calm.

He was alone on the beach, and the rhythm of the sea was invigorating. Then, suddenly, a solitary figure appeared out of the morning mist. It was Darnell. Dressed in a black spandex body suit topped by a yellow jacket that brightened the gray morning, she was running straight toward him.

Thad stood mesmerized as he watched her graceful movements. Her curvaceous body was synchronized perfection. Rivulets of perspiration glistened on her ebony face. His groin tightened instantly, and he silently reprimanded his body for its betrayal.

Darnell's mouth tightened when she saw the tall man standing on the beach. As she drew closer, recognition dawned. It couldn't be, but it was. *Thad Stewart!* Her groan was audible. Reaching him, she ran in place.

"What in the world are you doing here?" Her tone could chill ice.

Thad forced himself to ignore the hostility. "Good morning to you, too. In answer to your question, I'm here so that you can take me to this precious garage of yours and get my car repaired."

Darnell shot him a look that would have withered any other man. *Was he kidding?* She continued to run in place. "So you've suddenly changed your mind, surrendered, and decided to come back here and take me up on my original offer, huh?"

Thad's jaw twitched. "I just want to get my car repaired."

Darnell raised a suspicious brow. "I see, and you want that to happen today?"

Thad shrugged. "Whenever."

"Uh huh." She continued to eye him skeptically. "Too bad. Perhaps if you had given me the courtesy of informing me of your change in plans, I could have told you that Mr. Hazelwood's garage is closed on Sundays and Mondays. So if you'll excuse me, I'm not through jogging."

Her tone was dismissive, and Thad's patience was wearing thin. "Well, I wasn't sure about his being open today, and I didn't know about Monday. I guess we can go on Tuesday." He paused. It would take a day or two to have his car repaired, thus giving him adequate time to soften her up regarding the film. If he was really lucky, he might be able to talk her into reading the script before Tuesday, and save his car.

"I can follow you to the garage to deliver my car, get a rental to get around . . ."

Darnell scoffed. "Oh, really? So you plan on staying down here?"

Thad nodded, ignoring the sarcasm. "Sure do. That is, until the repair is done." He rubbed his hands together, buoyed by the possibility that he might be able to make his pitch without sacrificing his car. "Meanwhile, what can we do today?"

Darnell was amazed at his audacity. "Well, Mr. Stewart, since I didn't tell you to come here today—or any other day—I have no intention of planning my activities around you. As a matter of fact, if I recall, I told you I never wanted to see you again. So, I have things to do, and finishing my run is one of them."

That was it! This woman was simply rude! Thad crossed his arms and fixed her with a killer stare. Darnell remained unfazed.

"Now, if I thought that you were in shape to keep up with me . . ." she said as her eyes glanced down the length of his seemingly fit body, "I'd invite you to join me, but—" She shrugged, leaving the question of his ability hanging in the air.

Thad wanted to laugh out loud. This woman had nerves of steel, accusing him of being unfit. *Him!* Thad Stewart! He worked out every day. His stomach couldn't get any flatter! His waist couldn't get any trimmer! His body fat was practically zero. His biceps and his chest were both . . . both . . .

He fought to remind himself of his real reason for being here. Somehow, he kept his voice steady. "Despite what you think about me, *Ms. Cameron,* I assure you that I could keep up with you at any time, day or night. One day I'll accept your challenge, but I didn't come here to jog."

Darnell gave a contemptuous snort. She didn't believe for a minute that he could match her pace.

"Like I said, I have a run to finish. Excuse me." She moved past him and continued down the beach.

Thad bristled but remained silent. The sooner he accomplished his mission and got the hell out of there, the better.

She was such a lovely woman. Even at this distance, just seeing Darnell jogging down the beach took Moody's breath away. Excited, he had hastened his footsteps, knowing that he was only minutes away from finally meeting her in person.

He had noticed the man standing on the beach with his back to him, apparently staring out at the sea, and dismissed him from his thoughts. Moody's total focus was on Darnell. Just as he started toward the beach, she jogged up to the stranger and stopped. Moody froze, the muscles in his body taut as he watched and waited, poised to make a move.

After Darnell and the stranger exchanged a few words, she continued her morning run. The stranger watched her jog away, then turned and started walking in the opposite direction. Moody gave a sigh of relief. She was safe. The man was probably a fan—a lucky fan. If he had touched her in any way, he would have died on the spot. Coming to her rescue had not been in his plan, but he would not have hesitated to do so. He had been here a week, clandestinely studying her habits, and it worried him that she moved so freely around Carmel alone. That he would remedy. He would make her security a priority when he entered her life, assigning only his most trusted bodyguards to protect her. Meanwhile, it irritated him that a fan had interfered with his plan to *accidentally* bump into her. It was frustrating. He had timed it perfectly, but—

Moody turned and walked back up the path leading away from the beach. As was her pattern, she would be running for at least another hour. There was always tomorrow. Perhaps he'd have to readjust his plan. Maybe they'd bump into each other at the grocery store or at a restaurant. No problem; he had waited this long to meet her, and another day didn't matter. He planned to be on the coast for the entire summer. He had plenty of time.

An hour later, Darnell returned home to find Thad sitting on her three-tiered patio. His voice was strident as he explained how he got on her property.

"The gardener came by to drop off some tools, recognized me and let me in the gate, but that kid inside the house refused to open the door. I tried to tell him that it was chilly out here, but he wouldn't budge."

Darnell grinned. "That's my boy."

Thad was fuming. He had about reached his limit with this woman. She was much too full of herself. During their car wars, Ray had shared with him everything that he had learned about her in order to give him an edge in the negotiations. He couldn't deny that the woman was a fascinating study. She had earned quite a reputation in the business, and as far as he was concerned, it was a reputation that she well deserved.

"Ms. It" was the nickname Darnell had acquired in the entertainment industry, and it wasn't just a reference to her tremendous talent. While she had been on top of the music charts for years and had won nearly every award offered, to most of her fans, as well as people in the business, Darnell Cameron was a mystery. She was one celebrity who managed to keep her private life private, which wasn't an easy feat.

She rarely gave interviews, and the known facts about her were few. Her father was deceased, and she had been raised by her mother, Beverly Cameron, a CPA who owned a very successful investment firm in Chicago. Highly intelligent, Darnell spoke several languages and possessed amazing business savvy. In the process of emerging as a superstar, she had amassed a fortune. *Forbes* magazine touted her as one of the wealthiest entertainers in the industry, rivaling none other than Thad Stewart.

Unlike Thad, Darnell was a rebel in the industry. She shunned Los Angeles and the celebrity scene on which he thrived. Her quick mind and razor-sharp tongue had many in the media wary of her, but the public loved her rebellious spirit. Thad could appreciate the latter; it was everything else about her that he found annoying. As he sat on her patio with the morning chill whipping through his thin jacket, he gave serious thought to wringing her neck.

Mercifully, it was a plan that he didn't have to act on. She let him inside her house. There, she introduced him to her young cousin, Colin Reasoner, the boy who had refused Thad entrance. He watched Darnell with narrowed eyes as she praised the kid for obeying her directive not to open the door to anyone.

"This is my little sweetheart." She gave the adolescent boy a fond hug. "Colin, I'm sure you know who Mr. Stewart is."

The boy's handsome, cinnamon brown face broke into a grin at the endearment Darnell had bestowed on him. The grin faded when he turned to Thad.

"Yeah, I know, who he is," he drawled, dropping onto the sofa. "I've heard you and Mama talking." It was clear that he wasn't impressed.

Thad gave the boy a cursory nod and settled in a chair across from him. It was obvious that he knew Darnell's opinion of Thad and was trying to play her protector.

The kid had nothing to worry about. Thad wouldn't touch her with a ten-foot pole.

"I'm going to run upstairs and change," Darnell informed Thad as she headed toward the stairway. "Then we'll talk. I'm tired of arguing with you, so I'd like to settle this matter once and for all."

Thad raised a brow, encouraged by her words. Maybe some progress could be made. He watched her as she left the room, trying hard not to notice the soft sway of her hips. Despite her many irritating qualities, there was no doubt that the woman was built.

Upstairs, Darnell took a quick shower, then wrapped her wet body in a large, fluffy towel. As she dried herself, her thoughts turned to the man downstairs. What was Thad really up to? His presence here was highly suspicious. Over the past few months, they had fought like warring countries. From what she had learned about him, he wasn't the type to cave in easily. Something was amiss. For now, all she wanted to know was what she had to do to get rid of him permanently.

Frustrated, she dropped on the bed. Her eyes fell on the picture of Lance Austin on the nightstand. Ironically, it was on a date with Lance that she first heard the name Thad Stewart. At the time he had been a rising young comedian, poised for his age and very funny. Lance had said that Thad was going places. He had been right. Presently, however, he was in *her* place, and it was imperative that she get him out of her home and out of her life.

As she dressed, Darnell prepared herself mentally to go one more round with Thad. As she started out of the bedroom, her eye fell on the manila envelope lying next to Lance's photo. It had arrived by messenger earlier that morning. It was a script. According to her manager this was *the* script—the one that would assure her entrance into the movie world. She couldn't wait to start reading it and had planned to do so the rest of the day. The sooner she got rid of Thad Stewart, the sooner she could settle down and begin reading . . .

Darnell glanced at the title her manager had scribbled on the envelope—*Sensuous.*

CHAPTER 4

The staring duel between Thad and Colin had been ongoing from the moment Darnell left the room. Finally, Thad broke the war of silence. "How old are you, Colin?"

Colin answered pointedly, "Old enough to know what you've got on your mind."

Thad frowned, taken aback by the boy's candor. Just his luck; a smart-aleck woman *and* a smart-aleck kid. "You're out of order," he warned sternly. "You don't want me to tell Darnell that her little angel has some devil in him, do you?" He looked at him steadily until Colin muttered a half-hearted apology and diverted his attention to the television.

Restless, Thad rose and began wandering the room under Colin's watchful eye. Boldly, he meandered past the living room and down the hallway, grateful to escape Colin's unfriendly glare.

Evidence of Darnell's talent and popularity were apparent in every room he passed. Awards and citations were displayed on tables, shelves, and walls. Locating her office, he wandered inside.

The room was a kaleidoscope of color, furnished comfortably with overstuffed chairs and an array of gigantic floor pillows. On one wall was a fireplace, and placed on the mantel were framed pictures of what appeared to be family and friends. A built-in bookcase full of books took up a second wall. The third wall consisted of floor-to-ceiling windows with glass so clear that the room and the Pacific Ocean beyond seemed one.

Thad's eyes drifted to the glass-topped desk placed in front of the bookshelves. A picture caught his eye. Rounding the desk, he flopped down in the leather swivel chair behind the desk and picked up the picture.

He knew from the media that the man in the picture was Darnell's significant other—Lance Austin, a hotshot doctor, who was presently conducting AIDS research in South America. Reportedly, he and Darnell had been together for years. Thad studied the man closely. He would guess that some women might find the guy handsome. He looked a little too perfect as far as Thad was concerned.

"I hope you're enjoying yourself."

Thad looked up to find Darnell standing in the doorway. She had changed from her jogging outfit into a pair of jeans and a tailored shirt. Leather loafers had replaced her running shoes. Her hair was still in a ponytail, and she wore no makeup, but her smooth, dark skin practically glowed. She looked enticing. Thad reined in the hormones.

"I was just looking around." Thad placed the photo back on the desk.

"So Colin said." Darnell's voice was terse. "But I'd rather we return to the living room."

Without a word, Thad brushed past her. She was weary of this man, and for that reason she would simply concede the battle just to have him gone once and for all.

Following him into the living room, she gestured to a chair.

"Have a seat, and we'll talk." Darnell joined Colin on the sofa as Thad settled into a chair.

Darnell smiled at the boy warmly and threw an arm around his shoulders.

"Did you know that my cousin here is one of the brightest kids around? He wins every prize that they give out in his school. We're so proud of him." She hugged him to her and gave him a quick kiss. Colin threw Thad a triumphant grin.

Thad ignored both the grin and the comment. He had no doubt that the kid was smart, but if Colin thought that he was going to compete with him for a grown woman's attention, he was sadly mistaken. The grownups had important matters to discuss. He got straight to the point.

"Are we going to discuss the car repair or not?"

Darnell turned her attention to Thad. She stared at him long and hard, then turned to Colin. "Sweetie, do you mind going downstairs to watch television?"

Getting the hint that his presence was not needed, Colin rose and left the room. Darnell addressed Thad.

"I thought that the car issue was settled last week when I threw you off my property, but obviously not. I'm sick and tired of the entire situation, so let's settle this once and for all."

Thad nodded. "I agree."

"Then I'll tell you what. Since Hazelwood's will be closed today and tomorrow, and you don't want him to fix your car anyway, I'll pay your transportation cost for coming down here, and I'll write you a check for whatever you think it will cost to fix the car. I won't question it. You can take your car anywhere you want."

Thad knew that the answer he was about to give would frustrate her, and secretly delighted in the fact. "Then I choose Hazelwood's garage on Tuesday."

Darnell closed her eyes for a moment to regain her composure. She knew this man was up to something, but she conceded. "All right, I'll make the arrangements. When you bring your car back here on Tuesday, I'll pay to fly you back to the Bay area." *She would do anything to get rid of him!*

"I'd rather have you rent me a car so that I can drive home."

"No problem. I'll type up our agreement and you can sign it."

Thad rubbed his hands together eagerly. "Sounds like a plan to me."

"Good, then it's settled. I'll see you back here on Tuesday at ten-thirty in the morning. That should give me time to arrange everything." Darnell started to rise to see Thad out, but he settled deeper in his chair. It was clear that he wasn't ready to leave.

She frowned. What was he doing, taking up permanent residence? She watched as Thad placed his ankle across his knee and flashed her a charming smile. "So, what are we going to do the rest of today?"

Darnell was stunned. "We? Aren't you driving back to Tiburon?"

"Nope, I'm staying in Carmel until Tuesday, and since I'm here, I assume that you'll be entertaining me."

Darnell's eyes narrowed. "You *assume* wrong. I have plans for the day. I won't be able to *entertain* you." The nerve of the man!

Thad gave a prolonged sigh. "But I thought I might drive to Big Sur this afternoon. You can go with me."

Darnell raised a brow. Something was wrong here. She and Thad could barely stand to be in the same room together, and he wanted to take her for a ride. Hmmm, maybe he meant that literally. "Like I said, I have plans."

Rising, she walked to the entranceway. Thad followed her. He looked disappointed.

Colin appeared at the downstairs entranceway. "Goodbye, Mr. Stewart," he called. It was obvious that Colin was happy to see him go.

"Bye, kid," he threw over his shoulder as he stepped outside. He turned to Darnell. "What are you doing tomorrow?"

She raised both eyebrows this time. What *was* this man up to? She had no doubt that she would find out eventually. Placing a finger against her temple, she pretended to ponder his question. "Let me see, what am I doing tomorrow? Hmmm, when I'm fully awake, I'm going to get up, wash, slip into some clothes, and go for a run on the beach. Maybe you should do the same. Goodbye." She closed the front door firmly in his face.

As he headed to his car, Thad gave a wicked grin. He just might take the lovely Ms. Cameron up on her flippant little suggestion. He could do with a little exercise.

Besides, he had to soften her up in order to get her to read his script. What better way to do that than by joining her in her morning ritual? It looked as if this little project might not be as difficult as he thought.

The gates leading to Darnell's house opened, and the red Ferrari exited just as Moody was driving his rental car down his driveway. As the luxury sports car with its tinted windows turned and headed down the street, he briefly wondered who the occupant of the flashy automobile might be. He knew from last week, when he had nearly collided with the same car, that it didn't belong to Darnell. He knew her cars on sight. Besides, the color wasn't her style. Her taste was more refined. Perhaps it belonged to one of her band members or some other employee. It didn't matter. Presently, there were more important matters on his mind.

His right-hand man had called and informed him that the shipment from South America had reached its destination, but in transport a large quantity of product had come up missing. Millions would be lost if it wasn't found. The matter called for his immediate attention. He hadn't planned on making any trips back east so soon, but this one was necessary. He estimated he could take care of his business and be back here to resume his plan to meet Darnell within a week. These interruptions were frustrating, but hopefully this would be the last one.

By the time Moody reached the road leading to the highway, the red Ferrari had disappeared, and his curiosity about its occupant had been quietly dismissed

When Darnell descended the stairs the next morning, ready for her run, she was faced with an unexpected visitor. Thad Stewart sat in her kitchen entertaining her housekeeper, Mrs. Sharon.

"Good morning, Ms. Cameron." The grin on Thad's face was as wide as Darnell's eyes.

"What are you doing here?" Her glance swept the length of his long, firm torso. He was clad in a designer sweat suit and a white cotton T-shirt that defined every line of his muscular chest and arms. The expensive running shoes he was wearing were new. A stylish pair of sunglasses perched on top of his head.

Mrs. Sharon, a pleasant, rotund woman in her early sixties, looked up at Darnell with surprise. "I thought you two were running together this morning?" She eyed Thad suspiciously. Had the dimpled smile the handsome young man bestowed on her been one of deceit?

"We are." Thad spoke up quickly, trying not to look guilty about his little white lie. He eyed Darnell, undaunted by her hard expression. "Remember yesterday when you said that maybe I should go for a run on the beach? Well, here I am, ready to go." He spread his arms wide and flashed a smile as sparkling as the diamond stud earring twinkling at her from his ear.

At this point, it didn't matter to Thad whether Darnell wanted him with her or not. She was wearing another one of those spandex outfits. Hell yeah, he was going running!

"I don't remember extending an invitation to you." She was about ready to report this man as a stalker.

By the look on her face, Thad could almost hear what she was thinking. It galled him, but he decided that humility might be the best tactic for this one.

"Please, may I go with you?" He tried to turn on the charm. It didn't work.

"Cut the act. I'm not falling for it. If I thought that you could keep up with me, I wouldn't mind, but—" She allowed her skepticism to speak for itself.

"Believe me, it won't be a problem." Thad was insulted, but he didn't want her to know it.

Darnell studied him for a moment. This guy was bluffing. "Let me warn you, I'm not about to slow my pace for you."

"Like I said, no problem."

She gave a suit-yourself shrug. Placing her earphones over her ears, she adjusted her sunglasses, then walked past him and out the patio doors.

With a wink at Mrs. Sharon, Thad drained the glass of juice she had given him and, in a few long-legged strides, he caught up with Darnell. That was the last time that morning that he could make that claim.

He tried. He tried hard, but as fit as he was from daily workouts, he hadn't run on a regular basis in years, and it showed. During the first mile, he called upon the skills he could remember from his glory days on his high school track team, but by mile two, he knew he was in trouble. By mile three, he was in *serious* trouble. Years of partying and club hopping had finally caught up with him. Mile four was excruciating, and by mile five he had conceded defeat. Darnell left him lying face-up on the beach at mile five.

About an hour later, on her return trip, she found Thad where she had left him, sprawled in the same position. She thought about continuing her run and letting the tide do what she couldn't seem to do—make him disappear—but her conscience got the better of her. Stopping, she kicked his outstretched hand with the tip of her shoe. "Thad!" He didn't move.

Bending over him, observing his stillness, she frowned. Maybe he had passed out. She shook his shoulder gently. "Hey, are you okay?" No response.

Darnell dropped to her knees as her stomach began to flutter nervously. Oh, God! He wasn't dead, was he? She didn't mean for him to die. Sure, the thought of killing him had crossed her mind a time or two, but she hadn't been serious. With tentative fingers, she felt his neck for a pulse, then sighed in relief. He was breathing, but he still hadn't responded to her touch.

Darnell felt bad. The man was unconscious, and she had left him there on the beach unattended. What kind of person had she turned into? With care, she removed his sunglasses, and gently laid his head in her lap. She bent close to his ear, hoping that he could hear her. "Thad, are you all right?" She rubbed his brow with the tips of her fingers. Her touch was as light as a bird in flight. His smooth skin glistened with perspiration, giving it a soft, healthy sheen. His long eyelashes cast a shadow against his dark cheeks as they began to flutter in response to his name.

Darnell drew back a little, suddenly struck by how handsome Thad actually was. He wasn't pretty-boy handsome as some members of the press described Lance. No, Thad was a rugged, masculine handsome, with dark, deep set eyes, thick, straight eyebrows, a broad nose and a strong jaw line, all in a chocolate brown face accentuated by perfectly round dimples centered in the middle of each cheek. The combination had set many-a-female heart aflutter, but not hers, of course.

His lips parted. He sighed, and a sound escaped him. He was snoring. The man wasn't unconscious. He was asleep! Darnell jumped to her feet, dumping his head in the sand.

The impact of his head hitting the ground brought Thad's eyes flying open. "What the hell?"

With some effort, he sat up. Every bone in his body was aching. Hands on hips, Darnell stood glaring down at him.

In the twilight between sleep and awareness, he had been sure that he had died and gone to heaven. When he surrendered his pride and admitted defeat, Thad was certain that death would be better than the pain his attempt at jogging had caused. The sand had felt good beneath his exhausted body as he lay waiting for either his heart or his lungs to burst. Which came first didn't matter. All he wanted was a painless death. Instead, sleep had over-taken him and he was grateful, until he had been so unceremoniously awakened. He wasn't sure what had happened, but it didn't take a genius to see that Darnell wasn't happy.

"I must have fallen asleep," he said sheepishly. He rose and brushed the sand from his clothes and hair. "This salt air will do that to you." He stooped to pick up his sunglasses and placed them over his eyes.

Darnell glowered at him. "You are pathetic." She spat out the last word contemptuously. Flipping her sun-glasses down on her eyes, she turned to resume her run. Thad's hand on her upper arm stopped her.

"Hey, come on. I'm standing here humble in the face of defeat. No more running, okay? Walk with me."

Darnell scowled as she looked at the hand he had placed on her arm. He quickly removed it.

"Come on, walk for a little while. Pleeeease." He could only hope that his voice held the right amount of pleading. She didn't look concerned.

Darnell didn't feel sorry for him, no matter how pitiful he looked. She started toward the house, strolling leisurely at first as Thad limped beside her, trying to keep up. Then she picked up her pace.

As Darnell poised to resume running, Thad became desperate.

"Look at me, I think I might have pulled a muscle or something. I can hardly walk, let alone run. I might have to pitch a tent down here on the beach beneath your house. I don't think I can make it back to your place."

Darnell gave a victorious smile, buoyed by Thad's inability to keep up. That should teach him a lesson. But she continued walking.

Thad caught the smile. Too bad he didn't see it more often. He wondered if he could make her laugh.

Snapping his fingers, he reached into the pocket of his jogging pants, withdrew a leather wallet and hollered at her retreating back, "I'm not even going to try and walk back to your house. I'll just camp right here on the beach!" That caught her attention as she stopped and turned to look at him. Thad withdrew several bills from his wallet and held them up. "If I give you some money, will you go to the sporting goods store and buy me a tent and some camping supplies?"

Darnell shook her head at the absurdity of his request. She fought a giggle at the seriousness in his tone.

He continued. "I'll need a sleeping bag . . ."

The giggle was threatening to erupt.

"A kerosene lamp, some bug spray . . ."

Darnell couldn't hold the urge to laugh much longer.

"A portable grill would be nice, and some food, of course." He paused dramatically. "And I'll need a portable john."

That did it. Darnell collapsed into uncontrolled laughter. The man was a maniac. Thad limped up to her and stood gawking with a deadpan expression.

"Is there a problem?"

Recovering, Darnell wiped the tears from her eyes. "You're sick. Do you know that? You are totally loony tunes."

Thad tried to look confused. "I beg your pardon. I'm not crazy. I just need help buying the supplies. So here." He took her hand and tried to force the money into her palm. "Please, go get them for me. Bring them back to me, and I'll be grateful forever. I'll wait on the beach near the rocks."

He walked away from her with an exaggerated stiff-legged limp that brought a new wave of laughter from Darnell. Laughing hysterically, she caught up with him.

"If you don't take this money I'll strangle you." She tried to push the money back into his hand. Thad resisted.

Darnell's laughter enchanted him. To his surprise, he liked this carefree side of her. In the short time that he'd known her, he had never seen her like this.

As she recovered, Darnell felt self-conscious. She was amazed at the idea that she was enjoying herself with Thad Stewart, but gradually she turned serious.

"If you keep acting crazy, they're going to put you away for good." Placing the money firmly in his hand, she continued down the beach.

Thad followed her, disappointed that their moment of levity was over. "You know that's how I got into show business in the first place, *acting crazy.*" Picking up a large, sturdy stick that had drifted in with the tide, he began using it as a walking cane. "I started out as a standup comedian."

"Yes, I know." Darnell glanced at him as he stumbled along beside her, aided by his makeshift cane. "And from there, one magazine went on to dub you as 'The Sexiest

Man of the Year,' the irascible playboy with the million-dollar smile."

Thad blanched at the censure in her voice. "That's just media hype."

"I have no doubt about that, just like all of the women you've been rumored to have gone through." She shook her head at the thought. "Surely you want to leave a greater legacy behind than that?" Or did he? Did the man have any character? Was he committed to anything? Darnell quickened her steps, anxious to get home.

Insulted by her words, Thad was aware of Darnell's change in demeanor. A minute ago, she had seemed to be enjoying herself, but now she was back to her old self. The woman was schizophrenic. Besides, she of all people should be aware of the games played in Hollywood. Everything was for publicity or show.

He had never been comfortable being dubbed a sex symbol. He had worked hard to be respected as a legitimate actor and did not appreciate being thought of as some testosterone-driven clown. As for the rumors of his sexual exploits with women, for the most part they were without fact. He had never bothered to squelch most of them because they'd never seemed to be that important to him, until now. Darnell had made it clear that she thought less of him because of his reputation—among other things—and although that shouldn't matter, much to his annoyance, it did.

They continued walking the beach in silence, but as they drew closer to the path leading to her house he confessed. "I'm serious about my aching body having trouble getting up the steps to your house. Let's take that path over there. That's the way I got down here the other day."

Throwing a glance in the direction he was pointing, Darnell shook her head. "You go that way. I'm going this way. I'm in a hurry."

Thad was disappointed, but tried not to show it. "Where are you off to?"

Continuing to make her way toward the house, Darnell's words drifted to him from over her shoulder. "Not that it's any of your business, but I'm going dancing."

CHAPTER 5

While Darnell got ready, Thad kept Mrs. Sharon company in the kitchen. He was rewarded with two plump burritos and a plate of Spanish rice.

A short time later, Darnell reappeared in the kitchen, and Thad nearly choked on his meal. She was dressed in a form-fitting leotard with a colorful African-print cloth tied loosely around her shapely hips. Thad sat in a daze. Darnell had to call his name twice before his mind was clear enough to respond.

"What did you say?"

"I said, what are you doing here? I thought you left!"

Thad looked at her blankly. "Why would I leave? I don't have anywhere else to go."

Darnell gave a frustrated sigh. Lord, the man was like locusts. She couldn't get rid of him. Then Mrs. Sharon intervened and made it worse.

"Why don't you go to dance rehearsal with her?" she asked innocently. "I'm sure she won't mind." She turned to Darnell. "Would you?"

The look Darnell gave the older woman was deadly. Obviously, Mrs. Sharon wanted to be on the unemployment rolls.

Darnell's reaction didn't appear to faze the woman as she added, "You ought to go. It should be fun." Mrs.

Sharon smiled fondly at Thad. It looked as though he had won the admiration of another female.

Grinning as if he had won the lottery, Thad questioned Darnell.

"What is this dancing thing about?"

"I'm in an African dance troupe that performs for charity events in this area. It's called Nia, which is Swahili for 'purpose.' I'm on my way there now."

"I think they'd get a kick out of Thad Stewart sitting in on a rehearsal," Mrs. Sharon added, continuing to ignore Darnell's dagger stare.

"I'd think that your presence would cause enough of a stir among the dancers," Thad contended, silently blessing Mrs. Sharon for this tidbit about Darnell.

She shrugged. "They're used to me. I've been with the troupe for three years, so I'm nobody special in the group. When we perform, I go by the name Nailah when I'm introduced. Most people in the audience don't even recognize me."

Thad nodded. So the lady had a secret life, and he just might have a chance to catch a glimpse of it. Maybe progress was being made. "I'd like to tag along, if you don't mind. I'll even drive if you want me to."

Darnell's eyebrows shot up. "You have got to be kidding! You want *me* to ride in that conspicuous contraption of yours?" she asked, referring to his Ferrari. "That's a little too much for my taste. I'll take my car. You can follow me." She headed for the front door.

Thad leaped from the barstool. "Guess that means I'm invited," he mumbled as he passed Mrs. Sharon. She winked at him, and he grinned. At least he had one ally in the Cameron household.

An hour and a half later, Thad regretted his having attended the rehearsal. The problem wasn't the sensation his presence caused among the women dancers. It was the rehearsal itself that proved disturbing.

Darnell took pains to protect them both from speculative gossip about their having arrived together. As a cover story, she told the other dancers that he was looking at the troupe for a possible booking. At first Thad thought that she was being overly cautious, but by the time the rehearsal ended he was grateful that she had thought to avoid speculation because her performance shook him to the core.

Her shapely form glided through the African dance movements with the grace of a gazelle. With braids flying and hips swaying, she danced with unrestrained abandonment, gyrating provocatively to the vibrating beat of the accompanying drums. Thad was mesmerized.

He made more than one attempt to give the other dancers equal attention, but his eyes always strayed back to Darnell. She was an African queen—regal and magnificent.

After the rehearsal, he tried to collect his senses but found it all but impossible. So he thanked her for inviting him, muttered goodbye to the other dancers, then hurried from the building as if it was on fire. His plan to talk to her about the script was all but forgotten for today. Hot and bothered by her seductive perform-ance, he headed back to his hotel feeling as though he had been hit by a thunderbolt.

As Darnell drove home, she too was bothered by the day's rehearsal. The Nia Dance Ensemble was as much her sanctuary as the cliffside retreat she called home. She had never been self-conscious when executing the move-ments of the dances they performed, but today had been different. Under Thad's intense scrutiny, she had been more than aware of every movement of her body. His visual appraisal had been disturbing. Yet, it had also been intoxicating, and *that's* what bothered her. Never had her pulse raced so rapidly. Never had her heart beat so loudly. She had tried desperately to mask her reaction.

As she sped along the highway, Darnell tightened her grip on the steering wheel. She was more than a little annoyed, and it was all Thad's fault! She wasn't used to anyone leering at her. Before, she had always danced for the simple joy of dancing. Today, she had danced for him.

Shaken by that revelation, Darnell stomped into the house and up the stairs, passing Mrs. Sharon in the hallway.

"How did the rehearsal go?" she asked, noting Darnell's irritation.

"Fine," Darnell answered before slamming her bed-room door behind her.

Mrs. Sharon chuckled. It seemed that sparks were beginning to fly.

After a sleepless night of self-recrimination, Thad came to the conclusion that the safest recourse for him was to talk to Darnell about his script ASAP, then get the hell out of town. If she rejected the script and his pitch about it, so be it. If she accepted it, their lawyers would handle the negotiations. This woman had messed with his mind yesterday, and he didn't like it.

Bright and early Tuesday morning, he called Darnell and confirmed the trip to Hazelwood's Garage. He informed her that he needed to talk with her about something important prior to their appointment and that he also needed to finish with the garage business no later than noon. He had an important appointment in Oakland. He arrived at her house fifteen minutes early in a good mood, which quickly changed when Darnell met him at the door with a cordless telephone dangling from her ear. She held up a finger and mouthed, "This is business. I'll only be a minute."

Thad frowned. He had grown up with three older sisters, and he knew how long "a minute" could be. He had planned to pitch the script in the interval before going to the garage, and very much doubted that her conversation would be as short as she had stated. He was right. As the minute turned into two, ten, and then thirty, he glanced at his watch pointedly and repeatedly. It didn't matter.

With each ticking second, Darnell made it obvious that she would be talking on the telephone as long as it would take. She paraded up and down the room in front of him, leaving a trail of scented body oil with every step. Clad in a pair of shorts, her tousled cornrows held back from her face with an African-print scarf, she looked and smelled delicious. There was no doubt that she had alluring qualities. That couldn't be denied. It was her personality that stunk.

As Darnell's telephone conversation continued, she ignored every entreaty he made of her to respect his time. Desperate, he tried to suggest that she resume her conversation on her cell phone so that they could go. She ignored him. It was only Thad's good home training that kept him from strangling her. He was about to leave her house and never grace her doorstep again when she decided to hang up the telephone. One minute had turned into forty. Darnell was apologetic.

"I'm sorry it took a little longer than I'd expected," she said, leaving the sincerity of her apology open to question as far as Thad was concerned. "But, as I told you earlier, I've made all of the arrangements, and they'll take us whenever we get there." She could see from his expression how upset he was.

Slowly, Thad got to his feet. Without a word, he started toward the front door with her behind him. He was incensed. His momentary fascination with this woman yesterday had been an aberration. He was sure about that. His equilibrium was back on track, and she was going to pay for this. He didn't know how, but he had decided that her inconsideration was going to cost her.

CHAPTER 6

It was after noon when they pulled up to Hazelwood's Garage and Body Shop. Thad's schedule was shot, but at least one thing was going right for him today. Hazelwood's Garage turned out to be way above his expectations.

It was a small place, located on what could more easily be described as an alley than a street. Mr. Hazelwood turned out to be a pleasant man in his sixties, tall, slim and meticulously groomed. He was dressed in spotless gray overalls with the name of his business embroidered in red across his breast.

Thad had to admit that he was impressed. The man knew his business and was very professional in the way he handled his customers. The two men busily working in the garage with Mr. Hazelwood appeared to be well trained. The office walls were adorned with numerous awards for excellence, and there were other luxury automobiles being serviced. Thad breathed a sigh of relief, knowing that his car would be in good hands. He didn't even mind the smug look that Darnell gave him as he and Mr. Hazelwood spoke.

Things were going well at the garage until Thad saw the car that Darnell had rented for him to drive while his was being repaired. He was dumbfounded. The vehicle was a conservative black. It reminded him of a hearse.

"This is an old man's car. I know you don't expect me to drive around in this."

Darnell was taken aback by his ingratitude. "You said you have another car at home you plan on driving. Just use this one to get to Tiburon, and you can use the other one as transportation until yours is ready. Although I really don't see what's wrong with this one. It's new. It has tinted windows, and at least it's inconspicuous."

Thad was not persuaded. "Then if it's all that, you drive it."

His retort started a round of verbal sparring that had Mr. Hazelwood and his employees taking side bets on who would land the first blow. Finally, Mr. Hazelwood made an attempt to quell the storm. "I'm sorry to interrupt you folks, but I need to know if you're going to leave your car for that tune-up, Ms. Cameron. I mean, since you're already here, this would be a perfect time to do it."

"I don't know, Mr. Hazelwood," Darnell hedged, still upset by her exchange with Thad. "I'll need a ride home." She didn't notice the sudden light that appeared in Thad's eyes.

"I can give you a ride," he offered, his angry demeanor suddenly vanishing. "That is, if you don't mind riding in this rental car."

Darnell started to decline, but, anxious to move both temperamental celebrities out of his garage, Mr. Hazelwood spoke up.

"Sounds good to me. Especially since I can't spare anybody to take you home right now, Ms. Cameron."

Reluctantly, Darnell accepted the offer.

Once buckled into the car, Darnell sat stiffly, her arms folded across her chest. She didn't have anything to say until Thad passed her exit on the highway and headed toward Santa Cruz.

"Where are you going?" she demanded as they passed a second exit to her home.

"To Oakland," Thad stated calmly. "You're going with me."

Darnell went ballistic. He had to admit that the language she used was creative. She opted to avoid the most obvious expletives and, instead invented new ones in an effort to be more lady-like, he assumed. When she eventually stopped screaming at him, he explained to her how she had disrupted his time schedule.

"I have no choice but to take you with me if I want to get to my appointment before the day is over."

"And how am I supposed to get back to Carmel?" The chill in her voice was deadly.

"Maybe you can drive this car back," he drawled.

The car's interior was sizzling from the heat of Darnell's anger. "You're going to jail. I am with you against my will, which is kidnapping, and I'm putting you on notice that I'm filing charges as soon as we get to Oakland."

Thad shrugged nonchalantly. "You're going to put me in jail?"

"Did I stutter?" Darnell rolled her eyes at Thad as hard as she could. She was seething.

For a while, they rode in silence with Darnell staring out of the window. When they reached San Jose, Thad turned on the radio. Darnell's voice drifted from the dashboard and filled the car's interior. He hummed along with the familiar love song, occasionally singing a line or two. He had a beautiful baritone voice.

Darnell was unable to hide her surprise. "You don't sound half bad."

"Thank you." Thad was pleased by the compliment, considering the source.

"You'll have plenty of time to perfect your singing style in jail." Darnell crossed her legs and began swinging her foot. "It's good you have another talent. Your shattered acting career will need a new direction once you get out."

Thad laughed as his eyes followed the swing of her shapely leg. He shook his head in amazement at the woman's tenacity. "Lady, you are something else!"

Darnell followed his gaze, and Thad looked away guiltily, but it was too late.

"In your dreams," she hissed, glaring at him.

Thad chuckled. He had been caught red-handed. He gave an exaggerated shiver. "Brrr, it's cold in here."

"Not half as cold as it's going to be in jail," she shot back. "Get used to it."

Thad sighed. Despite their altercation at her house, in Hazelwood's garage, and practically everywhere else they had been together, he had hoped that their drive to Oakland would be a bit more amicable. This could be the opportunity he had been looking for to talk to her. "Come on, Darnell, loosen up. That's the third time you've threatened me with jail. It was *you* who wasted my time today. Now you're complaining when the tables are turned."

"But I didn't kidnap you."

"I didn't kidnap you, either. I'm merely taking you on a little ride since I didn't have time to take you home."

"Tell it to the judge." She shifted in her seatbelt, turning her entire body away from him. "This conversation is over."

Thad got the message, but he pressed on anyway. No matter how angry she made him, he didn't want to fight with her anymore. There were matters to be discussed. A truce was needed that wouldn't be broken five minutes later. He was ready to smoke a peace pipe—again.

"All right, do what you've got to do, but I bet you'll enjoy where we're going. I saw the artwork hanging all over your house, and this is a great gallery we're going to."

Darnell's head snapped around. "You're going to an art gallery?"

"Yep."

Darnell's interest increased. "So why didn't you just tell me where you were going and ask me if I wanted to go instead of abducting me like some Neanderthal?"

"I didn't plan on you coming with me, but my appointment was at three, and I had planned to be there on time, but that's shot to hell. I've got the opportunity to get a Romare Bearden original, and I need to get to that gallery."

That really piqued her interest. Darnell turned completely toward Thad. He smiled to himself, glad that they had finally found a common interest. He continued, "I can get it at a good price, too. The gallery owner is a friend of mine. I called her when I was at your house because I could see that I might be late. She's waiting for me. As a favor, she's even closing the gallery when I get there so I can shop in peace."

Darnell cocked her head, eyeing him suspiciously. Did he really know anything about art, or was this a line? She was serious about putting his butt in jail. "I wouldn't think you'd even know who Romare Bearden was. What do you know about art?"

"I've been an art collector for about six years. It's one of my hobbies. My attorney, Ray . . . remember him?"

Darnell nodded.

"He's the one who got me interested. He said it would be a good investment, and I got hooked. Bearden is one of my favorites. I have two originals already."

Darnell could no longer hide her excitement. "Really? What else does the gallery have? Any Varnetta Honeywood originals?"

Thad liked seeing this animated side of her. Her eyes were actually sparkling. He didn't know the answer to her questions, but it didn't matter. His mission was accomplished. They had found common ground. Another truce had been declared.

The art gallery was located near historic Jack London Square in a large, renovated warehouse. The building was made resplendent by its high ceilings and skylights, and there were a multitude of potted and hanging plants. Camelback sofas were placed strategically on each of its two tiers.

Thad introduced the gallery owner, Regine Lexy. He had stated that she was a friend, but Darnell quickly noted that Regine seemed to think of herself as a little more than that. Her greeting was less than enthusiastic as she limply shook Darnell's hand. A statuesque beauty, Regine stood at least six feet tall to Darnell's five feet, seven inches. In her early thirties, her olive skin was flawless. Her luxuriant brown hair framed an exquisite face dominated by hazel eyes that were reserved for Thad only. At first, she had seemed surprised when he arrived with someone. She quickly turned territorial as she inspected Darnell from head to toe.

"I didn't know that you and Thad were friends," she stated coolly.

"We aren't." Darnell turned her back to the two of them and began to inspect the artwork on the walls.

Thad could see from Darnell's stance that she didn't appreciate Regine's attitude. Inwardly, he groaned. He knew Regine, and as tough as she was, he doubted that she was a match for Darnell. The woman had no idea what she was in for if she pushed Darnell too far. He hadn't come here for a cat fight. All he wanted was a painting.

At one time, he and Regine had been "an item," according to the press. In reality, they had dated for a few months and then parted. She was a jealous, possessive woman, and their parting had been less than amicable. A year had passed since he'd seen her. He hadn't heard from her again until a few weeks ago when she called to tell him about the gallery and the availability of the Bearden painting. At the time, he had suspected that there might be more behind the telephone call, and given her present demeanor, he recognized that his suspicions had more than likely been correct.

Thad met Regine's questioning look at Darnell's comment with a shrug and changed the subject. "When can I see the Bearden?"

As Regine continued to hang onto him, engaging in chit-chat about people and places he had forgotten long ago, he watched Darnell out of the corner of his eye as she studied the paintings, lithographs and prints, seemingly oblivious to them both. He wanted to join her and regain the camaraderie that their common interest had created on the way to the gallery. He found that he enjoyed those rare times when the two of them got along. She was intelligent, introspective, and also pretty good with the one-liners.

Darnell was aware of Thad's scrutiny, but she chose to ignore him. After all, she was here against her will. Sure, she had enjoyed the rest of the journey with him after getting over the shock of being kidnapped, but that was then, this was now. She did not appreciate being in this gallery and being given the evil eye by the Wicked Witch of the West.

"We're going to see the Bearden, Darnell. Are you coming?"

She turned at Thad's inquiry. For a moment, she hesitated, wanting to tell him that she wouldn't think of interfering with his liaison with the exotic Regine. But the moment passed, common sense overruled, and she nodded. She joined Thad and Regine as they moved up the winding staircase to the second floor.

The trip to the gallery proved fruitful for them both. After viewing the Bearden, which Thad purchased on the spot, Darnell discovered a rare Varnetta Honeywood print. After making arrangements for delivery of their purchases, they prepared to head back to Carmel.

With a forced smile Regine held out her hand to Darnell. "Well, this has been a profitable showing. I hope that you are pleased with your purchase."

Darnell shook her hand graciously, returning her smile. Despite the cool reception she had received earlier, she had to admire Regine as a businesswoman. She was a whiz when it came to making a sale.

"I'm very pleased. Thank you, and good evening."

Regine had a less formal farewell planned for Thad. Standing flush with him, she kissed him tenderly.

Darnell sighed impatiently. Why didn't they just get a room?

"I'll wait in the car," she announced to no one in particular as she exited the gallery, slamming the door behind her.

Thad barely noticed her departure as he recovered from Regine's affectionate farewell. She had caught him off guard again, and he didn't like it.

"What are you up to, Regine?"

Ignoring his question, Regine had one of her own. "What are you up to? What's going on between you and Darnell Cameron?"

Thad frowned at the audacity of her inquiry but decided to choose diplomacy over confrontation. He'd had enough conflict for one day.

"You're a *friend*, Regine. We go way back and I value you as a person, so let me just say that I really appreciate the business we do together, and I want to thank you for the tip on the Bearden painting."

He left the gallery with her question unanswered. As he and Darnell drove away, neither of them noticed Regine's malevolent glare as she stood in the gallery entrance watching them.

Headed back to the Peninsula, Darnell still felt tense from her encounter with the gallery owner. She didn't care who Thad slept with, but she would have thought that he would have better taste than Regine Lexy. The woman was a phony! Deciding that Regine wasn't worth further thought, Darnell occupied herself with the passing scenery until Thad broke the silence.

"Do you think they recognized you, too?" He knew the question was frivolous, but he wanted her to talk. He wanted a return of the connection that they had found previously. He had really enjoyed it.

Darnell turned confused eyes toward him. "What are you talking about?"

"Those people in the car back there. They spotted me when I was coming down the steps of the gallery. I could tell they recognized me. They started to do a U-turn. That's why I took off so quickly. Didn't you notice?"

Darnell shrugged. "No, I didn't. She turned back to the window. The sun was setting. She was anxious to get home.

Thad frowned. Not the cold shoulder again. What had he done this time? He tried again.

"I don't think they saw you, but we can't be too careful. We wouldn't want anybody to think that we're together. Perish the thought!"

Mistaking his teasing for sarcasm, Darnell turned to him. Her generous mouth was set as her eyes skittered across his face. "Yes, perish it quickly."

Thad sighed. "Are you hungry? We'll be heading into the Santa Cruz Mountains. We can grab a burger first."

"Nope, I'm not hungry." Her voice was a monotone.

Thad had had enough. "What's with you? You run hot and cold more often than a faucet! And what was that little performance back there at Regine's?"

Darnell snapped her head around so fast that she thought it might come off her neck. Performance? Did he say *performance*? One of his girlfriends takes a dislike to her and he accuses *her* of a performance?

Her voice was granite. "If one was given, it was mutual. I suggest that you keep your mouth shut and your eyes on the road. There seems to be a slowdown ahead."

She was right. For nearly two hours Thad and Darnell sat in standstill traffic while an accident was cleared ahead of them. Thad was determined not to say another word to this wacky woman, and the sentiment seemed to be mutual as Darnell ignored him. Eventually, she scooted down in her seat, closed her eyes, and fell asleep.

It was dark when she awakened. Looking at the clock, Darnell stretched the kinks out of her body.

"It looks like we finally got out of that mess. How far are we up the mountain?"

Thad didn't answer. He was still irritated about their earlier exchange. Gripping the wheel, he kept his eyes on the road. *Women!* They were nothing but trouble. He didn't know why he continued to bother with them, especially this one. Forget the script! Forget everything! He had made every possible attempt to be civil to Darnell over the past few days, and what had he gotten for his kindness? Slapped in the face every time. If he hadn't been raised to be a gentleman, he would drop Darnell Cameron off on the side of the road and let her cute little butt hitchhike home.

He glanced at her with the thought in mind. She was looking at the speedometer.

"You're going a little fast in these mountains, aren't you?" Darnell looked up through the front windshield at the blackness ahead of them as they climbed the winding mountain highway leading to Santa Cruz. It was a dangerous trek in broad daylight, and at night it could be treacherous.

Thad grunted unappreciatively. On top of everything else, she was a backseat driver! Annoyed, but not wanting to frighten her or harm them both, he heeded her warning and slowed the car down a little. At that instant, there was a pop, and the car swerved to the left.

Darnell gasped, her eyes wide with fear. Thad fought for control of the car. With lightening reflexes, he turned the steering wheel left, right, left, and finally gave the wheel a sharp right. The car careened off the paved highway onto a gravel road, spitting rocks and dust in its path.

CHAPTER 7

Frantically, Thad fought to control the steering wheel, avoiding the brake until he had command of the vehicle. Finally, he brought the car to an abrupt stop. Thankfully, their seatbelts held them.

For a moment Thad sat immobilized as he uttered a silent prayer of thanks. He turned to Darnell, who was trembling but unharmed.

"Are you okay?"

She nodded, hugging herself in an effort to stop shaking. "What . . . what happened?"

Thad peered out the window into the surrounding darkness, pierced only by the glare of the car headlights. "I heard a popping sound. I think the tire blew."

Opening the door, he stepped out into the night and groped his way to the back of the car to confirm his suspicion. Reappearing a few seconds later, he reached through the open window and retrieved the car key. "I was right. It's a flat."

Feeling his way to the rear of the car again, he fumbled with the lock until the trunk opened, then, aided by the trunk light, he rummaged around inside looking for tools to change the tire. While she waited for him to return, Darnell's breathing gradually returned to normal. They had survived, thanks to God and thanks to Thad's skillful driving. She said a prayer of gratitude for both.

Thad reappeared and slid into the driver's seat, slamming the door behind him. He wasn't happy.

"What's wrong?"

He sighed. "No jack."

"No jack?" Darnell echoed. "This is a new car. What could have happened to the jack?"

"I wonder." He couldn't keep the sarcasm out of his voice. He glanced at the glowing clock on the dashboard. "It's not too late. We seem to be on an access road, not far off the highway. I hear cars going by. I'm with the Auto Club, I'll call for . . ."

He was about to reach for the console between the bucket seats when he remembered that he wasn't in his car. Did this car have a telephone? He flipped up the console. It was empty. He slammed it down. "So much for Plan A. Let's go to Plan B."

Reaching in his jacket pocket, he whipped out his cell phone. The flashing message on the screen and the look on his face told Darnell the problem.

"Low battery?"

Thad nodded. "Have you got your cell phone on you?"

Darnell opened her purse to withdraw it and was met with a surprise—no telephone. She sighed. "I changed purses. It must be in the other one. But I do have a small flashlight on my keychain." She held it up for him to see.

They began to consider alternate plans. Walking back to the highway to hitchhike wasn't a good idea. The flashlight they had was too small to be of much service, and standing on the narrow mountain highway was dangerous and unwise. Neither one of them remembered seeing an emergency roadside phone, and neither had any idea where the nearest one could be. The most prudent idea was to spend the night in the car. At daybreak, they could make their way to the highway and get assistance.

Thad hated to admit it, but this big car was going to come in handy. It was roomy, and they could stretch out. He felt guilty about the predicament they were in. She wouldn't be stuck in these mountains if he hadn't forced her to come with him. Look where it had gotten them. It got cold in the mountains, and she was wearing shorts. They weren't practical for mountain temperatures, and he was concerned.

"Are you cold?"

Hugging herself, Darnell rubbed her bare arms. "Yes, I am. I was thinking that we can turn the headlights off, and maybe we could keep the dash light on for a short while to get settled, then we'd better turn it off, too. We may need to crank the car for heat later."

Thad didn't want to tell her that it wasn't only the battery that they had to worry about. He had failed to buy gas on their way back to the Peninsula. His plan had been to stop in Santa Cruz to fill up. It was a decision he now regretted. He didn't know how long they could keep warm.

"May I use that flashlight?" he asked. Darnell complied.

With the aid of the small light, he made his way to the trunk once again, then returned to the front seat carrying a leather Louis Vuitton overnight bag. He had transferred it from his sports car to the rental car when they were at the garage. With the dash light still illuminating the interior, he opened the bag and withdrew a knit pullover sweater. He handed it to Darnell. "Put this on."

Darnell slipped it over her head. The garment was much too big. The sleeves covered her hands and flopped around limply as she tried to push them up her arms.

Thad laughed. "Here, give me your arm. Let me fold those sleeves for you."

Leaning toward her, he took her arm in his hands and meticulously began to fold the sleeve up her arm. Darnell shifted in her seat, unsettled by his closeness and the tantalizing smell of his cologne. She could feel herself growing warmer, and she knew that it wasn't because of the sweater.

Thad laid her right arm gently in her lap and started to roll her left sleeve. Darnell wanted to snatch her arm away, but how silly would that be? After all, he had done nothing to warrant such behavior except to escalate her heartbeat.

"I want to apologize for getting you into this situation," Thad said, breaking the silence between them. His head was bowed as he continued his chore.

Darnell was impressed by the sincerity in his tone. He didn't strike her as being a humble man, which made an apology from him a major event. However, that paled compared to the effect his voice was having on her. It was low, husky, and very sexy. She cleared her throat, unsure of her own voice. She hoped it sounded steady because she certainly didn't feel that way.

"Don't worry about it. You saved our lives tonight."

Thad lifted his head to look at her. The sleeve was folded, but he was still holding her arm, gently caressing it with his thumb. "Yes, but if I had taken you home in the first place, you wouldn't have been in the car when the tire blew."

Self-consciously, Darnell withdrew from his grasp. "That's true, but if I wasn't with you, you'd be out here in these mountains by yourself and wouldn't have anyone here to protect you."

It took Thad a second to get what she was saying. Then his booming laughter echoed throughout the car.

"That was a good one!" It was hard to believe that a short while ago he had been ready to toss her out on the highway from a moving car. Now, he was actually enjoying being with her. The mountain air must be affecting his brain.

With a sigh of regret, he got out of the car and moved to the roomier back seat. Darnell followed his movements.

"What are you doing?"

"It's too cramped up there. I need leg room," he explained, knowing that what he was saying wasn't entirely true. He wasn't about to tell her that he needed to put distance between them. Being so close to her was a bit too tempting. In spite of their constant differences, she did arouse the male in him. They were beginning to establish a camaraderie, and he didn't want to blow it.

Now settled comfortably in the back seat, he watched as Darnell shifted her position in the front seat, stretching her legs over the console and onto the empty driver's seat. She rested her sandal-clad feet against his overnight bag. He noticed that her toenails were pedicured and that the dark red polish matched that on her manicured fingernails. *Sexy.*

"Open the bag, and you'll find some clean socks inside. You're going to need something on your feet tonight when it gets cold."

Much to Thad's relief, Darnell did as he suggested. She needed to cover those toes. Actually, she needed to cover her entire body. Darnell Cameron was simply too sexy for her own good. She was also enterprising, self-sufficient, stubborn, and demanding. She was different than most of the woman he had been with over the years, that was for sure. He was a man used to having women cater to him. With Darnell, there was no fear of that happening. She took nothing from him, and strange as it might seem, he liked that about her. As hard as he tried *not* to, he was beginning to like her. Too bad the sentiment was not returned. But he wasn't a bad guy. She needed to know that.

"Hey, Darnell, I've got something to ask you."

"What?" Her tone was cautious.

Thad swallowed, surprised by his sudden anxiety about the question he was about to ask. "What do you think of me?"

Darnell paused. Where had that come from? If she didn't know better she would think that her answer really mattered to him. Dismissing that thought, she answered honestly, "I think that you're a selfish, self-centered, spoiled brat with no social conscience. You have an overinflated ego, but no self-pride. Plus, you have little regard for women except as sex objects, and . . ."

"Never mind!" Thad interrupted, angry and crushed by her harsh assessment. "I'm sorry I asked."

"I can only go by what I've seen so far and by what I've read."

"You, of all people, can't tell me that you believe everything you read in the media!"

"Of course not, but . . ."

"Well, maybe there are some things I've read about you that I choose to believe, too. Like, how you and that guy you're with . . ."

"Lance?" Darnell tensed. "What have you read about me and Lance?"

"That you're both eggheads and that you spend most of your time together reading medical journals and listening to opera."

Darnell snorted. "Oh, please!"

"Please what? Please believe it, or please don't believe it?" The temporary camaraderie had gone out the window. The malice in the inquiry was barely masked. "You're telling me that you believe what you've read about *me* but I'm not to do the same. That's hypocritical."

"So this playboy image of yours is a total lie?" Darnell was skeptical.

"I've had my share of women, I won't deny that, but if I'd had all the women that the media say I've had, then I wouldn't have time to walk and talk. I'd spend it all in bed."

"And you haven't?"

"No." Thad shook his head. "I haven't. And I don't know what you think that you've *seen* so far as my attitude toward women, but believe it or not, my parents raised me to respect women, and I do. I also like them. I have three older sisters, and I wouldn't want anyone to disrespect them. So I've taken pains not to treat any woman I've known like that."

Against the illuminating light from the dash, Thad watched Darnell assessing his words. He wanted her to believe him. Her devastating assessment of his character hurt. He had always thought of himself as a good person. People liked him. He liked himself. Why couldn't she? He wasn't some immoral playboy, and he didn't want her to think that he was.

It was at that moment that he made a decision. For the next few days, he was going to put his interest in getting her to do his movie aside. Instead, he would concentrate on the two of them getting acquainted. If they stayed on this continuous collision course, there would be no way for them to work together. His script was a sizzling love story, and it would hardly be believable if its two co-stars looked as though they hated each other. His voice filtered through the tense silence between them.

"I want to make a proposal."

Darnell drew back suspiciously. He hadn't been able to mask the pain in his voice at her scathing personality assessment, and while she hadn't meant to be harsh, just honest, she wasn't sure that he wouldn't retaliate.

"What kind of proposal?"

"We've spent weeks fighting with one another, but rarely have we listened to each other. It seems that we've judged each other by what others have said and little else. Let's throw out all that past garbage and try to really get to know each other."

Darnell started to speak, but he leaned forward, silencing her effort with a finger to her lips. "Just let me finish. I'm not trying to give you a come-on line. I just don't want to fight anymore. We're stuck here on this mountain overnight. So let's agree to try and get along. That's not too much to ask, is it?"

In the shadow of the dimly lit interior, Darnell studied him closely. He appeared earnest, and she had been unfair to him regarding his image. He was right. They needed to abandon their childish behavior and start acting like adults. If she were honest with herself, she would have to admit that Thad really wasn't that bad. He did have his moments, and he was right about the media. What did she have to lose trying to get along with him? She shook her head in agreement.

"All right. It sounds good to me."

Grinning, Thad stuck his hand out. "To the beginning of a brand new friendship."

She slipped her smaller hand into his and shook it. "To the beginning."

Moody slammed the telephone down on its cradle. He had product missing. A mistake had been made on the other end, and somebody was going to pay. Not only was this costing him money, it was interfering with his personal plans. What he thought would take a few days to solve looked as though it would take longer. This was time that he had planned on using to further implement his plans in Carmel, and he was angry.

Settling back in his chair, he allowed his thoughts to drift to Darnell. He had been so close to meeting her, and now it would have to wait. He wondered where she was, what she was doing. He would give anything to be wherever she was now.

Tossing the thought aside, he resolved that the most immediate need was to take care of the business at hand so that he could return quickly to the West Coast. With that in mind, he picked up the telephone and started dialing.

CHAPTER 8

Thad and Darnell spent the next few hours on the mountain trying to stay as comfortable as possible until daylight. They donned the remainder of Thad's clothing from his overnight bag to keep warm, and managed to temporarily relieve their hunger with a package of peanut butter crackers they found buried in his bag. In an effort to preserve the battery, they shut off all of the car lights and entertained each other in the dark. Thad did snippets of monologue from his old comedy routines, while Darnell treated him to a preview of songs she had written for her next CD.

"No wonder you can command an audience," he said after she had finished. "You're awesome."

"Thank you." She smiled, pleased by the compliment. "Your talent is pretty awesome, too."

"Aw shucks," he grinned, equally as pleased. "My talent is nothing compared to yours. All I do is imitate my father. He's hilarious. When we were young, he kept my sisters and me in stitches. I wanted to be just like him, so I became good at making people laugh, especially when I was in trouble."

"It sounds like you and your father are close."

"We are. My three sisters are much older than I am, and being the only boy and the baby of the family, I guess that made me kind of special."

Darnell grunted. "You mean spoiled."

Thad chuckled, "Okay, I admit it. I was a wee bit spoiled, but my dad and I were inseparable, and he kept me on the right path. I learned a lot from him. How about you? I've read that your father is dead, but were you two close when he was alive?"

Darnell shook her head. "No. He died before I was born."

"That's rough."

"Yes, I would have liked to have gotten to know him."

She sounded wistful. He wanted her to keep talking. "What did your father do for a living?"

"Construction."

"He was a construction engineer?"

"No, he never went to college. He was a construction worker. According to Mama, he was gone a lot. He did jobs all over the place for some man that he worked for."

"What did he build?"

"I don't know, houses, I guess." Darnell shifted in the front seat to get more comfortable. Thad certainly asked a lot of questions. "My mother adored him. She talks about him as though he walked on water. They were young when they got married, and they loved each other like crazy. She claims that I have his temperament."

"Hot one minute and cold the other?" He knew that she couldn't see the smirk on his face in the dark.

"No, deadly, and don't you forget it." Stretching, Darnell stifled a yawn. "It's getting late, and I'm tired. I think I'll try to get some sleep." She adjusted her body to make herself comfortable. "Goodnight."

Amused by her retort to his last question, Thad echoed her "Goodnight." He had hoped that they could talk longer so that he could learn more about her, but no matter. They were enjoying each other's company, and for now that was enough.

The next morning, a highway worker stumbled on the disabled car and got the surprise of his life when two of the biggest stars in the country tumbled from its interior. An hour later, Thad and Darnell were headed down the mountain, toward Carmel, laughing about their mountain adventure. Stopping in Santa Cruz, they bought breakfast from a drive-through window, then found a secluded place to park and enjoy their meals. The camaraderie between them felt good. Thad wanted to prolong the feeling.

Finishing his meal, he sat enjoying the pleasure on Darnell's face as she took a bite of her breakfast sandwich. From their many conversations during their night on the mountain he had learned that Darnell wasn't adventurous. She liked control. She didn't like surprises. Maybe it was time for that to change.

"Say, do they still have that boardwalk with the amusement park here in Santa Cruz?"

Darnell shrugged. "I don't know." Taking a bite of her sandwich, she looked up to see a mischievous gleam in Thad's eyes. Instantly, she knew what he was thinking. "No, Thad! We can't go to an amusement park!"

He grinned. "Why not?"

"Suppose we get recognized? We're still in the clothes we had on yesterday. We look a mess. We must smell like pigs . . ."

"We'll have fun," he said pulling the car out of its parking place. "Come on."

Darnell searched for excuses. "But . . . but . . ." She fought her rising excitement at the possibility. Yet, she had to be practical. "I've got to get home. Mrs. Sharon will be worried sick when she discovers that I haven't been there all night."

"Call her when we get to the boardwalk. I'm calling my housekeeper. He was expecting me yesterday."

The word *he* caught her off guard. "You've got a male housekeeper?"

"Yep, his name is Donald. I just promoted him to my assistant since my old one moved away. Donald's a jack-of-all-trades and he cooks, too," Thad said proudly.

Darnell wasn't sure whether to believe him or not. Thad Stewart, the chauvinist, had a male housekeeper. *That* was a surprise!

At the boardwalk they made their telephone calls. Thad let Darnell have the phone so that his very proper, and very efficient sounding housekeeper-assistant, could confirm Thad's equal opportunity hiring policy to her.

The rest of the day, they spent enjoying themselves. They rode every ride, played games of skill and pigged out on hot dogs and cotton candy. Thad won Darnell two stuffed animals, and she was as excited as a child at Christmas.

It was early evening when they arrived back in Carmel. At Darnell's doorway, Thad had another surprise.

"I'll pick you up at ten tomorrow morning," he informed her. "I've decided to stay in town another couple of days. I want to show you something."

She resisted. "Thad, I've got things to do."

"They can wait. You're on vacation."

"But I can't just run all over the place with you."

Thad pushed. "Why not? We're friends now, aren't we? Just dress casual tomorrow." With a quick peck on her lips, Thad left a stunned Darnell standing in her doorway. He had jumped into his car and driven away before she recovered.

The kiss had been unexpected. She wouldn't have believed that it had happened except for the tingling she felt in her limbs. Slowly, she exhaled. Being with Thad was like being caught in a whirlwind. It barely left her time to breathe. What had happened since yesterday morning when she left her house for a trip to the garage? How could her relationship with Thad have changed so quickly? She was actually beginning to like the man.

Entering the house, Darnell found Mrs. Sharon about to leave for the day. She raised a brow at Darnell's wrinkled clothing, mussed hair, and the two large teddy bears she was carrying.

"Good evening." Darnell passed her and floated up the stairway.

"Good evening." Mrs. Sharon smiled. From the looks of it, the sparks that she had so astutely observed the other day might be turning into flames.

Thad arrived at Darnell's front door at ten sharp the next morning. He was as animated as he had been yesterday, except today he was driving a yellow Porche.

"How do you like it?"

Darnell hedged. "Well, it is bright."

Thad ran his hand lovingly over the car's shiny hood. "I took the car you got me back to the rental company and exchanged it for this little baby. This is more my style."

"I would have never guessed," Darnell deadpanned.

Thad smiled. "I figured that you weren't a yellow car kind of woman, but you could use a little spice in your life."

"You don't call being kidnapped and sleeping in a car in the Santa Cruz mountains a little spice?"

"Okay, I'll admit that those things were a little unexpected, but today is well planned. I want to take you to Big Sur."

Her eyes widened. "Big Sur?"

"Have you ever been there?"

"No."

"Then you're in for the time of your life."

He was right. As they drove along the highway, enjoying the panoramic vistas, she found Thad's enthusiasm infectious. He reveled in the surrounding beauty, pointing out sights and sounds along the way. He had purchased a dozen books on the Big Sur area and seemed to have read them all overnight as he recited tidbits about the area and the scenic highway on which they traveled.

They stopped for lunch at Nepenthe Restaurant. "It was built in the 1940s as a honeymoon cottage for Orson Welles and his movie star wife, Rita Hayworth," he informed her.

Darnell had worried about having lunch at the tourist hangout, but Thad assured her that they wouldn't be recognized. Again, he was right.

He had chosen Julia Pfeiffer Burns State Park as the day's destination. It was one of several parks in the Big Sur area. His choice turned out to be perfect. Along the miles of scenic coastline, they discovered canyons laced with trickling creeks, groves of towering redwood trees, a fifty-foot, solid-rock tunnel and the magnificent beauty of Saddle Rock Falls, a cascading waterfall that fell straight into the ocean. It was breathtaking.

They took endless photos. Awed by the natural beauty, Darnell chastised herself for not having taken the time out before to enjoy such moments, and she was grateful to Thad for orchestrating this day. They ended their adventure at the waterfall.

By the time Thad pulled up to Darnell's house, the moon had made its appearance in a star-filled sky. He turned to find Darnell slumped against the seat asleep, her braids tousled in wild disarray and her sunglasses perched precariously on her nose.

Easing the glasses off, he threaded his fingers through the errant braids. With the lightest of touches, his knuckles skimmed the contours of her jaw. She was so beautiful, so tantalizing. Thad drew closer. The urge to kiss her was strong. All day he had wanted to taste those lips. This woman filled him with more conflicting emotions than he had ever experienced, and after today he could no longer deny what he knew to be true. He wanted Darnell Cameron. He drew closer. It wasn't just her body that he wanted. His lips caressed hers lightly. He wanted her admiration, her respect, her devotion. He wanted *her*.

She stirred. He drew back. *But* she belonged to someone else. That was a boundary that he had never crossed.

Darnell opened her eyes to find herself staring into Thad's eyes.

He greeted her softly. "Hello, sleepyhead. You're home."

She sat up groggily and surveyed the familiar surroundings. She felt a sense of loss at having left the beauty of Big Sur behind.

Thad escorted her to the front door. They stood in the doorway face to face.

"Today was great, Thad. Thank you so much. I haven't had so much fun in years."

"You mean you and your boyfriend don't do things like this?" He was fishing.

"Oh, there have been good times." She measured her words carefully. She wasn't about to let him know that she had never done anything remotely like this with Lance, but Thad was quick. His grin told her that he had guessed the truth.

"I'm determined that the good times will keep rolling. You're too young to be so serious. You need to lighten up. So if you think today was fun, wait until tomorrow."

"Tomorrow?" Darnell was receptive.

Thad grinned. "Yep, I promise you surprises galore."

With a wink, he left Darnell standing at her front door wondering what could possibly be next, and looking forward to it.

CHAPTER 9

Thad kept his promise, and for the rest of the week Darnell's world was filled with a whirlwind named Thad Stewart. They took a tour of the Hearst Castle, where some overzealous fans recognized them and put an early end to that excursion. He took her on a ride through the redwood forest on the Big Trees Railroad, an old steam train that carried its riders to Roaring Camp, an 1880s logging town. There were picnics nestled in hidden coves along the coast, a bike ride on the Monterey Pier, and a trip to the fabulous Monterey Aquarium. On each excursion, they engaged in discussions, from philosophy to celebrity, and they seemed to agree on nothing. At times, their raucous debates sounded more like battles between warring nations.

In Darnell's opinion, Thad was badly misinformed about nearly everything. He was stubborn and not easily swayed, but she had to admit that he was also quite intelligent. He proved to be a formidable debater, using his silver tongue well. His counterarguments on the topics discussed were insightful and well thought out. He was never reluctant to challenge her position on issues and rarely backed down. It was stimulating.

From kindergarten to college, Darnell had always been the special one, the gifted one. All of her life, she had worn those titles with an air of arrogance. Most people seemed intimidated by her intellect, but not Thad. He enjoyed it. She liked that about him. As a matter of fact, with each passing day she liked him more and more.

Thoughts of the adventurous week they had spent together were on Darnell's mind as she sat across from him eating dinner. At the end of their latest excursion, they had discovered a Jamaican restaurant in which they now dined. It was nestled on a nondescript side street in Monterey, not far from the Wharf. Over plates of jerk chicken and fried plantains, they talked. Thad's sense of humor was razor sharp, and he kept Darnell laughing. At his best, the man could charm the devil out of hell.

"You know, Thad, I realize that I sound like a broken record, but I've got to tell you again, I haven't had so much fun in my life."

Looking up from his plate in time to catch the dazzling smile that Darnell bestowed on him, Thad's pulse raced into overdrive. He was amazed at her girlish pleasure over simple things. Today, they had gone hiking in the mountains, and she had been like a kid in a candy store. He had been delighted at the pleasure it gave her.

"I'm glad that you've enjoyed yourself these past few days, Doe Eyes, I'm here to please." Thad returned to his meal, unaware that he had uttered the nickname that he had secretly bestowed on her.

Darnell blinked in surprise. *Doe Eyes?* Where had that come from? It was the first time he had called her that. Yet where she once would have challenged him for calling her something other than her name, she let it pass. What a difference a week had made. With a satisfied sigh, Darnell finished her meal.

Thad caught her sigh of satisfaction. She was happy and so was he. How he had kept his hands off her so far he would never know. But if he spent one more day, hour or minute with her he wasn't sure his chivalry would last. Darnell had cast her sensuous spell on him.

Sensuous. Yes, she was that. Ray had nailed it.

Last night, he had found himself lying in his hotel suite unable to sleep. Thoughts of Darnell consumed him—the way she looked, the way she smiled, everything she said and did. Darnell was unique, a rare gem, so different from the other women he knew. She was passionate about her beliefs, yet willing to listen to opposite opinions. She seemed to have no pretenses, and she was fearless—willing to try almost anything he suggested. And was she smart! Darnell was one of the most intelligent people he had ever met. She was not only articulate and well read, but she spoke three languages fluently. She took pride in her intellect. He *really* liked that.

Despite his media persona as a partying playboy, he was no dummy himself. Few people knew that he spoke two foreign languages, played the piano flawlessly, and had graduated from college magna cum laude. Information like that didn't fit the image. Until now, he had never met a woman who had kept him studying day and night to keep up with a mind so sharp, and he loved every minute of it. No, Darnell was nothing like the empty-headed Hollywood bimbos who constantly threw themselves at him. No, not Darnell.

Oh, she still knew how to irritate the hell out of him when she really wanted to, but she also knew how to excite him. As she sat across the table from him babbling about some political theory that she had formulated, he smiled at the friend he had come to cherish—the woman he had come to love.

Thad jumped, startled at this last thought. His action stopped Darnell in mid-sentence.

"What's wrong?" Her brow furrowed. "Did something scare you?"

"No, nothing," he stammered unconvincingly. "Nothing's wrong."

Avoiding her gaze, his eyes fell back on his plate. He didn't want her to see the desire that was becoming more and more difficult to conceal. When the small band that had been setting up when they first arrived began to play, he reached across the table and took Darnell's hand.

"Come on, let's dance."

It didn't take long for Thad to realize that the invitation was a major mistake. The song that the band played was a love song with a reggae beat, and he was quickly reminded of the sensual skill with which Darnell danced. Every movement of her limber body was calling him like a moth to a burning flame. The closer Thad got, the hotter the fire.

Darnell could also feel the heat. Consumed by the tantalizing beat of the music, she was lost in the joy of dancing until she opened her eyes. The look in Thad's eyes nearly singed her; it clearly said that he wanted her. Testing the waters, he moved a little bit closer, held her a little bit tighter. She didn't retreat.

Their bodies flush, the couple moved fluidly, rhythmically, in perfect synchronization. It was as if they were born to dance—together. The music soothed them . . . moved them . . . enticed them. And then the music stopped.

Darnell looked around the room to find that she and Thad had become the center of attention.

Someone whispered, "That's her, that's Darnell Cameron."

The ripple of a murmur followed. Someone else added, "And that looks like Thad Stewart." With those words, they both knew that their day was over.

Reining in his hormones, Thad tossed a wad of bills on the table, took Darnell by the hand, and led her through the restaurant and out the door. They walked to the car in silence, more aware of each other than ever.

With a racing heart and trembling hands, Darnell fumbled for the handle on the car door. Impatiently, she yanked, desperate to escape into the car's interior.

"Let me in!" she implored, not daring to look at Thad, who stood gazing down at her.

"That's what I'm asking you to do." Thad's voice was low, calm, in stark contrast to the storm racing through his body. Reaching across her he opened the door for her easily and watched as she slid into the passenger seat. Closing the door after her, he stood for a moment attempting to gather his senses. He had thrown the gauntlet down with his words and actions. What happened after this point was up to her. All he knew was that Darnell Cameron was an aphrodisiac, and he was becoming addicted.

The silence between them continued as they drove to her house, fully aware of the sexual tension between them. At her front door Thad uttered a polite goodbye and quickly left. Darnell gave an audible sigh of relief before going inside.

Safe in her room, she lay across her bed berating herself for allowing Thad Stewart to get close to her. What in the world was her problem? She didn't have the time or the inclination to become Thad Stewart's latest conquest. Thank goodness he would be picking up his car tomorrow and driving back to Tiburon. Meanwhile, she had things to do.

Spotting the *Sensuous* script lying on the nightstand, she picked it up. She hadn't even had time to sit and read it. Yes, indeed, she had plenty of things to do, and Thad had become a distraction. The man had taken up too much of her time. She had to focus. The spell he had cast over her was temporary. Once he left town, things would get back to normal. That was how she liked things in her life, nice and normal.

CHAPTER 10

"What do you mean that you didn't get a chance to ask her? You were in Carmel for a week!" On the other end of the telephone line, Ray sounded incredulous. "What in the hell were you doing?" He paused. "On second thought, don't answer that. I don't want to know."

Thad sighed. "It wasn't like that, man." And it wasn't, but he had no way of explaining to Ray how it was.

Less than twenty-four hours earlier, he had picked up his sports car from Mr. Hazelwood and driven out of the Monterey Peninsula like a bat out of hell. He had been running scared. Darnell Cameron was evoking emotions in him that he had difficulty comprehending. Lust he could rationalize, but this tug at his heart whenever he was near her was different from anything he had felt for a woman before. Nevertheless, he tried to provide Ray with an explanation.

"I've been trying to soften her up a bit, get her to like me. You know we haven't been getting along . . ."

"That's no revelation," Ray said with a sigh of disgust. "But how long does it take to ask one simple question? Man, if you ask me . . ."

"Which I didn't."

"Yeah, but I'm going to tell you anyway. I think you're just using the movie as an excuse to get in the woman's panties."

Thad grew defensive. "I'm just trying to get the job done, Ray. That's all."

"Uh huh," Ray sneered. "And when do you plan on getting this job *done?*"

"Well, uh . . ."

"It's not that hard, Thad. Just ask the woman to read the script and consider doing the movie. All she can say is yes or no. We'd like to start production in this century."

Ray hung up, frustrated and skeptical. Thad knew that he had the right to be. Time was money, and he was wasting time. It was all too unsettling. He had taken the coward's way out—escape. He was more of a man than that. He had to face Darnell. As far as he was concerned, the script had become secondary. At this point, Darnell Cameron and what he was feeling for her had become the primary concern in his life. He had to see her again.

It was done. The missing product had been traced to its source, an associate of his contact in Columbia who had objected to the liaison that had been brokered by Moody. Unfortunately for the fellow, his solution had been to try and steal product to set up his own personal deal. The result had been the loss of his life as well as those of his entire family. The Columbian cartel had mercy on no one and left no loose ends.

The crisis was over, and Moody was glad. It would take a little while longer to clean things up here on the East Coast before he could get back to the Monterey

Peninsula and continue executing his plans. Soon—very soon—he would be near her again. This time, nothing and no one would stand in his way.

Thad was gone. Darnell had expected to hear from him the day that he picked up his car, but she didn't. He had left Carmel without a word.

She had been annoyed at herself for feeling disappointed. After all, much to her surprise, they had become friends, and that was darn near a miracle considering where they had started. She had never expected it to happen.

She had been in her room berating herself for missing him when the buzzer at the front gate rang. It turned out to be a delivery person holding the largest box of flowers that she had ever seen. As she lifted the box lid, she gasped at the two dozen yellow roses laying in an array of colorful tissue paper. Written across the gold-trimmed card were two words—For You. There was no signature, but Darnell wasn't surprised. That was Thad—unpredictable.

A few hours later, another box of yellow roses arrived. There were three dozen this time, again with no signature. There were three words scribbled on the card this time—For You, Again.

As Darnell retired that evening, she glanced at the flowers displayed on the fireplace mantel and smiled. Thad Stewart had turned out to be a much different man than she had thought. His thoughtfulness in sending the roses had touched her, and a few days later when she went to the beach for her morning run, there he was, sitting on the water's edge waiting for her.

It was hard to ignore the skip of her heartbeat as she watched Thad slowly stand to his full height and flash that dimpled smile. He looked almost boyish as he spread his arms and yelled, "Surprise!" It was indeed.

"What are you doing here?"

Thad took a step closer. Could it be possible? Was she glad to see him? He knew that he was glad to see her. His heart had been racing all the way to Carmel. He kept his hands jammed in his sweatshirt pockets so that she wouldn't see them shaking.

"I'm here to go jogging," he answered evenly. He wanted to tell her how hard it had been to stay away.

Darnell cocked an eyebrow. "Oh, I see. You couldn't go jogging in Tiburon?"

Thad shook his head. "I don't have a jogging partner in Tiburon."

For some reason, the seriousness with which he answered her question struck Darnell as funny. She laughed. "You can't get enough, can you?"

Thad watched the way her eyes crinkled when she laughed, the way she threw her head back, hunched her shoulders and put her entire body into the joy of the moment. How he had missed her.

"No." His voice was husky. "I can't."

His words stopped her laughter. Her heart began to thump against her chest, and her mouth felt dry. But she kept her calm façade. "And you think you can keep up with me?"

Thad nodded, unable to trust his own voice. With a shrug, Darnell began to stretch. Thad joined her, and then further surprised her when they started jogging and he kept up during the entire distance. Although winded at the end, he didn't seem any worse for his efforts, and his grin was as wide as the ocean when Darnell complimented him on his improvement.

At the house, Mrs. Sharon welcomed Thad happily. They teased each other as he settled his frame at the table in the kitchen while Darnell went upstairs to take a shower.

"Are you going to join us?" asked Mrs. Sharon as she moved about the kitchen fixing breakfast.

Thad shrugged. "Thanks, I'd like to, but I'm all sweaty from the jog. I'll tell you what, I've got some sweats outside in the car, and I'll go get them and freshen up, if you don't mind. Then I can really chow down."

When he returned to the kitchen with his overnight bag, Mrs. Sharon led him to a bedroom suite located near Darnell's office. "You can clean up in here," she said, directing him inside. "This is Mr. Austin's room. There should be some toiletries in here."

Mrs. Sharon was out the door before it registered with Thad what she had said. *Mr. Austin's room?* He was so shocked by the revelation that for a moment he stood speechless. He couldn't believe what he had heard. Repeating her words in his head, he turned them over carefully and examined them. Lance slept in a separate bedroom from Darnell and on a different floor. What was that about?

He wanted to go to Mrs. Sharon and ask so badly that he had to force himself to stay in the room. As he stood under the shower, a million questions raced through his head. Was there trouble in paradise? He could only hope.

He knew that the resentment he felt against Lance Austin was irrational, but he didn't care. Lance had Darnell's heart, and he envied that. He wanted to respect their relationship, but he was finding that increasingly difficult to do.

Despite his reputation with the ladies, he had never made a move on another man's woman. He'd known as he was headed to Carmel that morning that his attraction to Darnell had spiraled out of control, but his need to see her again was so strong that reason hadn't been a consideration. He wasn't sure what to expect and had been thrilled by the positive reception. Never had he expected to hear anything like the statement made by Mrs. Sharon about Lance. He had the distinct feeling that what she divulged hadn't been accidental. It looked as though this trip would reap more benefits than he had imagined.

After his shower, he hurried to get dressed and rejoin Mrs. Sharon. Maybe she had some additional information she might like to share.

When Darnell returned to the kitchen, she found her housekeeper fussing over a refreshed and invigorated Thad. He was helping Mrs. Sharon make pancakes, and she was grinning from ear to ear. It was obvious that he had lost none of his appeal with the ladies.

After piling their plates with fluffy pancakes and sausage, Mrs. Sharon left Darnell and Thad alone to enjoy their meal. The mood was upbeat, charged with expectation. For Thad, it was the perfect time for him to bring up his movie script. He wanted to get it over with. After that, they could move on to other things.

"You know, Darnell, I want to ask you something."

She gave him a crooked smile. She had wondered what was behind his sudden reappearance. "Oh, yeah? What do you want to ask me?"

"Well, there's this script . . ."

The ring of the telephone stopped him in mid-sentence.

"Excuse me. I'm expecting a call." Darnell went to answer the telephone. "Hello?" Pause. "Hi, Lance. How are you?"

Thad went still. Silverware in hand, he turned toward Darnell. Her tone was casual, but the smile she wore lit up her face.

As she spoke softly on the telephone, she moved across the room, farther and farther away from Thad. Slowly, resentment began to build. So much for the two of them sleeping separately. He wanted to snatch the receiver from her hand and hang up on her super doctor. Suddenly, as if propelled by that thought, he marched across the kitchen and did just that.

Darnell stood stunned. She looked at Thad, then at the telephone receiver now back on its cradle, unable to believe what had happened. Her attention returned to him.

"Why did you do that?" She sounded like a small child who had been reprimanded. "He was calling all the way from South America!"

Pausing for a moment, Thad tried to formulate a rational explanation for his actions. He knew the real reason, but at the moment an alternative would do.

"Every time I come here, you've got a telephone hanging from your ear," he hissed. "I'm not playing second fiddle to a phone again. In short, lady, you're just rude, and I'm sick and tired of it."

Darnell was taken aback. "I'm sorry, *Mr. Stewart,* if I've offended you, but I still don't think that gives you the right to hang up on my boyfriend."

Boyfriend? The word cut him like a knife. Feeling justified in his indignation, Thad headed toward the door. If she wasn't going to admit that she had been in the wrong, then there was no point in remaining here. His voice was steel.

"I see that we're getting ready to get into an argument, so I'm heading back to Tiburon. You can think about what I said and call me later with an apology."

Darnell exploded as she stalked after him through the house to the front door. "An apology? An apology for what? You snatched the phone out of *my* hand. You owe *me* the apology!"

Thad hovered over her menacingly. "When hell freezes over!" With that, he slammed the front door firmly behind him.

Tearing out of her driveway, he nearly collided with a car slowing to turn into the driveway belonging to the house across the street. Blowing his horn at the culprit who dared block his way, Thad drove down the street, tires screeching, without looking back.

The car charging out of Darnell's driveway startled Moody as it came within inches of sideswiping his vehicle. Moody shouted an expletive at the retreating car as it disappeared down the street. He recognized it as the same one that had cut him off weeks ago under similar circumstances. Whoever was driving was reckless.

He had turned into his driveway when he started to become concerned. He didn't know if the driver had been angry, impatient, or simply irresponsible. He stopped the car and let it idle as he studied the house across the street in the rearview mirror. Had there been a problem at Darnell's house? Maybe he should go see if everything was all right. This would be the perfect opportunity to introduce himself. What luck!

After picking his car up at the airport, he had returned to his West Coast residence to resume his plan. He had never expected to have an opportunity so quickly. Besides, he needed to assure himself that everything was all right at her house.

Parking the car, he climbed out and walked across the street. He was about to push the buzzer at the entrance gates when they opened unexpectedly. A car appeared. He recognized Darnell's housekeeper as the driver. The gate closed behind her. Both Moody and Mrs. Sharon looked surprised to see each other. She rolled the driver's window down a crack.

"May I help you?" She surveyed the well-dressed man standing before her. Middle-aged, he was of medium height, with a smooth, light brown complexion framed by straight, dark hair that was streaked with gray. His eyes were dark, and the smile he flashed was friendly. Yet, she was wary. He was a stranger appearing at Darnell's gate. She was a celebrity, and although her fans adored her, that didn't mean that they all meant her well. Undetected, Mrs. Sharon pushed the car button that would alert the security patrol of potential problems. They made their appearance whenever summoned. Meanwhile, she observed the man cautiously as he spoke.

"Hello, I'm Mr. Waters, your new neighbor across the street. I came over to introduce myself and to see if everything was okay over here. I was turning into my house, and this car came tearing out of the driveway over here and almost hit me. I was concerned."

Mrs. Sharon relaxed a little. She had heard about the man who had rented the house across the street. This was him. Impressive. He appeared cultured and well-spoken. He seemed nice enough.

"No need for concern, everything is fine." That's all he had asked, and that was all she was telling him. She had heard the fight between Darnell and Thad, and there was no need to spread the woman's business.

Moody pressed. "I've been told that the singer Darnell Cameron lives here. I was wondering if she was available. I'm a big fan, as well as a neighbor. Is there a chance that I can introduce myself to her personally?"

Mrs. Sharon shook her head. "No. I'm afraid she's not receiving visitors today."

Although disappointed, Moody decided on retreat. He might need the housekeeper as an ally. His friendly smile broadened. "I understand, but nice meeting you, Mrs.—" He knew her name but didn't want her to know it. The lady was smart; she offered no further information.

"Nice meeting you too, Mr. . . ."

"Waters."

"I'm sorry, Mr. Waters. Thank you for stopping by." Case closed, Mrs. Sharon continued on her way just as the patrol car appeared. She stopped to inform them that the problem had been resolved, then headed down the street.

Moody smiled to himself as he crossed the street under the watchful eye of the security patrol. He knew that the housekeeper must have summoned them. The company had provided him with the same safety device when he moved into his house. It was good to know that they would respond in such a timely manner. However, Darnell was in no danger from him. On the contrary, it was his plan to see that she was protected every day of her life.

CHAPTER 11

"I don't care what you think, Ray! I want you to send that letter, and I want it sent today! I want her to have it in her hot little hands by tomorrow morning. She destroyed my property. She owes me some money, and I want it!" With that, Thad hung up on Ray, not giving him a chance to respond. He didn't want to hear that he was making a big mistake. Even two days after storming out of her house, he was still angry with Darnell, and he wanted to savor that anger.

Stalking through the house, he looked for his favorite sunglasses, but couldn't find them. Grabbing another pair, he headed out the door. Maybe a good run was what he needed to work off some of the nervous energy he was feeling. In the time since he left Carmel, nothing in his life seemed to work.

Thad ran along the Bay shoreline, forcing himself not to think about Darnell Cameron. As he passed an early morning sun worshipper stretched out on a blanket, a radio resting beside him, Darnell's voice interrupted the early morning calm. The sound settled like a dull ache in Thad's pounding heart. She had sung that song to him the night they had spent together in the mountains. He had been the first person outside her recording studio to hear it. It had been a humbling experience, but *she* wasn't humble. Darnell was spoiled, selfish, conceited, and rude! He would have thought that her mother had raised her to have better manners! Anger flared anew.

The woman would have to get on her knees and beg for his forgiveness if she ever wanted to see him again. With that thought, Thad ignored the pain of missing her, picked up his pace, and continued running.

Returning home, he showered, ate, and wandered his large house aimlessly, finally drifting upstairs to settle on the balcony outside his bedroom to read. It was a book that he had been discussing with Darnell, and he wanted to finish it so that he could discuss it with—

His mind raced across a long list of acquaintances and a very short list of intelligent friends. Other than Ray, who else did he know who read anything besides the show business newspaper *Variety*? Certainly not any of the women he dated. He doubted if the majority of them could read. Why did he date those airheads anyway? Sure, they were long on looks but definitely missing key elements of gray matter. He would be insisting on some intellect when it came to choosing women from now on. Darnell had said that he could do better.

Thad sat straight up. Oh, no! He was quoting her now! He fell back in the chaise lounge and groaned. Had she brainwashed him? What next?

With a heavy sigh, he wandered back into the house and flopped, belly first, onto his oversize bed. He had to admit that Darnell was brilliant. He had gained a lot from his acquaintance with her—more than he had from any other woman he had known. Thad rolled over on his back and stared at the pattern on his cathedral ceiling. He closed his eyes, disgusted with himself. He was thinking about that woman a little too much. There was no denying that he had wanted her at one time, but that was in the past. Peace and quiet had prevailed since he left her house, and he was enjoying it. Of course, he did miss her a *little* bit. It was normal to miss a friend. After all, she had been the only woman friend he had ever had outside his family.

He had never thought about having a female friend before, which Darnell would say was another one of his flaws. He could see her now with those graceful fingers curled into fists planted on her hips as she told him about himself. She was something.

Thad swallowed hard. He remembered when they were in Big Sur; she had climbed on some rocks and stood in awe as she viewed her surroundings. She had slipped trying to climb down, and he had caught her before she tumbled to the ground. Her firm breast had pressed against his chest. Those curvaceous hips had molded against him—

Thad's eyes flew open. He shook his head to clear the vision of her face, the feel of her body, the smell of her hair, of everything about her. He had to get her out of his mind. Getting to his feet, he stumbled to the bathroom and threw cold water on his face. He wanted the voice inside his head to stop repeating her name. He wanted it to stop reminding him that there would never be another woman in his life like her.

Darnell awoke from a fitful night's sleep with a headache. She hadn't been feeling well and had avoided going jogging yesterday, but she was determined to forge ahead on this day. She was rarely sick and took pride in the fact that since her career began, she had never missed a performance.

Pushing herself up in the bed, she glanced at the clock on her nightstand. It was six forty-five. Her body had become a human alarm clock, thanks to Thad Stewart. She shuddered at his name. He used to call around this time just to bug her. Thank goodness that was over.

She sighed. For a while, she'd thought she had found a friend. She had been wrong. The man was mentally unbalanced, and if she lived to be a hundred years old she would never understand him. She still didn't know what she had done to deserve being treated so rudely the other day, but that was ancient history, and so was he. Ignoring the feeling of loneliness that had plagued her since his departure, she got out of bed to get ready for the day.

She had taken her bath and was dressing when Mrs. Sharon knocked on the bedroom door. She entered at Darnell's request and handed her an overnight express envelope.

"I just signed for this. It's for you. I thought it might be important." Handing the envelope to Darnell, Mrs. Sharon started to leave, then turned.

"I forgot to tell you. The other day after Thad left, some guy who said that he had moved into that house across the street came over to see if everything was all right. I forgot his name."

"Oh?" The envelope she was holding held Darnell's attention, and she was barely listening to Mrs. Sharon.

"I told him there was no trouble. Things were fine."

"All right."

Knowing that she was preoccupied, Mrs. Sharon closed the door quietly behind her. Meanwhile, Darnell turned the envelope over in her hand, her brow furrowed in question. She noted the return address. It was from Thad's attorney.

Reluctantly, Darnell opened the envelope, and as she read its contents, she began to see red. It was a bill for $64.86, and with it a letter stating that this was the balance for the cost of one pale yellow, silk blend sweater, ruined a few weeks ago by Darnell Cameron. The letter demanded payment immediately and threatened action in Small Claims Court if it was not received within forty-eight hours.

That cinched it. Thad was certifiably insane! What else would have possessed him to pursue such foolishness?

Beside herself with indignation, Darnell was unable to sit still. Donning a skimpy jogging suit, she left the house and started to run the beach, trying to ignore her aching head. She didn't get far. She felt dizzy and nauseous. That did it! Thad Stewart was making her sick.

Returning home, she took a shower, then wrapped herself in her favorite robe. After a short nap, she felt a bit better. Going downstairs to the kitchen, she fixed herself a cup of steaming hot tea and plotted her revenge on Thad.

She knew that he would expect her to reduce herself to ranting and raving like a lunatic, but she refused to give him that satisfaction. She could ignore his childish antics, but knowing Thad, despite the resulting media circus, he probably would take this little stunt to Small Claims Court just to win some small victory.

She sipped and thought. Okay, he could have his $64.86. She would pay more than that to get rid of him. She would simply drive to Tiburon and tell Mr. Stewart face-to-face what she thought of him, mincing no words. It would take all of her self-control, but she would remain calm, and it would be *she* who would have the final word.

Darnell gave a satisfied chuckle. It would be worth the drive just to see the look on his face when she told him off. As the day progressed, however, her delight soon became secondary.

She had traveled through San Francisco and was approaching the Golden Gate Bridge when the headache returned. It was dull at first, and she dismissed it as being caused by tension from the traffic congestion she had encountered on her drive from the Peninsula. By the time she had crossed the bridge, her headache had intensified and her stomach roiled. Desperate, she took the nearest exit. It took her through the tourist hamlet of Sausalito in search of a pharmacy. Maneuvering the crowded streets proved difficult and dangerous as dizziness overcame her. Pulling into the nearest parking lot, Darnell brought the car to a stop and slumped against the seat. She could no longer dismiss how she was feeling. She was sick. She needed help, and she needed it now.

Thad jumped, reacting to the ringing telephone. He had been on edge all day. He knew that Darnell had received the bill by now and, knowing her, she would be contacting him to let him know exactly what she thought of his actions.

He was surprised that he could think clearly enough to react to anything. Yesterday, Ray had called to inform him that he had followed his directive and sent the letter. Then he had raked Thad over the coals for his "childish" behavior.

"Man, what you're doing is weak. Anybody would think that you're a jealous lover or something," he tossed out before they were disconnected. The comment didn't upset him. His astute friend hadn't told him anything that he didn't already know. Thad had figured out a long time ago that he was jealous of Lance Austin.

During the time he and Darnell had spent together, she hadn't mentioned Lance, but he was a silent presence between them. Thad knew the man only through what he had read, and the media made Lance sound as though he were some genius saint. Well, if he was *that* smart, he would have married Darnell a long time ago. It was clear that Lance was crazy, or even worse, a fool!

Darnell was unique. Unlike too many women in his life, she wasn't easily swayed by his charm or dimpled smile. She demanded things from him that no woman in his life had ever demanded—intellectual prowess, pride in and knowledge of his heritage, political and spiritual awareness. He respected the woman and he knew in his heart that he would do anything to gain her respect.

Last night, he had been plagued by erotic dreams of Darnell, and he had awakened with his body aching with want and need. The fact that he couldn't get her out of his head hadn't improved his disposition one bit. It had only been two days since he stormed out of her house, but Lord, did he miss her. He missed those flashing eyes, the way she tossed her head and sent those sexy braids flying in all directions. He missed the smell of the exotic body oil she wore. The aroma drove him insane.

It wasn't fair! He had found a woman he could love, and she belonged to somebody else.

The thought of loving her had crossed his mind once before, that night in the Jamaican restaurant, but he had dismissed it. Now, here alone with that thought, it was something he had to examine. Did he love her? He *could* love her. Yes, he *did* love Darnell Cameron! He was hooked on a woman who had a long, solid relationship with another man—a woman who, after the stunt he pulled, would never want to see him again.

It was the insistent ring of the telephone that brought Thad's thoughts back to the present. He sighed. It was probably Darnell. She would be hopping mad and would let him know it, but at least he would hear her voice, even if she was screaming at the top of her lungs. Reluctantly, he picked up the receiver.

"Hello, Stewart residence."

"Thad?" The voice on the other end was female, thin, weak, and yet familiar.

"Yes?" He tried to place the voice.

"Help me."

Recognition! Fear gripped him. "Darnell?"

"Yes. Please come. I need you."

CHAPTER 12

Thad gathered Darnell to him gently as he removed her from his car. Weakly, her arms circled his neck. He groaned.

"Darnell, you're burning up. I shouldn't have listened to you. I'm calling an ambulance. You need to be in a hospital."

Her "No" was barely a whisper as her head moved against his shoulder in protest.

She had insisted that he take her to his home, stating that she didn't want the publicity her hospitalization would cause. Reluctantly, he had complied, breaking the same speed records on his return home that he had broken as he headed to Sausalito to find her. Luckily, as he was going to find Darnell, he passed his neighbor David Alan, who was out jogging. He was a doctor and had agreed to meet Thad at his house when he returned home. If it hadn't been for David's assurance that he would be available, Thad would have taken her to a hospital whether she wanted to go or not. As he looked at her now, he hoped that he hadn't made the wrong decision.

Thad called David from his car phone as he neared their neighborhood. He was relieved to see David pull into the entrance to the driveway as Thad carried Darnell up the steps.

Donald, returning home from an outing, had just opened the front door when he looked around and was startled to see his employer behind him, carrying a woman. Thad looked frantic. Needing no explanation, Donald stepped aside.

"Show Dr. Alan to my bedroom," Thad bellowed as he darted past him into the house.

Thad's adrenaline was pumping as he raced up the stairs. Stepping into the massive bedroom, he glanced down at Darnell in time to see her eyes roll up into her head. She went limp in his arms. He froze.

"Oh, God!" He couldn't breathe. He placed her on his bed, just as the doctor entered the room carrying his medical bag.

Pausing, David stood for a moment assessing the situation. One look at Thad's face and the unconscious woman on the bed brought him swiftly across the room. Thad hovered anxiously at the foot of the bed as David examined Darnell.

"Is she all right? Is she going to be all right?"

David looked from Darnell's sweat-drenched face to Thad's worried one. He tried to sound reassuring. "She'll come around."

Weak with relief, Thad gripped the four-poster bed for support. His eyes never left Darnell's face.

She began to stir. Her eyes opened slowly and focused on the dark-haired stranger sitting on the bed beside her. He was wearing stylish wire-rimmed glasses and was dressed in a white knit shirt and white shorts. For a brief moment, Darnell wondered if she was in heaven.

"Hello." His voice was soothing as he smiled down at her. "I'm Dr. Alan, but there's no need to introduce yourself. I know who you are. I'm one of your biggest fans. So I'm going to make sure that I take special care of you."

A weak smile made its way to Darnell's lips before she closed her eyes and slept. Thad resumed breathing.

What in the world was going on? How had the actor Thad Stewart gotten into the picture? Moody was literally stunned by what had occurred.

He had been watchful and worried since returning to his West Coast home. Yesterday, he had been on the beach waiting for Darnell for their planned *accidental* meeting. He was determined that it would take place that day. His patience had run thin. He had waited for quite some time, but she hadn't appeared for her run. He had been very disappointed.

Undaunted, Moody had returned to the beach this morning. This time, Darnell did make an appearance, but again there was a change in her routine. She started to run but seemed to have changed her mind as he glanced up in time to see her climbing the path toward her home. She was too far away for him to reach her. Frustrated, he had returned to his house, but his luck had changed this afternoon.

Feeling confined, he had gotten in his car for a trip into town when he spotted Darnell's sports car ahead of him on the road leading to the highway. He decided to follow her.

He had thought that their drive would take them into town or maybe to Monterey on some errand. He was ecstatic, thinking that this would finally give him the opportunity to bump into her and start a conversation. Instead, he found himself on an unexpected trip to San Francisco, but she didn't stop there.

They crossed the Golden Gate Bridge and took the exit into Sausalito, which had been clogged with sightseers. Moody maneuvered the crowded streets skillfully, undetected by Darnell, but he was confused as to where she was going and the reason why. Perhaps a short getaway for a change of scenery? He wasn't sure, but he kept following. When she pulled into the parking lot of an upscale strip mall and parked, his confusion increased as she remained in the car. Parking across the street, far enough away so that she could not see him, he sat watching and waiting. She didn't get out of the car.

Twenty minutes passed, and a bright red Ferrari raced down the street and screeched into the parking lot. Alert, Moody sat up and peered through the windshield. He recognized the red car as it pulled up next to Darnell's Mercedes. It had nearly run over him—twice. Moody unlocked his car door. A man leaped from the car and rushed to Darnell's vehicle. Moody's hand slid behind him for the gun that he wore in his back holster. By the time the man lifted Darnell up in his arms and placed her in the passenger seat of his Ferrari, Moody was across the street with the gun concealed in his jacket pocket.

Moving steadily but not wanting to attract unwanted attention, Moody was still unsure as to what was happening, but his heart was pounding loudly. What was happening with Darnell? He could see that she wasn't putting up a fight at being transferred to the other car. Had she been expecting this stranger? And why had she not walked to his car on her own?

By the time he reached the sidewalk separating the parking lot from the street, the man had gotten back into the Ferrari and was pulling out of the parking lot. Darnell was at his side. Hand in his pocket, Moody stood at the exit of the lot. He would have a split second to assess the situation and make the decision as to whether the stranger would live or die. He stood tensely as the car came to a halt only inches from him. The window was down. The driver slowed briefly to check traffic before pulling out. It was in that moment that Moody peered at the face behind the steering wheel. He knew that face! Caught off guard, he hesitated and his grip on the gun relaxed.

The car turned onto the street as Moody stood immobilized, watching as it became a blur in the distance. Through the back window, he could see the faint outline of Darnell's head against the headrest. There were no screams of protest, no resistance to having been abducted. She had gone willingly, and her supposed abductor was no dangerous stranger. It was none other than Thad Stewart, a man who had entertained Moody and his cohorts for years.

Long after the car had disappeared, Moody stood frozen in place, trying to comprehend what had happened. His Darnell had been carried away. She was now in Thad

Stewart's hands. What he couldn't understand was how that had happened, and most important of all, why?

He was there. On the occasions in which Darnell opened her eyes from her feverish illness, Thad was always there—sitting by her bedside, stroking her hair and reassuring her of a speedy recovery. She would awaken and see him sitting beside her bed, asleep, awakening at her slightest stir. Or, he would be lounging on the balcony outside the bedroom, reading, yet alert and at her side at the hint of any movement. He attended to her every need.

When the doctor diagnosed her illness as the flu, Thad hired a private nurse to be at her disposal. Introducing her as Catina, he assured Darnell of the woman's discretion. She was a friend. Neither of them would have to worry about her revealing their arrangement to the tabloids.

Thad also called Mrs. Sharon and informed her of Darnell's infirmity. Her mother was not contacted at her daughter's request. She was out of the country on vacation, and Darnell didn't want anything to disturb her. Voicemail and text messages would handle any communications from Bev on her daughter's cell phone. Mrs. Sharon was to make an excuse for her employer if Bev called the house.

It was on the third day of her confinement that Darnell fully awakened. Catina, an attractive woman in her early forties, was entering the room with a food tray when she noticed that her patient was wide awake. For the first two days of her illness, she had only stirred from her slumber to take medication, quench her thirst and hunger, or take care of bodily needs.

"Hello. How are you feeling today?" she asked, flashing a friendly smile.

Darnell stretched, gave a wide yawn, and returned her smile. She liked this woman. Her boundless energy was a spirit booster. "I feel much better. Thank you."

"Good. I'm glad to hear it." Setting the tray aside, Catina hurried to help Darnell as she pulled herself into a sitting position. The nurse fluffed the bed pillows behind her back for support, then went to the window and pulled the cord that opened the vertical blinds covering the windows. Daylight streamed into the room. Catina moved quickly as she walked back across the room, picked up the tray, and settled it on Darnell's lap.

"I've got some homemade soup for you, chicken noodle, and there's Jell-O for dessert."

Darnell looked into the bowl of chunky liquid and shook her head. "I'm not hungry."

Catina ignored the comment and handed her a spoon. "Dr. Alan said you've got to eat. You haven't eaten much of anything in three days."

Darnell glanced at the soup. It looked good, but her stomach still felt queasy, and she had no appetite. With a weary sigh, she pushed the bowl of soup away, settled against the pillows, and looked around the bedroom. It was the first time that she had felt well enough to do so.

It was a beautiful room, decorated in muted tones of beige and pale yellow. The furniture was expensive and tasteful. The huge four-poster bed in which she lay dominated the room. Original paintings by African-American artists adorned the walls. Fresh flowers—long stemmed yellow roses—rested in heavy cut crystal vases on shelves and tables throughout the room. She inhaled their fragrance.

"Whose room is this?" Darnell asked.

"Mr. Stewart's."

Darnell nodded. Catina's reply didn't surprise her. The room was meticulous, just like the man. There was a place for everything, and everything was in its place. Thad was the kind of man who knew how to take care of things, just as he was taking care of her in her illness. She stole a glance out of the doors that led to the balcony.

"He's not here," Catina said knowingly.

Darnell's eyes slid back to the nurse. She looked at her innocently. "Who?"

The woman wasn't fooled. "Mr. Stewart will be back shortly. He had to run over to the center in Marin City."

"The center?"

"Yes, the center." She paused expectantly, surprised by Darnell's inquiry. "You know, the one Mr. Stewart built for the kids in Marin City," she prompted, trying to jog Darnell's memory. " The new community center."

"Oh! *That* center." Darnell dropped her eyes, not wanting the woman to know that she didn't have a clue what she was talking about.

Sensing Darnell's confusion, Catina shrugged. "I guess he doesn't talk about it much. I shouldn't be surprised. He doesn't like to talk about all of the things he does for people. He does so much."

"He does?" Darnell couldn't hide the surprise in her voice.

Catina, who had resumed fussing with the pillows supporting Darnell's back, stopped short. "Yes, he does. He donates a lot of money to charities all across the country and—" She shrugged. "But like I said, that's something he doesn't talk about." She paused thoughtfully for a second before proceeding. "I really don't mean to pry, Ms. Cameron, but how long have you known Mr. Stewart?"

Darnell wasn't one to discuss her business, even with someone who seemed as nice as Catina. Her answer was short. "Not long."

Her reply left no room for further discussion. Getting the message, Catina nodded and continued her duties while Darnell considered the tidbits of information that she had shared with her about Thad. He had never said anything to her about having contributed in any way to any community. As far as she knew, it had never been publicized that he had a commitment to any cause except pleasuring the opposite sex. This made Catina's revelations about him even more amazing. It certainly heightened Darnell's curiosity. Thad had to be the most complex person she had ever met. The contradictions in his life were as mind boggling to her as her growing attraction to him.

She had started to Tiburon to give the man a piece of her mind and to sever all ties with him once and for all.

Yet, when she fell ill, she'd had no doubt that when she called him he would come for her. What a paradox.

Where her trust in the man came from, she didn't know. Maybe it was the confidence and skill he had displayed in handling the car in the Santa Cruz Mountains, or perhaps the care with which he'd planned each activity they did together. Whatever it was, he had come through and she admired that about him. She could tell by the way that Catina talked about Thad that she admired him, too.

Darnell put the tray aside. Catina eyed the untouched meal, then looked at her disapprovingly.

"Mr. Stewart is not going to like this. He's been beside himself with worry about you. I've never seen him so upset."

Darnell raised a surprised brow. "Really? Why?"

Catina looked at Darnell as if she were half-witted. Surely, this woman was aware that Thad Stewart was in love with her. Everything he did and said indicated that fact.

"If you don't know, then it's not my place to tell you. Now, Dr. Alan told me that you had to eat to get your strength back, and you're going to eat!"

Darnell noted the determination in Catina's command, but it wasn't going to work. "I'm not hungry," she answered with equal determination.

The two women glared at each other, both sensing that the other's will was as strong as her own. Catina sighed, deciding to try another tactic.

"Believe me, Ms. Cameron, my husband's homemade chicken soup is a taste you won't forget."

Darnell's voice rose in surprise. "Your husband's soup?" Darnell glanced at the third finger of Catina's left hand. She wasn't wearing a ring. "Who's your husband?"

Catina followed Darnell's eyes and anticipated the unasked question. "My husband is Donald Chapman, Mr. Stewart's assistant, and I don't wear a wedding band because I'm allergic to gold."

Darnell's eyes registered her surprise. She couldn't picture this petite, attractive woman married to Thad's staid, straight-laced assistant. At least that's how she pictured Donald. She hadn't met him yet.

"How long have you and Donald been married?"

"Four years," Catina answered, tucking the covers in at the foot of the bed. "Ever since he got out of prison."

The latter information was delivered so matter of factly that Darnell doubted what she had heard. She tried not to convey the shock she felt, but she could hardly believe it. Prison! Old straight-laced Donald was a criminal?

Preoccupied with straightening the bed covers, Catina didn't notice Darnell's reaction. She turned back to her and indicated the abandoned soup. "I'm telling Mr. Stewart about this."

"Telling me about what?" The deep voice resonated throughout the room, drawing the attention of both women.

Thad was leaning casually against the doorframe. His arms were folded across his chest, and his attention was fixed on Darnell.

Her eyes swept his towering frame. He was dressed in white linen slacks, a black double-breasted sports jacket, and a white shirt tucked neatly in his pants. He looked as though he were posing for the cover of a magazine. Darnell felt her pulse quicken as she became aware of her own appearance. She gave her hair a cursory swipe. Then, in an effort to hide her discomfort at his sudden appearance, she set her mouth firmly and met his gaze. She had come to do battle with this man, not to go weak over the sight of him. There were matters to be settled here, and she would not let his movie star looks sway her . . . except, of course, she was already swayed.

CHAPTER 13

Catina looked from her stubborn patient to Thad. "She refuses to eat, Mr. Stewart, and that won't do."

"No, it won't." Thad shifted his weight from the doorframe and stepped into the room, his eyes still on Darnell. With feline grace, he moved across the room, removing his jacket as he did so.

Catina shifted uncomfortably. The electricity between Thad and Darnell increased with every step he took. Tossing his jacket onto a chair, he tore his gaze from Darnell momentarily and took the tray from Catina. "Thank you. I'll call if I need you." Relieved, she stole silently from the room.

Thad placed the tray on the coffee table in front of the sofa. His heart was doing its usual drumbeat. He had become used to its beating double-time whenever he was near Darnell. His spirit soared at the sight of her awake and alert. Her large, dark eyes were bright and shining with fire, no longer dull with fever.

"Good morning, Doe Eyes."

Darnell could not repress the flicker of pleasure she felt at the tenderness in his greeting. However, before she could respond, her surprise turned to shock as unexpectedly he scooped her up into his arms.

"What are you doing?" She kicked her feet in protest. "Put me down!"

Having reached the sofa across the room, Thad plopped down on it with Darnell still in his arms. He pulled a comforter from the end of the sofa and wrapped it snugly around her as she twisted and turned in his lap. Thad held on.

"I suggest that you sit still," he muttered. His ability to speak was being seriously challenged by his body's response to her movements. "If not, we both might get more than we've bargained for."

Feeling the evidence of truth against her bottom, Darnell instantly stopped. Her chest heaved in indignation.

"You . . . you . . . if you ever . . ."

Thad pressed a quieting finger to her lips. "I don't want to fight with you, Darnell." He dipped the spoon into the chunky liquid. "David said that you have to eat to regain your strength." He held the spoon close to her lips. "Please, just eat something."

Darnell shook her head. "I'm not hungry," she managed to whisper.

He wasn't having it. "You have to eat. Now open."

His last words were a seductive whisper that sent tremors up her spine. She wanted to turn away, resist him, but she didn't. She was too preoccupied by the drumming inside her chest from his closeness.

His eyes looked tired. Red lined the rims, indicating a lack of sleep. The man had been worried about her. He had proven his concern and continued to do so. The least she could do was be grateful. She opened her mouth and let him slip the spoon inside. Instantly, Thad regretted that she had complied with his request.

Darnell's generous mouth wrapped around the spoon, and he watched in fascination as she savored the brew. She slid her tongue from her mouth to lick her lips—slowly, very slowly. His aching groin tightened. Relinquishing the spoon to her, he hoped that might solve the problem. It didn't. A few more swallows and licks, and he was about to explode.

It was Darnell who placed the soup bowl on the coffee table in front of them, then looked up at him. Her own control was just as tenuous as she fumbled for something to say.

"I . . . I want to let you know that I'm grateful for everything you've done for me, Thad. We haven't always been civil to each other, but when I called, you came. I don't remember if I've said it since I've been here, but thank you."

He looked at her thoughtfully, reading the sincerity in her eyes. "Did you doubt that I would come for you if you called?"

For a moment, they held each other's eyes. Darnell knew that her next words could change the course of their relationship—again—but she whispered them anyway.

"No, I didn't. I didn't doubt it at all."

Thad leaned forward. He was going to kiss her. She knew it. Her respiration increased. She closed her eyes a split second before Thad slid her from his lap and abruptly stood.

"I'll tell you what," he said, disregarding her look of astonishment. "Since you seem to feel better today, why don't you get dressed and come downstairs? Maybe we can find something more substantial in the kitchen that might whet your appetite." Not waiting for a reply, he hurried from the room.

Outside, Thad leaned against the closed door and took a deep breath. The urge to kiss her had been so strong that he still didn't know how he fought it. All he could do was run like a scared rabbit. This woman had become much too important to him. He wanted her more than he had ever wanted anyone, but there was a reality that had to be faced. He wasn't the man that she was in love with.

Having regained some semblance of self-control, he pushed away from the door and started down the stairway just as David was coming up the stairs. Trailing behind him was his wife, Heather. What was she doing here?

"David?" Thad gave him a questioning look. The doctor tossed him a sheepish grin.

"Hey, Thad. Uh, I hope you don't mind." He nodded toward the leggy blonde following close on his heels. "I know you said that you didn't want anyone to know she was here, but Darnell is Heather's favorite singer, and I . . . uh, well . . ."

Thad sighed in annoyance. He understood that David was a newlywed with a younger wife who had him wrapped around his finger, but there were limits. "David, you promised."

"Oh, come on, Thad." Heather spoke up quickly, seeing an opportunity slipping by. "I'm not going to tell anybody."

Thad frowned skeptically. Discretion wasn't one of Heather's strong points. The last thing that he wanted was a media circus. "Heather . . ."

"All I want to do is say hello and maybe get an autograph," she pleaded.

"I don't know if Darnell is well enough." He turned to David, who looked caught in the middle.

"I'll tell you what," David said, his eyes silently pleading for Thad to go along with his suggestion. "I'll go in and examine Darnell, and if she's up to it and says it's okay, Heather can come in just for a minute and meet her. Let's make it her decision."

Reluctantly, Thad agreed.

Darnell perked up when Dr. Alan entered. She felt better than she had in days, and a clean bill of health from him would be her ticket out of here.

"Hello, Doctor." She greeted him with her brightest smile.

David returned her friendly greeting. "Hello. You certainly sound chipper today."

Darnell sat up in bed as high as she could. "That's because I feel great. If you ask me, I'm all over the flu."

David chuckled. "I think I'll be the judge of that."

After a brief exam, he agreed. "Yes, you do appear to be doing much better."

"Which means I can go home, right?"

"It means that you still need to take it easy for a while . . ."

"But I can get up and get out of here, right?" Darnell pulled the covers back, ready to get dressed now.

Amused, David raised his hands to halt her actions. "Whoa! You still need to rest and gather your strength."

Darnell's face fell. "But you said . . ."

"I said that you're better, but you still need rest."

"I can rest at home," Darnell pouted.

David raised a brow. "You seem awfully anxious to leave here."

"I am." Darnell didn't offer any further explanation and the doctor didn't appear to want one. But there was something that he did want from her. He asked her to greet his wife and to give her an autograph.

Darnell gave him a sly smile. "I'll tell you what. You wash my back, and I'll wash yours."

A deal was struck. An hour later, Darnell descended the staircase. The doctor had given her a clean bill of health, with a warning to take it easy for the next couple of days. She had translated that to mean that she was free to do whatever she wanted as long as it was within reason. She had decided to take a short walk along the beach. The day was sunny and warm, and she refused to be cooped up any longer. So, after taking her first leisurely bath in days, she had donned a pair of sweats borrowed from Catina, and she was intent on going outside for the first time in three days. As Darnell approached the front door and reached for the handle, she met an unexpected obstacle.

"And just where do you think that you're going?" Thad moved to block her way.

With those words, the truce that had been declared over the past few days was over. Thad was dead set against her going outside. Darnell was just as insistent about going. The ensuing argument was a loud one. Then, seemingly out of nowhere, a bulk of a man appeared in the foyer.

"What's going on here?" It was Donald, Thad's housekeeper-turned-assistant and Catina's husband. To Darnell's surprise, he was far from the staid, proper figure that she had envisioned.

Donald looked like a model for a bodybuilding magazine. Golden brown and bald, he was at least six and a half feet of muscle and biceps. He was a handsome man, but he was also intimidating. He looked dangerous. Remembering what Catina had said about Donald being an ex-con, unconsciously Darnell moved a little closer to Thad as she was introduced to the giant of a man. It was while Thad was preoccupied explaining the reason for the altercation to Donald that Darnell took the opportunity to slip out the front door before Thad could stop her.

Fifteen minutes later, she stormed along the beach like a soldier doing a goosestep. She was angry. Thad had already found a million ways to infuriate her, and he was now on number one million and one. She refused to look behind her as he trailed her like some watchdog. She didn't need a babysitter, and had told him that when he caught up with her and demanded that she wear his oversized jacket. He insisted that it was too cool on the beach for her not to wear one and that he was afraid of a relapse. She had been touched by his continued concern, but when he refused to let her walk the beach alone she wasn't amused. She didn't like how he had dismissed her earlier that day and needed to be away from him. She had to have some time alone to think about why it mattered.

Darnell's shoulders drooped as her goosestep slowed to a saunter. She knew that it wasn't his solicitous behavior that was disturbing her. It was because she wanted him, and she wasn't sure what to do about it.

Some distance behind her, Thad strolled along, amused by Darnell's angry stride. He hadn't responded to her verbal tirade. He had decided that their sparring was going to stop once and for all. He knew that the tension between them wasn't spurred by anger. It was sexual tension. They both knew it. It was time for them to lay their cards on the table.

Remembering the separate sleeping quarters at her home for her and Lance, he wanted to know exactly what was going on between them. Of course she could tell him that it was none of his business, but he *had* to know. If there was no chance for him, so be it, but hiding his feelings for her was becoming more and more difficult. They were strong, and they were deep.

A jogger whizzed past him, jolting Thad's thoughts back to the beach. He looked up in time to see Darnell about to round the corner of the only rock formation on the otherwise flat beach surface. Her stride had slowed, and she appeared to be deep in thought.

What occurred next seemed to happen in slow motion. The jogger approached Darnell, and in passing unexpectedly bumped into her. Caught by surprise, Darnell made an attempt to keep her balance but failed. She lost her footing, and Thad watched helplessly as she fell against the large jagged rocks, then crumpled to the sand like a rag doll. The jogger continued running.

Thad rushed to Darnell, fighting the urge to chase the hit-and-run jogger and beat him senseless. She was sitting up rubbing her right arm when he reached her side.

"Are you all right?" He took her arm and gently examined it.

"Yes, no thanks to that idiot. If I hadn't been wearing this ugly coat of yours I could have broken my arm." She looked at the large rip on the coat sleeve where it had caught against the rocks. "Sorry."

"No problem." Thad helped her up and looked down the beach to where the jogger had disappeared. "If you had hit your head on those rocks instead of your arm, you might not have walked away so easily. On top of that, he didn't stop to apologize."

"The 'he' was a she," Darnell informed him as he rubbed her aching arm, "and she better be glad that she didn't stop. I would have done her some serious harm." The look on Darnell's face confirmed that serious harm would have been inflicted. It seemed that *both* women had been lucky.

Returning to the house, Darnell perched on a stool in his bright blue kitchen while they both examined her arm. The skin hadn't been broken, but there was some discoloration. Thad was still seething about the incident, and it took some convincing from Darnell to keep him from calling the authorities to track the jogger down.

Neither Catina nor Donald was home, so Thad offered to fix Darnell a meal. By now she was famished, and she readily took him up on the offer. As Darnell sat watching him, she was amazed at the skill with which he prepared broiled chicken breasts, corn on the cob, and spinach salad. He did it with the same meticulous attention to detail that he put into everything he did. Whatever the task, Thad gave it his undivided attention, including being with her. She liked that about him, and she liked *him*, a lot.

It was the sound of her sigh that drew Thad's attention. Sitting on the edge of a kitchen stool with her elbows resting on the island, she looked pensive. He wondered what she was thinking. Could it be about him?

Cued by his silence, Darnell looked up. The intensity of Thad's gaze made her uncomfortable. She lowered her gaze and reached across the island to retrieve several tomatoes, a chopping block, and a knife.

"Here, let me work for my meal."

She started chopping as he returned to his own task. For the moment, her gesture stifled the rising tension between them. They worked in silence until Thad spoke.

"Darnell, I hung the telephone up on Lance because I was jealous." He made the statement as if answering a question she had just asked.

She continued slicing, not looking up. "Oh, really?" She didn't know what else to say.

Thad glanced at her as he shucked the corn. "Sending that bill to you was immature, and I'm sorry. I should never have done that."

Darnell tried to concentrate on her slicing. "No, you shouldn't have."

Thad dropped the corn he had been shucking into a pot. "What I should have done was call you and tell you how much I missed you and how I wanted to see you again."

With shaky hands, Darnell placed the tomato slices in the bowl. Then, wiping her hands with a paper towel, she looked up at him steadily. "I missed you, too."

Thad picked up the pot of corn and placed it on one of the burners built into the island. His hands trembled as he placed the lid on the pot. Completing his task, he came around the counter to stand within inches of Darnell. She tilted her head expectantly. Fear and doubt laced her dark eyes.

Taking her chin in his hand, he sought to erase both their doubts and lowered his mouth to hers. She made no move to resist as gently, tenderly, Thad's lips melded with hers.

The tension in the house was palpable. Each member of the household staff could feel it. Mr. Waters had come back home a few days ago in a very foul mood. Since that time, they had heard him pacing back and forth from the sitting room to the bedroom suite like a caged animal. He took his meals in his room and barely spoke to the staff. They heard the sound of shattering glass one evening. The maid later reported having to clean up shards of broken crystal—remnants of a broken vase. The housekeeper added it to his bill.

It appeared that the reserved and refined Mr. Waters had another side to his personality—possibly a lethal one. So, unsure as to what had caused this metamorphosis, the staff moved throughout the house like silent shadows, uncertain how to respond to their temporary employer's behavior or what to expect from him next.

CHAPTER 14

A sweep of his tongue across her lips sent shock waves careening through Darnell's system. She opened her mouth slightly to allow him entrance, and instantly he took control. Deepening the kiss, he stroked her tongue. Darnell groaned with pleasure. By their own volition, her hands snaked upward, encircling his neck, drawing him closer. Only the need for oxygen forced them to part.

For a moment, neither of them could speak. Thad stood shaken. He had kissed women before, but the magnitude of what had passed between them with this kiss amazed him. Surely, Darnell had felt it. Gently, he pressed her cheek to his heart so that she could feel it beat for her.

"We shouldn't have done that," she whispered, sounding unconvincing even to herself.

Threading his fingers through her hair, his eyes swept her passion-swollen lips. "Yes, we should have, a long time ago."

Darnell shook her head vehemently. She couldn't do this. She couldn't fall for Thad. They were like fire and ice, day and night.

Thad lifted her chin, forcing her to look at him. He could almost hear what she was thinking.

"It'll be all right," he pleaded. "Don't think about anything but us." Once again he took possession of her mouth with a kiss almost desperate in its intensity.

Darnell's knees nearly buckled. Yet, with a half-hearted effort, she tried to release his hold. She couldn't let this man into her life. "No, Thad," she implored, trying to pull away.

"Yes, Darnell." Thad's voice was filled with quiet certainty.

His heart raced like the wind when he was near her, and her very touch caused him to tremble. No woman had ever made him feel this way.

He loosened his hold on her. "Talk to me, Darnell. Tell me how you feel about what's happening between us. Tell me how you feel about Lance."

Closing her eyes against the hope in his voice, she gave a troubled sigh. Why did he have to bring up Lance's name? Her head was swimming; her legs were shaking so badly that she doubted if she could remain standing if Thad weren't holding her. That's how Thad affected her, in ways that Lance never had.

"He and I have a special relationship . . ."

"Do you love him?"

"A long relationship . . ."

"Do you love him?"

"He's easy, familiar . . ."

"But do you *love* him?"

"Yes, I do."

He inhaled the pain of those words.

She continued. "You and I are too different, Thad. I mean, your impulsiveness, your zest for life is so different from the person I am. I'm reserved. I like order. There has to be a progression for me, step one, step two . . ."

Her voice drifted off in her struggle to explain. She looked away. She had never been so confused, so unsure of herself in her life.

Reluctantly, Thad released her, his hopes sinking. She *was* in love with Lance, but what was she saying about him, about the two of them—Thad and Darnell?

"I'm not sure whether I should be flattered or not by your description of me. Could you explain a little bit more, especially about us?"

Darnell's legs finally gave away. She sank onto a kitchen stool. At this moment, she wasn't sure what she meant or how to explain it. All she knew was that in the heat of Thad's presence, words were at a premium. How ironic.

She made her living forming words and music that explored the mysteries of passion. Yet here she was in the face of insatiable desire struggling to form a coherent sentence.

"You're disrupting my life, Thad, and it's an orderly life, considering my career." Darnell threw her hands up in frustration. "I don't know! I made plans for my life. I used to know where I was headed . . ."

She *used to* know? Thad's hope sprang anew. He grasped at straws. "So are you saying that I scare you?"

She bristled. "I'm not afraid of you."

Thad smiled inwardly at her denial. It was a little too defensive.

"Well, Doe Eyes, you scare me."

Darnell's eyes searched his face trying to find a hint of untruth in his words. She saw none.

He stroked her cheek, soothed her anxiety. "Being with you over these last few weeks has turned my whole world upside down. I'll never be the same. The question for now is, where do we go from here?"

The heat from his touch overwhelmed her. Where indeed? It was an honest question that called for an honest answer, but it was one that she was not prepared to give.

"I'm tired, Thad. I can't talk about this anymore. I'm going upstairs." With that, she left him.

Thad knew that Darnell wasn't ready to face the possibilities for the two of them, and it hurt, but she was right about the differences between them. Not the external ones, but the internal ones that were keeping them apart. While she was in emotional control, he was a man out of control. He wanted her. He needed her. He loved her. He could no more hold back the flood of emotions that she evoked in him than he could hold back the ocean tide. That made him a desperate man.

Over the past few weeks, he had come to recognize Darnell's course of action when she didn't want to face an issue. She ran scared. That meant that she would be leaving him soon, and he didn't want that to happen. They needed more time together, time in which they both could learn to face their fears and doubts about one another—time in which she could see for herself how very good they could be together.

Where do we go from here? The words echoed in Darnell's head hours later as she lay resting in bed. Where *could* they go? Why couldn't Thad just go away? Why did he ignite such a firestorm within her? This feeling she had for him was so new. She couldn't understand it, or explain it. And what about Lance? She had made him a promise, one that she now realized was fueled by the ignorance of youth. Nevertheless, she had given him her word, and it was a promise that now was in serious jeopardy.

It had taken exactly six months for Darnell to realize that her initial infatuation with Lance was not the all-encompassing love she had hoped it would be. Only their parents and the outside world continued to hold that illusion, and the two of them liked it that way. Their being thought of as a loving couple proved beneficial to them both. She became an asset to his career, and he proved an asset to her in other ways.

They were compatible, and they looked good together. He kept the wolves at bay. Most men were intimidated by Lance's pretty-boy looks, and women were often green with envy imagining the fervor such a man could elicit. But looks can deceive. Although they had tried in the beginning, there had never been any passion between them. Passion had only been a word to her until Thad Stewart entered her life.

Night had fallen when Darnell startled awake. Groggy from her nap, she peered out the balcony doors.

The lights of San Francisco twinkled in the distance like diamonds against black velvet. The sight was alluring. She could learn to like this.

Abruptly, Darnell sat up in bed. She had to leave here! Her relationship with this man had become much too complex. Tomorrow, she was going home.

Opting for a quick shower, she decided that although it was early still early, she would retire because she would be leaving this house with the sunrise. Donning a clean nightgown provided by Catina, she returned to the bedroom and found her jovial nurse bustling around the room.

"How are you feeling?" She flashed Darnell one of her infectious smiles.

Darnell returned her smile as she crawled back into bed. "I'm all right." That was only a partial truth, but it would do for now. "Is Thad around?"

Catina nodded. "As a matter of fact, he's on his way in here to see you."

As if summoned by her words, Thad appeared. He was carrying a cup of steaming hot chocolate. Darnell stiffened. She didn't notice the look that passed between Thad and Catina as the nurse left the room.

Thad's eyes swept Darnell's body, clad in the modest cotton nightgown, then returned to her face. She looked weary but refreshed. He placed the cup on the nightstand beside the bed.

"I thought that this might help you rest, but from the look of it, you had a good nap. Are you going back to bed so early?"

"Thanks for the hot chocolate." Darnell was touched by his thoughtfulness. "And yes, I am going to bed early. I thought I'd better get as much sleep as I can because I'll be leaving for home early tomorrow morning." Their eyes met. She jutted her jaw out defiantly, anticipating his reply.

Thad nodded. "I figured as much." With those words and a curt "Goodnight," he turned and left the room.

Astounded, Darnell stared at the closed doorway. She had expected resistance, not indifference. For a moment, she didn't know what to think or do. A confused sigh was her only recourse. Tempted by the aroma of the hot chocolate, she took a sip from the cup, still preoccupied by Thad's unexpected reaction to her announcement. Obviously, it didn't matter to him one way or the other if she left, so she was out of here. The man was a chameleon. One minute he had practically made love to her, and the next he didn't seem to care whether she existed.

Fighting her rising disappointment at his lack of reaction, Darnell drained the cup. She set the alarm, turned off the lamp, and crawled beneath the covers. Finding the remote, she turned on the wide-screen television hanging on the wall. By this time tomorrow, she would be at home. It was for the best.

As the oversized screen cast eerie shadows in the darkened room, Darnell's last thought as she drifted off to sleep wasn't of the distance that she wanted to put between them, but the memory of being in Thad's arms.

During the night, she dreamed that she felt those arms around her, lifting her, holding her close to him. The heat of his body was as vivid as the scent of his cologne. She sighed and mumbled his name. A brush of warmth against her lips softly answered her call.

Darnell's slumber was disturbed briefly by a familiar sound. What was it? An airplane engine? Disoriented, she tried to open her sleep-laden eyes, but heavy lids wouldn't allow it. She drifted back into oblivion.

Much later, she felt as if she were levitating. Her mind seemed disconnected from her body. Darnell managed to open her eyes. Through lid-heavy slits, she tried to focus. She seemed to be surrounded by a sea of white. Everything around her was white. Was she in heaven? Suddenly, Thad's face appeared and seemed to hover above her. Gently, his hand swept her hair away from her face. His knuckles grazed her cheek. The pad of his thumb brushed her lips.

Darnell felt as if she were watching him from outside her physical body. Finally, unable to hold her eyes open any longer, sleep overtook her. In the twilight of semi-consciousness she heard tender words soothingly whispered in a voice that sounded just like Thad's.

CHAPTER 15

"Now let me get this straight," Darnell repeated incredulously, still reeling from his revelation. "You drugged me?"

"No! I didn't say that." Thad held up his hand to stop. "Drugged is a relative term. It was just a sleeping pill. Uh, well, maybe two. But David said that Catina could give one to you if you had trouble sleeping. She only doubled it because I asked her to. She's a nurse, and she wouldn't have done it if it hadn't been safe."

"Then, in the dead of the night, you kidnapped me from my bed . . ."

"Uh-uh." Thad shook his head vigorously. "I wouldn't use the word 'kidnapped' so loosely. I picked you up so that I wouldn't have to awaken you. You've been sick, and you *do* need your rest."

"Then you put me on a hijacked plane . . ."

"What?" Thad sprang to his feet, indignant. "The plane we flew here on is my plane. It cost me a fortune! I didn't hijack anything!"

"Then you brought me here to Aruba."

Thad nodded his head in agreement this time. "Okay, you're right there. I brought you to Aruba."

"To be with you."

Looking guilty, Thad dropped back down into the chair opposite Darnell. "Uh, yes, I guess you can say that."

Still unable to believe the man's gall, Darnell sat back, crossed one leg over the other, and held Thad's eyes. "For what purpose?"

Thad didn't falter. "To keep you from running away. That's what you were planning to do, so that you wouldn't have to face what you're feeling for me."

His insight disarmed her. Getting up from the chair, she walked to the patio doors leading out to the white sandy beach and the turquoise sea beyond. When she awakened, he had informed her that they were in Aruba, housed in a ten-room villa. The estate belonged to him and it came with everything—a swimming pool, tennis court, sauna, exercise room, and private beach. A housekeeper, a cook, and a chauffeur were at her disposal. It seemed as though he had spared no expense, overlooked no detail to see that she was catered to, and he had done it all in less than a single day. She had to admire his audacity. Who but Thad Stewart would have thought of doing something like that?

Thad watched her reaction cautiously as she stood looking out toward the sea. She appeared to be taking the news well. She seemed calm. He had expected a different reaction from her about his desperate attempt to keep her with him. He had asked the house staff to remove all of the breakables from the bedroom she occupied because he had fully expected to do some fancy footwork to avoid flying objects. He had never expected this quiet acceptance. Every day, Darnell revealed a new side to her personality.

Joining her at the patio door, he placed his hands on her shoulders. She didn't shrug them away.

"There are times when I can be a selfish man, Darnell, and when it comes to you I'm even moreso. I want you to myself for a while. I also want you completely recovered from your illness, and a warmer climate will help do that."

"That's a rational assessment."

He felt encouraged. "I know that you're going through a lot because of me, and I want you to have time to think about how I feel about you . . ."

"Thad—"

He turned her to face him. "My feelings for you run deep, Darnell. *But*, I swear to you, while we're here, I won't pressure you. I won't touch you unless you want me to. And I'm a man of my word."

Thad took a step backward as if to emphasize his point. "I've spoken to Mrs. Sharon. She knows you're here. She'll forward any messages that you might need. I've got a doctor I know here on standby, and I brought all of your medication. We'll be here for four days." He took another step back. "So, I want you to rest and enjoy yourself. But if you want to fly back to the States, I'll have the pilot take you back today."

He paused, waiting for a comment. There was none, and he couldn't read her expression. He continued, "I'd be a liar if I said that I didn't want you to stay, because I do. Whatever you choose to do, it's all right. We're friends first, and I don't ever want to lose your friendship." With that, Thad exited the room, leaving Darnell alone.

Making the decision to stay in Aruba wasn't a difficult one. She had always wanted to visit the island. As for Thad, she would sort that out later. Until then she might as well enjoy herself, and with him there was no doubt that she would.

The fun started only a few hours after their arrival. After a refreshing nap, she decided that she needed to go shopping. The only clothes she had were the ones she had been wearing when she arrived in Tiburon and the night-gown and sweats that had been borrowed from Catina. Going in search of Thad, she was told by the housekeeper that he was not available, but that if she needed to go into town to shop, the chauffeur was at her disposal. Summoning the chauffeur, she was about to climb into the car when out of the corner of her eye she spotted a bright orange moped whizzing up the driveway leading to the ocean-side villa. It came to a stop within inches of the Mercedes Benz. When the driver removed the helmet and tucked it under his arm, to her surprise it was Thad.

"Hi, there!" He flashed a dimpled grin that could melt ice. "Where are you off to?"

Glad to see him, she returned his smile. "I'm going into town to buy some clothes and a swimsuit."

Thad frowned. "Don't tell me you're going in that conspicuous contraption?"

She recognized the description instantly. That's how she had described his car once when they were at each other's throats.

He winked, seeing that she recognized the reference. "Aren't you afraid someone will recognize you? This is tourist season, you know."

Darnell cocked her head, knowing where this conversation was going. "No, I didn't know that. Do you have another suggestion as to how I can get into town?"

Thad rubbed his chin thoughtfully. "Oh, I might." Picking up a second helmet attached to the moped, he held it up to her. "You got the nerve?"

He knew and she knew that she might not have had it before she met him, but she certainly had it now. He shook his head in amusement as she pulled the helmet over her neatly combed hair, pulled her pants legs up and straddled the moped. She wrapped her arms tightly around his waist.

"Ready!" she informed him, feeling both apprehensive and excited by yet another new experience with this man.

"Hold on," he tossed over his shoulder as they sped down the driveway, out the gate, and down the paved road toward town.

The ride was exhilarating as the warm breeze whipped through their clothing, helping cool their bodies, both of which were overheated by their contact.

Despite the helmet, Thad could smell Darnell's perfume, which made concentrating on the road ahead difficult. Her arms around him and the feel of her body against his caused his stomach to quiver. What had started out as fun was becoming unexpectedly erotic.

As her cheek rested against his broad back, she inhaled the scent of the woodsy soap he had bathed with earlier that day. He wasn't wearing the cologne she liked so much, but it didn't matter. He smelled all male.

Thad took her to the island's capital, Oranjestad. The hour or so that Darnell had planned to spend buying a few things to wear while on the island turned into a marathon shopping spree. For hours, she and Thad darted in and out of the many colorful boutiques lining the capital's downtown shopping area. She discovered that he loved to shop as much as she did, and they spent the rest of the afternoon buying clothes and gifts for family and friends.

Thad voiced concern about her overexerting herself, but she dismissed that possibility. She was having too much fun.

Night found them still in town, dining in a posh restaurant where Thad introduced her to an island specialty, Aruban fish cakes. As he watched Darnell devour her fourth one, Thad cast all doubt aside that her health had improved.

The entire day was perfect—the ride into town, the day spent with her shopping, and the return of her appetite all let him know that bringing Darnell here had not been a mistake. She was happy. Even having been recognized this afternoon by a few tourists in one of the boutiques hadn't quelled the good mood she was in. He had never seen her so animated, and he didn't want anything to spoil this day or her mood. He was as happy as she was and couldn't resist teasing her.

"You know, you wouldn't be in this fix of not having clothes when you need them if you kept an overnight bag in your car like I do. You'd have everything you need when you need it."

Darnell squinted at him, recognizing the teasing tone in his voice. "Oh, yeah? Well, hopefully I won't be kidnapped again, so I won't need to do that. Anyway, what about you? You bought as many new clothes as I did. Didn't you bring clothes with you to Aruba?"

"Nope! Don't have to."

"So what do you do, keep a full wardrobe on the island? Borrow clothes from friends? It looks like you've got a slew of them around here. It seems that everybody in town knows you. Are your movies that popular here?"

He shrugged and threw his hands up immodestly. "Hey, what can I say?

Darnell sneered at him playfully. "Conceited much?"

Thad smiled, his eyes twinkling devilishly. "So I've been told." Thad ducked as she threw her napkin at him in mock offense as, once again, her own words came back to haunt her.

The next day, they planned an early exploration of the island. As they whipped along the narrow roadways on the moped, Darnell clung to Thad confidently, trusting him. She had come to a decision last night as she lay in her snow white bedroom thinking about nothing but him. She wasn't going to fight her attraction to Thad anymore, and was absolutely delighted about her decision.

She couldn't pinpoint when her feelings toward Thad had changed. Perhaps it had happened on the mountaintop in Santa Cruz, or by the waterfall in Big Sur. Maybe it was when he came for her in Sausalito. She knew that it was before that wild moped ride yesterday. No, she couldn't be specific, but she did know that with the morning sunrise came the realization that her feelings for Thad wouldn't go away. For once in her orderly, well-planned life she was going to let fate have its way. So, as they sped along, carefree, Darnell tightened her grip around his waist and enjoyed the ride.

The first stop on their sightseeing adventure was the Ayo Rock Formation. It offered spectacular views of the island amid boulders that weighed tons. They tried to translate the hieroglyphics etched on some of the boulders, laughing hysterically at their interpretations. Their next stop was the Natural Bridge, a coral reef constructed by time and nature. While crossing the bridge, they passed Bushiribana, a historical landmark, and a vestige of the gold rush of an earlier era.

By midday, they had worked up an appetite and they stopped for lunch at an unpretentious eatery in the town of San Nicolas. Thad was as well known here as he had been in Oranjestad. Darnell was amazed.

"Where in the world aren't you known?"

Thad chuckled. "Well, movies get around. I guess CDs don't."

Darnell stuck her tongue out at him, feigning indignation. He loved teasing her. She was such an easy mark. "Actually, I have a confession to make."

She looked at him warily. "What?"

Thad took a sip of his virgin piña colada, then settled back casually. "Only a few people know this, but I own this restaurant and the one we ate in yesterday."

Darnell's jaws went slack with surprise. "You're kidding."

Thad laughed at her expression. "I own quite a bit of real estate on the island. I love it here, and I love the people." He took another sip of his drink. "So I guess I'm not as shiftless as you think I am."

Darnell's fork paused in midair. It was clear that the words she had spouted so carelessly weeks ago had bothered him. She could hear it in the catch in his voice. "I never thought you were shiftless, Thad. I never doubted your potential, and I'm sorry about what I said."

He smiled. Her words pleased him more than she would ever know. "No problem." Thad stood and held out his hand. "Come on, let's go. There's more of the island to see."

For the next few hours, Thad continued to introduce her to the sights and sounds of Aruba. He took her among the island natives, where she was fascinated by the musical cadence of the local language, Papiamento. Wherever he went, people knew him, and he always seemed to be at home. He was a man who was comfortable wherever he went. His smile was infectious, and his manner so relaxed that others seemed to glow in his presence. Thad enjoyed people, and they enjoyed him.

In casual conversation with one local, she was informed that Thad had financed a low-income housing project, two schools, and a medical clinic in the poorest of the island's communities. They had passed each of them during their romp on the island, yet he had never said a word to her about his generosity. Darnell was beginning to appreciate the man more and more.

To end their day, Thad suggested that they go for a swim at the beach. They ended up on a quiet stretch of beach near Thad's house. There they stripped down to their swimming apparel. He wore a bright red pair of bikini swim trunks, and Darnell a yellow one-piece swimsuit. They frolicked in the ocean for an hour, challenging each other to races and playing water tag. As the sun began to set, they lay side-by-side beneath one of the windswept divi-divi trees that characterized Aruba's landscape. The ocean breeze and the shade provided by the tree were both soothing.

Darnell lay on her stomach, enjoying the warmth of Thad's body next to her own and trying to calm the tremors of physical awareness his presence was causing. She had tried to ignore the chiseled perfection of his sculptured form in his swim trucks, but found that next to impossible. She had enjoyed previews of his broad chest beneath the T-shirts that he wore while on the island, but void of the apparel his well-defined pecs were arresting. His slender waistline tapered into a perfect V to his trunks, which were more than filled with that which nature had generously bestowed on him. There was no denying it. The man had a magnificent body. Even his legs were beautiful. How good could one man look?

Beside her, Thad was fighting his own battle for self-control. He had helped her pick out the yellow latex swimsuit she was wearing, thinking himself clever in having avoided the sight of her in a two-piece or a bikini. He knew that his heart couldn't take it. Neither could it take a form-fitting one piece.

Closing his eyes as he lay on his back, Thad enjoyed the serenity of nature and basked in the joy of being with Darnell. Meanwhile, Darnell was unable to resist the lure of the man beside her. She turned to face him. Propping her head in her hand, she stared down at him. Thad opened his eyes and stared back at her. The tension between them mounted.

Darnell reached out and stroked the hairs on his chest. Thad caught her hand in his and placed a kiss on the tip of her finger. Darnell's breathing nearly stopped, and so did Thad's. Suddenly, she turned in the direction of the road, distracted by the sound of brakes screeching to a stop.

Pulling himself up on his elbows, Thad jerked his head around angrily to see what had interrupted perhaps the most important moment of his life. It was a tour bus, and tumbling out of it were dozens of chattering tourists.

Falling back against the sand with a frustrated groan, he harbored murderous thoughts against the busload of camera slinging intruders. After today, he knew that he would never see tourists in quite the same light.

Darnell sighed, her own frustration mirrored in the sound. "We'd better go. Somebody might recognize us."

With that, they gathered their things and headed toward the villa. The day was over.

On their return to the house, Thad walked her to the door of her bedroom and bid her goodnight. As he turned to leave, she stayed him with a touch.

"It seems that I'm forever telling you how much fun I've had."

He tweaked her nose. "No problem, Doe Eyes. I aim to please."

"I guess I've been so single-minded about my singing career that I forgot what enjoying life was all about. That is, until you came along." She drew his face down and placed a tender kiss on his lips. "Thank you," she whispered.

Reeling from surprise, Thad drew a ragged breath. "Stop tempting me, Darnell. I promised not to touch you, and you're not making it easy."

She gave him an impish grin. "*You* made the promise, I didn't." Backing into her bedroom, Darnell closed the door. For a moment, she stood on the other side trying to force herself not to open it again and steal another kiss. Yep! There was no denying it. She had fought the good fight in the battle of resistance against Thad, and she had lost. She wanted the man, and she wanted him soon.

On the other side of the closed door, Thad stood in a daze. He doubted seriously if the cold shower he planned on taking would do any good. Recalling the feel of her luscious mouth, he mapped the path of her lips against his own. No, a cold shower wasn't what was needed tonight.

Thad Stewart was a dead man! He planned on doing the deed personally. There would be no more restless days and nights walking the floor waiting for Darnell to come home. Her absence made it painfully obvious that the dimple-cheeked movie star had somehow convinced her to be with him. How she had gotten caught up in that trap, Moody didn't know. He had been thorough in his study of her, and Stewart hadn't been in the equation. Something had fallen between the cracks, but he'd handle that slip-up later. His major concern was finding out if she was still with him.

It wasn't that hard finding out where he lived. A few inconspicuous, personal calls to Hollywood contacts who owed him favors got him the information that Thad's primary home was in Tiburon. A trip to that affluent bayside hamlet made his efforts almost pedestrian. It took less than an hour for one proud resident to point out the street on which superstar Thad Stewart lived. It seemed that Stewart hid in plain sight. So much for movie stars wanting their privacy. His next step was to make the decision as to how he would get inside the house to see if Darnell was there with Stewart. Was she all right? She had appeared ill, and he was concerned. He was desperate for information. It was sheer luck that garnered him the answer to his question.

While sitting on an isolated bench on the beach near Stewart's house hoping to catch a glimpse of Stewart and even Darnell, he overheard a snippet of a conversation. A couple jogging near him was engaged in a quiet disagreement in passing. It seemed that the man was concerned that the woman might tell someone that Darnell was at Stewart's house recovering from the flu. The moment was surreal.

It didn't take much longer to find a way to Thad Stewart's front door, posing as a deliveryman. Nobody was home when he rang the doorbell. The only decision left to be made was where and when he would kill Stewart. He was certain that whatever the relationship between the two superstars was, it was recent and could not have had time to blossom. Perhaps it was simply friendship, but from what he had observed in the way Thad had cradled Darnell when he placed her in his car, it was far from friendship on his part, and Moody wasn't willing to take that chance. No erstwhile playboy was going to have Darnell Cameron. She deserved better than that.

He would do the hit personally. There was no need to get anyone else involved. The fewer people who knew his business, the better. No one would ever trace the hit to him. There was no connection between him and Stewart, and if he did it right, Thad's death would look like an accident. The actor would be mourned for the blink of an eye, and then another one would come along to take his place. There was probably someone already waiting in the wings. The important thing was that Darnell would be free from making the mistake of her life. Actually, he would be doing her a favor.

CHAPTER 16

It was their last day on the island, and Darnell regretted she would have to leave Aruba. This place was magic, and Thad was the magician.

She didn't know the plans for the day, but that evening they were to go into town for dinner and dancing. It would be a special evening; he would make it special. He had a way of doing that. Darnell smiled at the thought.

After wandering through the house looking for Thad, she found him sitting in the room adjoining his bedroom suite. Like the other rooms in the house, this one was decorated in white, except there was a splash of red as an accent.

Thad was sitting in a swivel chair with his feet propped on the top of a wooden desk. Preoccupied with what he was reading, he didn't notice Darnell enter the room. Quietly, she took a seat on the sofa opposite his desk. He looked relaxed.

She had been watching him for a few minutes before he lowered the script and rubbed his eyes, his brow furrowed in thought. Sighing, he looked up and started in surprise at seeing Darnell. His face softened.

"Well, hello. I didn't know you were here."

Darnell's heart fluttered at his dimpled smile. "You were busy reading. I didn't want to disturb you." Getting up, she crossed the room to his desk.

As he watched her, Thad could feel his groin begin its familiar tightening. He was glad that he was sitting down. This woman could turn him on by simply walking into a room. Her shapely brown legs peeked at him from beneath a pair of white cotton shorts. The crisp white blouse she wore was tied in a knot beneath her breasts, revealing a flat stomach marked with a perfectly round mole located only inches from her navel. Thad's mouth went dry.

Darnell perched on the edge of his desk and nodded toward the script in his hands. "That must be interesting. What's it about?"

Thad couldn't think. Darnell was wrecking havoc with his senses. Wetting his lips, he swallowed. "What . . . what did you say?"

She leaned closer, which only made his situation worse.

"I said, that script must be interesting. What's it about?"

He followed her gaze, still disconcerted by her nearness. "Oh, this?" Closing the script, he quickly stuffed it in the desk drawer. "It's nothing."

Darnell frowned. "Nothing? Nobody writes a script about nothing. It must be about something interesting. It was holding your attention."

"It's about love." Thad's voice was barely audible.

Darnell stilled. Her eyes locked with his. "Love?"

"Yes, the love of a man for a woman he can't have."

Her heart hammered in her chest. "Why can't he have her?"

Thad's voice was steady. "Because she belongs to someone else."

This was it—the moment of truth. Darnell swallowed. "But people don't belong to people, Thad. They can only belong to themselves. If someone wants to be free, it's their choice when they take their freedom."

The room was thick with anticipation. Expectation. Thad was direct. "Are you willing to take yours?"

Darnell reached down and touched a finger to his cheek. "I'm already free."

Thad was too preoccupied with the feel of Darnell's finger traveling slowly down his cheek to examine her words. As it glided across his mouth and outlined his lips, he enjoyed the tortuous sensations. His body grew hard. Silently, he waited and watched as uncertainty danced across her features, then melted away, replaced with a look of resolve. Slowly, she inched her way across the desk, closing the space between them. When her body was within mere inches of his, she hesitated. Thad took the initiative and opened his arms to her. Instantly, she slipped into them.

Settled on his lap, Darnell encircled his neck with her arms and brought her lips to his. Thad's tongue delved into her mouth with such deliberate tenderness that it left her senses yearning for more.

Thad was delirious. Darnell was actually here in his arms where he had longed for her to be. But what did it mean? Was it simply for the moment, or could he hope for more? His mind begged for answers. With Herculean effort, he broke the kiss. His voice was ragged with desire.

"Darnell, I've got to tell you something." He felt her tense. "I've never dealt romantically with another man's lady, and I don't want to start now. I need to know what's between you and Lance, if there's a problem . . ."

"There's no problem."

"But you said that you love him."

"I do."

Thad sighed. "You're driving me crazy. Don't do this to me. Please don't play with me."

Darnell smoothed his worried brow. "I wouldn't do that, Thad. You asked me if I loved him, and I told you the truth."

He believed her. But something was missing in what she was saying. It didn't take him long to guess what it was.

"You love Lance, but you're not *in* love with him, are you?"

"No, I'm not."

That spoken revelation from the heart released them both. He crushed her to him.

"You didn't make this easy for me."

Darnell caressed his face. "You're Thad Stewart, movie star. If something comes too easy for you, I don't think that you'd want it."

"Smart lady," he breathed against her succulent mouth. He captured her lips with another soul-wrenching kiss, then moved down the slope of her neck where he languished, inhaling her, enjoying her. While one hand explored the delicious dips and curves of her body, his other hand freed her voluptuous breasts from the confines of a lacy bra and proceeded to massage her nipples, teasing them, taunting them until they were hard, ripe, and ready. Slowly, his fingertips snaked up the leg of her shorts, past her bikini panties. Arriving at their destination they entered and found paradise.

As Thad's expertise intensified her pleasure, fire ricocheted through Darnell's system, and her own wandering hands searched desperately for a haven. They threaded through his hair, flittering down the planes of his broad shoulders. They skated across his muscled forearms and chest—wanting, needing, and pleading for an anchor while afloat in a sea of desire. Darnell threw her head back in ecstasy, shattering the serenity of the snow white room with her moans of pleasure.

The shock wave had barely passed when Thad lifted her from his lap and carried her into the adjoining bedroom. Darnell felt much as she had the night that she was brought to Aruba—disembodied. Through the misty fog of desire, she lay on the bed watching Thad undress. Her eyes skittered across his body, stopping at his manhood. He was definitely ready for her, but was she ready for him, and for this? For the first time, she felt apprehension.

Slipping on protection, Thad knelt on the bed over her, anxious to claim her as his own. The fear in her eyes surprised him.

"Don't be afraid, Doe Eyes, I'd never hurt you."

The gentleness in his voice calmed her fears, and she relaxed. Between seductive kisses, he slowly disrobed her until she lay naked before him. For a moment, Thad was immobile as his gaze swept the length of her body, drinking in every magnificent dip and curve. Then lowering his body to lie beside her, he feathered kisses along her enticing length, taking special care to encircle that sexy mole near her navel with his tongue. He lifted feverish eyes to her.

"Tell me what you want, baby. Tell me what pleases you."

He watched as passionate eyes turned to ones filled with confusion. Darnell remained silent, so he took control. There was nothing he wouldn't do for her. He would give her anything she wanted, anything she needed. With that in mind he devoted himself to one purpose, giving total pleasure to the woman that he loved.

Threading his hands through her hair, Thad kissed her soundly before claiming a taut nipple as his own and suckling until both became hardened pebbles. Simultaneously, he caressed her precious folds. For Darnell, all coherent thought ceased to exist. Bolts of lightning snaked straight to her center, and her world tilted out of control.

Fighting his rising excitement, Thad prepared himself to enter her. He wanted the memory of their first union to be a special one for them both. Gently, he parted her thighs as Darnell watched him through lazy eyelids.

He was a large man, and he could feel her discomfort. He had prepared her well, but she was still tight, and his initial contact was nearly his undoing. Lovingly, he caressed her.

"I adore you, Doe." His breath sizzled against her ear. "You have no idea how deeply I feel for you." He plunged ahead, deeper. She winced. He stilled. "What's wrong?"

Darnell's expression mirrored her discomfort. It couldn't be what he was thinking. "You're not a . . . a . . ."

She shook her head vigorously against the pillow as her body begged for completion. "Thad, please!"

"Please what, angel?"

"Hurry!" A tear slid from beneath closed eyelids.

"Just relax, Doe Eyes." Seductively, he licked the heated teardrop. "The last thing I want to do with you is hurry. Just stay with me."

She did, and her body began to respond to Thad's gentle command. He was close to the edge. Every muscle in his body was stretched to its limit. He fought for control, but found it elusive as he plunged into dementia, burying himself deeper and deeper within her, losing reason with every thrust.

Darnell's hips undulated wildly. Her nails dug into Thad's flesh. His name tore from her throat with such intensity that it became indistinguishable from her screams. She climbed the pinnacle as spasms of ecstasy rocked her. She was a shooting star flung into the universe, until finally she exploded into a million tiny pieces.

With the sound of his name resonating in his consciousness, the force of Thad's completion shook his world off its axis. His body shuddered uncontrollably as a rainbow of colors swam in his head.

Later, weak and spent, Thad realized that his union with this woman had been much more than an incredible sexual experience. Reaching for her hand, he placed it against his heart—on the spot where she was nestled. The tingling in his limbs and the sensation of dizziness that lingered were testimony to the magnitude of what had occurred between them. For the first time in his life, he had made love and given himself to a woman completely. He had surrendered his mind, body, and soul to Darnell Cameron.

She snuggled up against him with her eyes still closed. Her skin glistened like satin with the sheen of their love-making. He placed a kiss in her hair as he softly whispered her name.

"My Doe." His lips brushed her forehead. "I love you."

Darnell stiffened, then rolled away from him. Her body missed his warmth.

Thad allowed the retreat, but repeated the words that he had been longing to say. "I've fallen in love with you, Doe, and I have no doubts about it." He paused for a moment, hoping against hope that she would repeat the same words. There was silence.

He continued. "I'm not asking you to make a commitment right now. All I ask is that when you know how you feel about me, about us, you'll let me know."

Darnell nodded, fighting back tears, knowing the words that Thad wanted to hear, unable to say them. Speaking carelessly was a mistake she didn't plan on making. Time would define what she felt about him. Meanwhile, she would enjoy the moment.

As Thad pulled her body against his, they lay spoon fashion, reveling in each other's warmth. As the shadows of the day gradually descended, sleep claimed them, and for the moment the anxieties of both were soothed.

CHAPTER 17

While Darnell slept, Thad rose from the bed, still shaken from the power of their lovemaking. He entered the bathroom, wondering how he could have allowed one woman to gain so much control over his emotions.

Running bath water, he watched the tub fill as he thought about his encounter with Darnell. Her response to him had showed an innocence that surprised him. As assertive as she was out of bed, he had expected that she would be the same when they made love, but she had been reserved. That is, until her passion was unleashed. He had not been disappointed. Her response to him had been everything he had hoped and more. Still, it made him even more curious about her relationship with Lance.

He was experienced enough to know that it had been a while since Darnell had shared herself. She had been dating Lance for ten years, and he knew in his heart that Darnell was a one-man woman. He seriously doubted that she had satisfied her need with anyone else, but how long had it been since she and Lance had made love?

What could have possibly happened between them? What was wrong with Lance? How could he not touch her? Wasn't the man human? Darnell certainly was. Her passion was undeniable. Had their relationship grown stale after all those years? Did they no longer want one another? There was something wrong. He could feel it.

There was one thing that she had made clear. She did care about Lance, but she was not in love with him. Thad grinned. That meant that the door was wide open for him, and he planned on moving through it like a tornado. For the first time in his life, Thad Stewart was in love, and he would fight for her with every breath that he took.

Darnell lay in the bed, staring at the ceiling, listening to the sound of running water coming from the bathroom. But the man in the next room wasn't the man who was on her mind. She was thinking about Lance. He had told her once that the day would come when she would find someone she cared about more than him. She had denied that it would ever happen. Emphatically, she had declared that her career came first and that it always would. There was no time for romantic entanglements. Lance had laughed at her declaration and attributed it to her youth. He had made her promise that when the time came and she did find that special someone, he would be the first to know. She had made that promise to him, certain that it was one she would not have to keep. She had made a second promise as well—to keep a secret that she had yet to reveal. She'd always thought that she would be able to keep both promises because she had never planned on falling in love.

Darnell sat up in the bed. Love? Was it possible? Nearly every song she wrote and sang was about that feeling of euphoria when a person finds that special someone. It was the feeling that she was now experiencing. She had never known that such heated passion between two people was actually possible. She knew now because she was living it.

She could claim that what had happened between Thad and her had been unexpected, but she knew better. Their feelings for each other had been building steadily. Thad's reputation with women was notorious; she had never planned on surrendering to him. She had willingly, thinking that after it was over she could walk away. She hadn't expected the profound intensity, the tenderness, the sensation of completeness that Thad aroused in her. They came as a surprise.

Thad entered the bedroom, interrupting her thoughts as he scooped her up into his arms. She yelped.

"Why do you keep picking me up?" Darnell laughed, kicking her feet daintily. "I can walk, you know."

Thad beamed as he moved across the room. "And it's a sexy walk, too."

Entering the bathroom with her in his arms, he approached the large claw-foot bathtub and submerged her in fragrant bubbles. In one graceful movement, he settled behind her, pulling her between his legs. The water felt good to her sore, love-spent body.

She sighed contentedly as she settled back against him. "And I know how to take a bath, too."

"I know." His silken voice caressed her. "But there are baths and there are *baths*." He pressed his lips against her temple. "Now, the average man sits back on his bottom and relaxes in an ordinary bath. But as we both know, I'm not your average man." Gently, he turned her to face him, fitting her delicious frame against the curve of his body.

"I see." Darnell wrapped her legs around him.

Taking a bar of scented soap between his long fingers, Thad worked up a soapy lather. "Now, the ordinary bath would include contact with a washcloth, which, of course, is meant to remove the dirt from the average body. But—" He began to massage the soft flesh at her neck, the concavity of her shoulders, moving down her body slowly—so very slowly—to her chest, where he teased each turgid mound. Darnell's head fell limply against his shoulder as his steamy breath evaporated into her ear. "As we both know, yours is *not* an average body."

Expert hands snaked down her flat midsection to briefly taunt her navel, then spiraled in circular motions to linger in the bushy apex at her entrance.

"And, as we both know, there's nothing *average* about you at all."

Soap slick fingers moved from her silken thighs to take command of the secrets within, where they began to work their magic. Darnell mewed like a kitten. She lost all control over her limbs, as she relinquished all that she was to him. The result was spontaneous combustion.

As Darnell recovered from her release, she lay limply in Thad's arms. Looking at him in wonder, she caught a look of pure male satisfaction on his face. Inwardly, she smiled. He had the right to be smug. His erotic bath was driving her to madness, but she had a few tricks of her own. She might not be as experienced as he was when it came to lovemaking, but there were a few things she did know. Reaching down, her hands moved slowly along the planes of Thad's muscular thighs, then across to his inner thighs where she gently began to knead the sensitive flesh.

Thad stilled, inhaling sharply. When Darnell's hand moved to encircle his manhood, already throbbing out of control, he gasped. "You little devil."

When her warm hand started to manipulate his manhood, his speech slurred and his eyes glazed. It was Darnell's turn to smile smugly.

Thad held on desperately, exhaling in ragged gulps, his sides heaving. His knees weak, he panted, "No, Doe! Please, not yet!" But Darnell was relentless as her hand made its point.

His head fell forward involuntarily, and she captured his lips for a kiss that left him drugged. When they parted, both of their bodies dictated that it was, indeed, time for a union. Darnell placed the protection on him much too slowly, as Thad traced a loving finger down her cheek.

"I love you, Doe Eyes," he whispered, "and I've never been in love before." They were his last words before passion consumed them and reason vanished.

Darnell pulled Thad's oversized T-shirt over her head and smiled at the sound of the shower running in the bathroom. Their attempt at bathing together had proven to be so arousing that they had been forced to separate. Never in her staid, perfectly planned life had she been so uninhibited, and she had enjoyed every minute.

She had read long ago that Thad was reported to be an "excellent lover"—now she could testify to that fact—but rumors and gossip had never reported what a very special human being he was.

I've never been in love before. She would always remember those words. He was a major movie star, a heartthrob. It was hard to believe that some woman hadn't captured his heart.

He had also told her that he wasn't quite sure what to do with the feelings that he had for her.

"I'm not sure if I'm saying the right thing when I'm with you," he said as he wrapped her in a towel and dried her body. "Or if I'll do the right thing, but I sure am going to try, and I want to thank you."

"Thank me for what?"

"For sharing yourself with me, and I'm not talking about just your body. You can't imagine how that makes me feel."

He was proud that she had chosen him as the man with whom she made love, and he'd made it plain that from now on it would be his kisses, his caresses, his passion for her that she would always want and need. Darnell was touched by his declaration and gave him a kiss of gratitude that left him drugged. Falling in love with Thad had not been in any plan that she had for her life, but right now it felt wonderful.

Dressed, Darnell wandered from the bedroom to Thad's office, the memory of their steamy bath together still fresh. Strolling to the patio doors, she opened them and inhaled. The shadows of the evening were beginning to appear over the horizon. The day was half over, and she and Thad had yet to make an appearance outside of these two rooms. She didn't care. Right now she was walking on sunbeams, drifting on clouds. The rest of the world had ceased to exist. She was a woman in love.

Moving to Thad's desk, Darnell fiddled absently with the fastidiously placed items. Then, remembering that he had been reading a script earlier, her curiosity peaked. She slid open the middle desk drawer in which she'd seen him place it earlier. Withdrawing the script she read the title—*Senusous.*

Thad couldn't bathe and dress fast enough. He didn't want to miss a moment with Darnell. Not finding her in the bedroom, he hurried into the sitting room and found her at his desk reading a script. He knew instantly which one she was reading. She glanced up at him as he entered, but continued to rifle through the script. He took a seat across from the desk.

Completing the page that she was reading, she looked up at him steadily, pausing as if to gather her emotions before she spoke.

"There's a note I found inside the cover page from your attorney that says I'm perfect for the role in this script." She indicated the note written in red in the margins. "It also says that you are to *get me* any way you can." She tossed the script on the desk in front of him. "Do you want to explain to me what all of this is about?" Her expression was unreadable.

Thad reached for the *Sensuous* script and grinned. In his excitement about the possibility of their working together, he didn't notice the questions in her eyes or the coolness in her voice.

"It's a script I wrote! If you'll finish reading, I think you'll see that you would be perfect for the role. That is, if you like it. Just read it and let me know what you think."

Darnell's eyes narrowed. "Let you know what I think, huh?"

"Yes! I know you'll like it!" Exhilarated, Thad leaped from his seat and began pacing the room as he explained his plans for the script's subsequent production. Finally running out of steam, he settled back in his seat and turned glowing eyes to Darnell for her reaction. The glow dimmed quickly at the look on her face. It was not enthusiastic. He frowned. "What's wrong? You don't like the idea?"

Closing her eyes against the confusion she saw in his eyes, Darnell told herself to calm down and not jump to conclusions. She could hear that the dreams that he had been harboring for so long were also her dreams. They were reflected in every word that he said, and she hoped against hope that what she was thinking wasn't true. It couldn't be! But she had to know. The doubts that she harbored had been like a weight on her soul from the moment that she read that note, so she was blunt.

"Just how far were you willing to go to get me to be in your picture, Thad?"

The furrows in his brow deepened. "What do you mean? I don't under—" The meaning hit him. For a moment, he couldn't speak. He simply stared into her incredible eyes, stunned. If she had taken a knife and plunged it into his flesh, it couldn't have hurt him more.

Darnell saw his pain and instantly regretted having posed the question. "Thad, I—"

"No!" He held up his hand and slowly rose. "Don't say it! Because if you think so little of me that you believe that I would use you like that—after making love to you, after confessing my love for you—then there's nothing else to be said." He started for the door, then looked back at her. His voice was hard. "Pack your things. I'll have the pilot fly you back to the States today."

He turned to leave. Darnell moved quickly across the room and planted herself firmly in front of him, halting his progress.

"Thad, I was wrong to think that you would use me sexually, so please don't go, and I don't want to leave this island without you."

He glared down at her, not bothering to mask how much she had hurt him. Darnell winced. Her careless tongue had done this damage, and his rigid stance showed her that his acceptance of an apology might not be enough to bridge the sudden distance. Desperate, she kept talking.

"I should never have questioned your integrity, and I know that the words 'I'm sorry' aren't enough. You know me well enough by now to understand that trust isn't one of my strong points. Yet I have come to trust you more than you know." Tears threatened to flow. She swallowed. "For me to even think anything like that, and worse to say it when I know how much I lo—" Darnell caught herself, hoping that he hadn't noticed her slip of the tongue. He had.

"When you know how much you *what*, Darnell?" His stance had relaxed and his voice held a challenge as he watched her struggle with her words. Was she about to say that she loved him? "Exactly how do you feel about me? Do you care about me at all?"

Darnell stepped closer to him. "Yes, I do. I care for you more than you may ever know. That's why hurting you hurts me."

Thad searched her face and saw the sincerity, but those weren't the words that he wanted to hear. She couldn't—or wouldn't—say them. Perhaps her love for him simply wasn't there. Still hurt and angry, he set her aside gently and left the room.

"I'm not going home without you," Darnell shouted after him, but he kept walking away from her.

Darnell sat alone in Thad's office, re-reading *Sensuous*. The sun had set by the time she finished. Every word she read held new meaning for her, knowing that they were his.

The story was about a man and woman so in love with each other that the realities of the world around them ceased to exist. The result was heartache and a new awakening for them both. His writing was magical, passionate, introspective, and insightful, as was the man. In *Sensuous,* Thad had revealed his vulnerability and his sensitivity. Both were qualities that Darnell had come to love and admire in him, and she was not willing to let them or him go.

With script in hand, she went looking for Thad and found him sitting on the patio outside his bedroom. She sat in the lounge chair beside him. He didn't acknowledge her presence as he continued to stare out toward the sea. Darnell sat quietly for a few moments, gathering her thoughts before she spoke.

"I've read *Sensuous* before today, Thad. I have the script at home."

He didn't respond, but she continued divulging her own plans for the script and the future. "So, as you can see, our dreams are similar. I think that if we combine those dreams, we would be a quite a team."

Quite a team. Under other circumstances, Thad would have been turning cartwheels, but now he heard her words with a heavy heart. "You don't trust me, Darnell. There's no future for us at all without that."

The truth in his words couldn't be denied. "Despite my foolish lapse in judgment earlier, I do trust you, Thad, and I hope that you believe that. Even when we were at each other's throats, you showed respect for me." She swallowed the lump in her throat for the second time in less than an hour. "You've respected my privacy, too. I know that you're curious about Lance and me, and well—"

She paused, hoping that he would interrupt her nervous chatter. He said nothing.

She sighed. "It's a complicated situation, and right now, I can't tell you any more than that."

"You and he aren't secretly married, are you?" Thad asked jokingly to break the tension, but his pulse didn't stop racing until she shook her head no.

"But as I've said, I do love him, and I don't want to hurt him."

"And our being together will hurt him."

"It will complicate matters."

Thad silently reflected on her answer before continuing. "Then I'm asking you again. How do you feel about me, Darnell?"

She looked him in the eyes. "I told you that I care for you deeply."

Thad's stomach lurched. Again, the wrong words. "That's good to know," he said sarcastically.

Darnell ran a hand down his muscled arm, relieved that he didn't withdraw from her touch. "I need time to get some things taken care of in my life, Thad."

His eyes searched her face. "And then?"

"We can go from there. That is, if you can forgive me for doubting you earlier."

For the first time in hours, Thad smiled. This was about as humble as Darnell would get, so he'd take it. Taking her hand, he pulled her to her feet, then bent and kissed her on the tip of her nose.

"I guess I can manage to forgive you. Just don't let it happen again."

She gave a mock salute. "Yes, sir."

It was hard to believe that a few months ago she couldn't wait to get this man out of her life. Oh, he was still a bit arrogant, but she had to admit that she was as well. He was still a little too self-centered too, but it was a flaw in character that she also possessed. It seemed that the two of them might be more alike than she had been willing to admit in the past, but there was no denying that this man had crawled inside her heart with a quiet persistence, and her life would never be the same.

As Thad pulled her toward the doorway with one hand, Darnell gripped the *Sensuous* script in the other one. A letter that had been tucked between the pages fell to the floor.

"Wait." She tugged on his hand. "I dropped your letter."

Thad turned to see her bending to retrieve a small blue envelope. "Oh, that. I used it as a bookmark. It's just a note from some crazy fan. I get nut notes like it all the time."

"Oh, yeah?" Darnell raised her eyebrows in mock suspicion. "Then you don't mind my reading it?"

"Ummm," Thad grinned broadly. "Do I detect mistrust or jealousy?"

Darnell wrinkled her nose. "Never the former, but maybe the latter." Slipping the matching blue linen notepaper from the envelope she read aloud.

"*My Dearest Love.*" Darnell raised a brow. "Oh, la la!" She continued, "*I think that it's time for you to know something that I have been trying to tell you for a long time. I love you. Your deep, sexy voice. Your wide, dimple-cheeked smile. Everything about you makes me happy.*" Darnell smiled inwardly in silent agreement. "*My love for you knows no boundaries. There is nothing I wouldn't do for you. We will be together someday.*"

"No signature, but hot stuff," Darnell teased. "Wish I had somebody as hot for me."

With one tug of his arm, Thad brought Darnell's body flush against his and placed a quick kiss on her lips. "You do."

"I don't give a damn what Wochev thinks!" Moody huffed as he stared out the window at Darnell's house. "The problem with that shipment was solved. It came from the Columbians, and the subject is closed. He's got nerve. Some little lackey rips the merchandise off, and he says he doesn't trust *me!*" His voice rose as his anger escalated. This whole week had been a nightmare, and he was fed up.

Darnell's unexplained absence over the past few days had already sent him over the edge. He had waited for days on the beach near Thad Stewart's house watching and waiting for him. By the third day, his anger had build to the point of fury. A cruise or two past the actor's home had revealed that it was occupied. A muscular man collected the mail, and there was a petite woman who came and went occasionally, but no sign of Darnell and Thad. Frustrated, he had gone back to Carmel, and with each day that passed his anger had increased.

Now his second-in-command was calling him with some absurd rumor about the head of the Russian cartel doubting if the entire missing shipment had been found. It seemed that the culprit who had been caught confessed to having siphoned less than was reportedly missing. Word was that others from his cartel might be involved with the rip-off stateside, but Moody was about to put an end to that preposterous gossip.

"Listen, Russ. The subject is dead. Don't repeat this ignorance. We don't need to defend something that didn't happen. Let it rest!" Abruptly, he pushed the disconnect button on his cell phone and started to throw it across the room. Thinking better of that idea, he jammed it in his pocket. He didn't have time for this.

"Where is she?" His anguished cry bounced off the walls of the room.

Burying his face in his hands, he massaged tense muscles. He had to calm down so that he could think. He had to regain control of his emotions and plan his next step—the death of Thad Stewart.

Taking a deep breath, Moody removed his hands from his face and looked out the window again, just in time to see the back of a car pull through the open gates of Darnell's estate. Although it was late, the car taillights put him on alert. They were quite distinctive to the knowing eye. They belonged to a Ferrari, and he could see that the car's color was red. It looked as though the answer to his question about Darnell's whereabouts had just been answered.

CHAPTER 18

Thad couldn't wipe the grin off of his face. As he sat in Ray's office trying to listen to what his friend was saying to him, his thoughts kept drifting back to Darnell and the time they'd spent together in Aruba. After their return from the island, he had driven her home and she had invited him to stay for dinner. He had accepted, discovering that leaving her at all was difficult.

The time that they had spent together had been indescribable, and so was she. Gone was the contentiousness of their prior relationship. It had been replaced by a growing closeness, one that Darnell wanted to keep private for as long as possible. Thad wouldn't have objected to having her all to himself for a while, but he knew that more than the press was involved in her reasoning. She also wanted to keep their relationship private because of Lance. At dinner, she had informed him that she would tell him personally about their relationship because she didn't want him to read about it in some trashy tabloid.

He knew that she was right, and he had tried to temper the feelings of jealousy that Lance Austin aroused in him. Yet he didn't like the thought that she had to see Lance again. There was too much history between them. Everyone thought of Darnell and Lance as a couple, but things would be different now. He was Darnell's man, and nobody was coming between them.

Thad was jolted out of his contemplation when Ray snapped his fingers in front of his face. "Uh, did you say something, Ray?"

"I said the building is on fire."

Thad frowned in confusion. "The building's on fire?"

Ray gave a disgusted sigh. "Man, where is your mind? Get a grip! That woman has you walking around here in a fog."

"Woman? What woman?"

Ray folded his hands on his desk and looked Thad squarely in the eye. "Do I look like a fool to you?"

Thad chuckled. There was no pulling the wool over Ray's eyes. "Aw, man, I was going to tell you about Darnell. It's just that we need to keep this kind of quiet right now. You know, the celebrity bit and all."

"So you were going to keep it from your best friend that you've got a thing going on with one of the sexiest women on earth? I'm wounded." Ray sounded more amused than hurt. "But I do have one question. How serious is it?"

"It's more than a *thing*. I can tell you that." Thad looked past Ray, visualizing Darnell. "I'm in love with her."

Ray didn't seem surprised by the revelation. "I wondered how long it would take for you to admit the obvious."

Thad frowned. "What are you talking about?"

"I'm saying that the way you two have been going at each other's throats, it was inevitable that the heat would turn into a fire. I knew that it was only a matter of time before you would be hooked. Better you than me."

"Your day is coming, and I hope that I'm around when it comes."

Ray scoffed. "Don't hold your breath. But you know you won't be able to keep this quiet for long. You're two of the country's hottest celebrities, and that's news. The press is going to be all over both of you when this breaks."

"Yeah, I know, and she hates the press. We'll just try to keep this quiet as long as we can."

Ray nodded, started to say something, then thought better of it. He began to shuffle papers on his desk. Thad caught the gesture.

"All right, man, you've got more to say, so say it."

Ray put the papers down. "I was wondering . . . from everything I've heard and read, Darnell's been hooked up with that doctor what's-his-name for a long time. I've never known you to make a move on another man's lady."

Thad bristled. "She said they're just friends." He rose from his seat and crossed the room to the small bar in the corner of Ray's paneled office. He poured himself a soda, then looked back at Ray. "They're just friends," he repeated, not sure if he was providing information or trying to convince himself.

Moody was torn. When the red sports car left Darnell's house, he wanted to follow Thad Stewart and eliminate him as a problem for good. He was just that enraged. Yet he longed to see Darnell again, to be near her. His plans to meet her hadn't changed because of Stewart's interference. He had learned long ago to let nothing interfere with his plans. The man was a minor inconvenience easily solved. He couldn't possibly mean anything to her. Dismissing him, he chose to try once again to make contact with Darnell.

A week had passed since Darnell and Thad had returned from Aruba, and today was an important one for her. This was the day that her mother would meet Thad. He would be pulling up to her house any minute, and Ray would be accompanying him. The three of them planned on discussing the possibility of her co-producing *Sensuous* with Thad; at least that was the excuse he gave her for bringing Ray along. However, she suspected that Ray was serving more as Thad's moral support for his meeting Bev. That was good, because he would need it.

To say that her mother wasn't happy about her daughter's budding relationship with the actor would be putting it mildly. Lance could do no wrong as far as Bev was concerned, and when Darnell broke the news about her blossoming feelings for Thad Stewart, her mother had been less than receptive.

She had broken the news to Bev over dinner when she came to Carmel for a visit after her mother's return from her vacation in Africa. She had chosen one of Bev's favorite restaurants, hoping that a delectable meal might cushion the blow about what she had to tell her.

Darnell was visibly nervous all through dinner, and Bev noticed. She knew that her daughter was sometimes edgy in public. Rarely was she able to dine without interruptions from eager fans. However, they had lucked out this evening. There were just a few tourists asking for autographs. This particular restaurant was a local hangout, and they were a breed of their own. They could care less about celebrities, so Darnell felt comfortable here; therefore it was obvious that something else was wrong.

"You've been kind of out of it this evening," Bev said. Her concern about the daughter in whom she took such pride was evident. "Are you still worried about Lance? I know he's a long way away, but he'll be back before you know it. I bet that's all he can think about, getting back here to you and your being here waiting for him."

Darnell almost groaned aloud at her mother's choice of words. She could kick herself for taking the coward's way out and bringing her out in public to break the news. Her hope had been that she wouldn't make the scene in public that she knew that she would make in private. She swallowed.

"That's what I want to talk to you about, Mama. Lance and me."

Bev had been finishing her favorite dessert—apple pie. A frown crossed her attractive face, so much like her daughter's. She didn't like the tone of the words, *Lance and me*. Putting her fork down, she sat back in her chair to observe her child more closely.

"What's on your mind, Darnell? What is there to talk about?" Her look was suspicious.

Darnell shifted in her chair. This was not the time to lose her nerve, even under a glare that used to stop her in her tracks when she was a little girl. Darnell steeled herself.

"I've met somebody else, Mama."

Bev's jaw grew slack. "I beg your pardon?" She couldn't believe what she was hearing. Had her daughter said that she had been creeping out on Lance?

"I've known him for about three months . . ."

"Were you messing around with him before Lance left?"

"No, after. This man and I hated each other at first, but as time passed . . ."

"You and this Romeo grew closer."

Darnell nodded. By this time, she had twisted her linen napkin into a wrinkled blob. Pleasing the woman who had helped make everything in her life possible was the most important thing on earth to her. She hated disappointing her.

Darnell and her mother were close. Her mother was the most important influence in her life. Darnell took pride in the fact that she had never caused her mother one moment of concern. She liked pleasing her, but Bev had taught her to live her life well and on her own terms, and pursuing a relationship with Thad was quickly becoming one of those terms.

"Who is this man?" Bev's eyes had narrowed, a sure sign that she wasn't pleased at the way this conversation was going. "Do I know him?"

"Yes, I think everybody knows him." Darnell couldn't hide the smile in her voice. "It's Thad Stewart, the actor."

"What?" Bev looked as if she had been struck in the face. "Are you crazy? What is your problem?"

Throwing her napkin on the table, Bev jumped up from her seat. In the restaurant, conversation stopped, forks paused in midair. The headwaiter hurried over to the table in a panic, certain that the food or the service was the cause for this sudden commotion.

Darnell assured him that everything was fine as he urged Bev to be seated, then scurried away as she eyed him as if he were a lamb ready for slaughter. Breathing hard and with nostrils flaring, Bev plopped back down in the chair and slammed two tightened fists on the table, waiting for an explanation from her daughter.

Darnell held her mother's steely gaze, unimpressed by her attempt to intimidate. Well, so much for avoiding a public display. She forged ahead.

"I have strong feelings for Thad."

"Strong feelings!" Bev snorted. "Like lust? Because from what I hear, that's all Thad Stewart's got going for him. I've heard and read that he's *very* good in that department."

"You can't believe everything you read in the paper. You of all people should know that. There's much more to Thad than his sexuality."

"Oh, really!" Bev spat out the words contemptuously, leaving no doubt about her feelings about the man.

She went on to recount every playboy exploit that she had ever read or heard about him, expressing her disappointment that the child in whom she had instilled such high standards would stoop so low as to "play around" on a good man like Lance.

The criticism hurt, but Darnell remained poised, refusing to allow her mother the satisfaction of a temporary victory. Their eyes continued to lock. Bev was livid.

"What has Lance done to you for the last ten years except love you and be there for you. He's done everything he could for you."

"Mama, please! Anything either of us got out of our relationship has always been mutual. He got as much out of being with me as I got out of being with him. But it's about Thad now, and the beginning of a new relationship with him. I'd like you to meet him."

Bev stiffened in reaction to her request. "So I'm suppose to be a coconspirator in this deception? Is that what this is about?"

"No, I'm only asking you to meet the new man in my life. I think that you'll like him. He's funny and charming. I've invited him to come to Carmel next weekend, and I'd like you to come, too. I'm asking you to do this for me, Mama, because I love you and because your opinion is very important to me."

Bev was hesitant. "It sounds to me like you've already made up your mind about him. I don't know why you want my opinion." There was a long pause as she considered the invitation. "But I love you, too, and I want you to be happy." She agreed to the meeting.

Now, the time for their first encounter was at hand and all Darnell could do was hope that this first meeting between her mother and Thad would at least be amicable. As far as she was concerned, that would be a small victory. Meanwhile, she had taken precautions to assure some pretense of civility on Bev's part at their meeting. She looked across the living room to where Trevor Reasoner, Colin's younger brother, sat at the piano, picking at the keys.

Darnell had turned the meeting between Bev and Thad into a cookout and had invited her cousin Nedra, her husband Sinclair, and their three children to share steaks grilled outside by the pool. With the Reasoner family and Ray, there should be enough people present to prevent Bev from making a scene—again. Yet her beautiful, vivacious mother was an independent spirit, and she was full of surprises.

Thad's heart was pumping overtime in anticipation of seeing Darnell again. It had been a week, and as far as he was concerned, it was a week too long. They had spoken on the telephone every day, sometimes twice a day, but nothing could replace his seeing her. He had chattered about her so much on the drive to Carmel that Ray had threatened his life if he didn't stop talking.

Darnell had been coming down the stairway when they entered the house. Stopping at the last step, she and Thad stood grinning at each other like two entranced teenagers, unsure of what to do next. She was the first to break the silence.

"Hello. Glad to see me?"

That was his cue. Thad closed the gap between them and stood before her. Placing his hands around her trim waist he lifted her from the bottom step as Darnell's arms encircled his neck. He brought her down to the floor slowly, her body pressed intimately against his own. "Hello," he whispered huskily as his lips grazed her lips, "and, yes, I'm very glad to see you."

As she floated to the floor, Darnell's body temperature rose. She was oblivious to everything around her until a loud "ah hmmm" coming from the upper stairway caught her attention. Withdrawing from Thad's arms, she turned to look for the source. Her mother stood looking down at her.

Thad's eyes followed Darnell's. There, midways up the stairs, stood a woman so breathtaking in her majesty that he gasped. Behind him, he heard a similar reaction from Ray. Darnell smiled. Her mother usually had that effect on people, especially men.

Bev Cameron *was* a beautiful woman. She stood nearly six feet tall, and at fifty her earth brown complexion was flawless. Her curvaceous figure rivaled that of her daughter's—ample breasts, small waist, and shapely hips. She wore her hair natural, sculptured close to her head. Strands of gray threaded through the dark tresses that ended in a stylish triangle at the nape of her neck. Finely chiseled cheekbones dominated her heart-shaped face, giving it an exotic appearance. Although her eyes were darker, they were just as large and as expressive as her daughter's eyes and held the same fire. At the moment that fire was aimed at him.

Darnell took a fortifying breath. "Mama, this is Thad Stewart. Thad, this is my mother, Beverly Cameron." Behind them Ray loudly cleared his throat. Darnell turned to him, embarrassed that she had forgotten his presence. "Oh, I'm sorry. This is Thad's friend, Ray Wilson. Ray, my mother Beverly."

Bev's eye's shifted over Darnell's shoulder to where Ray was standing. Recognizing his name as that of Thad's attorney, she was ready to intimidate him with her stare. This man had helped cause her daughter a lot of distress after the car accident. She glared at him coolly, but his gaze didn't waver. Their gazes held fiercely, except the light in Ray's eyes didn't spell discord. They were afire with interest. Bev shifted her attention back to Thad.

Flashing his most gracious smile, he thrust his hand out as Bev reached the bottom of the stairs. "Nice to meet you, Ms. Cameron." She nodded and took his hand. Her handshake was firm and self-assured.

Mrs. Sharon showed the two men to the separate bedroom suites in which they would spend the night. After getting settled, they joined the other guests by the swimming pool. As the day progressed, Darnell watched attentively as her mother interacted with each person in attendance; that is, everyone except Thad and Ray. She pointedly ignored both men.

Darnell was incensed. Bev had taught her the value of being gracious to guests, and right now her mother was far from following her own advice. Yet while Bev was ignoring the two men, the other guests were offering them their full attention, especially to Thad. He was at his charming best with the Reasoner family. Thad's easy-going personality even appeared to be softening Colin's stance.

Excited by his presence, Nedra approached Darnell, almost effusive in her praise of Thad.

"Girlfriend, I think that man is a keeper," she gushed as she and Darnell sat watching Thad romp in the pool with the Reasoner children. "If you don't want him, I know plenty of women who could use a good man."

"Well, our relationship is more or less professional right now." Darnell tried to sound nonchalant. She hadn't shared her growing feelings for Thad with Nedra yet.

Nedra laughed in her face, and she was still laughing when she sauntered away to join her family. It seemed that Darnell and Thad's effort to be discreet about their relationship wasn't working, and Thad certainly wasn't helping the situation. Every time he came near, he touched her, and each time her body reacted.

Later, the two of them sat at a table by the pool enjoying their meal. He reached across and took her hand. Immediately, heat began to snake up her arm. Darnell tried to withdraw her hand

"You do know my mother is watching us, don't you?"

"Yes, I know." He tightened his grip. "Like a hawk."

He watched Darnell's face flush as he concentrated on making lethal circles in her hand. "But my man Ray will be putting a stop to that."

"What?" Darnell's head snapped up. "Ray?"

Thad nodded. "Yep."

"How?

He gave her a mysterious smile. "You'll see. The man should be making his move soon."

Darnell looked over at where her mother was relaxing on a lounge chair, watching them from behind dark glasses. As if on cue, Ray walked toward Bev, took a seat on the lounge chair beside her, and started talking to her. Darnell's mouth dropped open.

Thad clucked her chin. "Shut your mouth, sweety, you might draw flies."

"I *know* he's not trying to *talk* to her!"

"Why not?"

"Because that's *my* mother, and he's *your* attorney!"

"*And* they're also a man and a woman," Thad chuckled. "Don't worry, I'm sure that they both can take care of themselves. I know for a fact that one of the Cameron women can."

Darnell smiled, remembering their verbal sparring sessions. It seemed such a long time ago. "I'm glad we got past that."

Thad nodded in agreement. "Now if we can get past your mother not liking me, maybe we have a chance of making it together." His words were said lightly, but there was a hint of sadness in his voice.

There was a moment of silence as they mused on that truth. Darnell's tone was reflective. "How does that make you feel, Thad, my mother not liking you?"

He laced his fingers through hers. "I can understand it. A man with a reputation as a player is in love with her daughter. Meanwhile, her daughter's ex-boyfriend . . ."

He paused. "Or, shall I say, her best male friend looks as though he's being replaced." He sighed. "I guess I never had a chance with your mother."

Pushing her plate aside, Darnell gave Thad her full attention. It was time to tell him the other reason she had extended an invitation for him to come to her home today. "I need to tell you something."

Thad's eyes skittered across her face in an effort to gauge the seriousness of what was about to be said. "Yeah?"

She swallowed. "I'm making plans to fly to South America to see Lance."

Thad's face hardened. "Oh, really. And may I ask why?"

"Like I've told you, I plan on telling him face-to-face that I've found someone that I'm crazy about."

His face softened slightly, but he still didn't like her going away. "And you have to go to South America to tell him that?"

"Yes, I do. I love Lance, and I owe him at least the courtesy of talking to him in person."

Thad couldn't disagree. As much as he would like for Darnell not to have any contact with Lance, he knew that she was right. Ten years of friendship couldn't be callously dismissed, and he was proud that she wasn't the type to do so. He marveled at the irony of it all. Only months ago, he had wondered how anyone could love this woman. Now he wondered how anyone could not.

The rest of the day went well. At sunset everyone at the cookout decided to take a stroll together along the beach. Mother and daughter walked arm-in-arm in silence until Bev spoke.

"I know that you don't want to hear this, Darnell, but I'm going to say it anyway. I think that this is the height of impropriety, your cavorting here with some playboy actor while your *fiancé* is in South America trying to find a cure for a fatal disease! I can't believe that this is the child I raised!"

Darnell sighed patiently at her mother's melodrama. The woman could be quite the actress when she wanted to be.

"Mama, you know good and well that Lance is not my fiancé. It's obvious that our relationship has never matured to that level. How many times have you asked me about that?"

Her mother dropped her defiant glare. There had been too many times, and while this might not be the right place, it was the right time to get brutally honest with Bev about her relationship with Lance. It was the only way that both of them could move forward. She looked around to see if anyone was within earshot. They were walking far behind the Reasoner family and way ahead of Ray and Thad. No one could hear what she was about to say. Darnell took a breath and plunged onward.

"The truth is that in a lot of ways, Lance and I are not compatible. I love him, but love can be an unpredictable emotion, and the two of us are not *in* love. We're simply used to using each other."

Bev gasped. Darnell continued.

"It might not have been right, but we felt it was necessary for what we each wanted to achieve in our careers, and out of it came a great friendship. He'll always have a special place in my heart, just not in my future."

As they continued to stroll, Bev stared at her daughter long and hard. Her voice wavered as she spoke. "I don't even know you, Darnell. I gave birth to you, and I don't know you." She bit her bottom lip to contain her emotions, hoping that her daughter would offer a retraction of her words in the ensuing silence. She didn't. Bev took her stance.

"I'll never accept this. Never!"

"I'm not asking you to, Mama. I'm just letting you know where things stand."

"And where *do* they stand?"

"I think I'm in love with Thad."

The muscles in Bev's jaw twitched angrily. "And just what are you going to tell Lance?"

"That I'm tired of using him and of being used. It's time for both of us to move on. Mama, you were the one who taught me to go after what I want in life. You said that I should be relentless and not give up until I get it. I want Thad, and he wants me."

Bev refused to relent. "You've slept with him, haven't you?"

Darnell fought a blush, refusing to give credence to her mother's inquiry as she looked at her steadily. "I'm a grown woman, Mama. I love you and I respect you, but what I do or don't do with a man is my personal business." With that, she slid her arm out of Bev's and hurried to catch up with her cousins.

On an elevated bluff above the beach, hidden from view to those traipsing the sandy shore, Moody stood watching the scenario unfold below. He couldn't move. He was paralyzed. He had become so the moment he saw her.

It had been an unexpected surprise. From the upstairs window, he had seen the parade of cars that passed through Darnell's front gate, including Thad's. He surmised that she was having a party and decided that she would be occupied for the rest of the day. He had opted for an evening stroll along the beach. He never made it.

He saw Darnell as he started down the road leading to his destination and had been frozen in his tracks. She wasn't alone. Her mother was walking with her. The intensity of his reaction had surprised him. His heart was still palpitating. His hands still shook as he removed his sunglasses and wiped the moisture from his eyes.

As he watched Darnell pick up speed and scurry up the beach, he noted that Thad increased his gait as well. On trembling legs, Moody turned and headed back toward his house. He couldn't bear to see another man go near her. He had experienced more than enough for now. It was best that he retreat.

Thad watched as Darnell hurried down the beach toward the Reasoner family. He had been watching mother and daughter converse. He could tell by their body language that the discussion between them was tense. He had no doubt that it had been about him. He felt bad. Her mother meant a lot to Darnell, and he didn't want to be the cause of a breech between them. He valued family. His was very close. There were enough obstacles to his blossoming romance with Darnell already; a family feud wouldn't improve matters.

Increasing his pace, he caught up with Bev and fell into step beside her. He noticed her stiffen, but decided to get straight to the point.

"I know that you don't like me, Ms. Cameron, but there's one thing I want you to know."

Her sudden stop caught Thad by surprise. He continued walking for a second before he realized that she wasn't beside him. He returned to her. Out of the corner of his eye, he noticed Ray's bemused expression as he gained on them, then made a detour around them, making it obvious that he didn't want to get caught in the fray.

Bev stood with her arms folded across her chest as she looked at him, but her stance wasn't one of defiance. It was resignation.

"You don't have to say a thing to me, Thad. It's in every look that you give her, every movement you make toward her. You love my daughter. Even a blind man could see that. I won't be coy with you or play games. I'm not sure I like you or this situation, but as she has informed me, it's her life—and she's right." She started to walk away, then added, "By the way, I like your cologne."

Thad grinned at her back as she trudged through the sand, shoulders squared and head high. Bev Cameron was a tough cookie just like her daughter, but at least there was one thing that she did like about him.

CHAPTER 19

The day had passed smoothly without Bev confronting Thad, and he had Ray to thank for that. He had occupied most of Bev's time and attention as he made it quite clear that he was interested in Darnell's lovely mother. Bev made it just as clear that she had no interest at all in Ray. Humbled but not defeated, he had backed off graciously.

Thad was grateful to him anyway; Ray's intervention had helped the day go smoothly. What he had with Darnell was so new, so fragile, that if he couldn't have her mother as an ally, he didn't want her as an enemy. For now, he was fine with the silent truce between the two of them. However, the night hours didn't pass as smoothly as the daylight hours.

As Ray lay sleeping peacefully in the suite next door, Thad stalked his own spacious bedroom suite restlessly. Knowing that Darnell was here in this house, sleeping only one floor away, kept him awake. Finally, before he could stop himself he climbed the stairs, telling himself that he was just checking on Darnell to make sure that she was getting her rest. Yet with every step closer to her, that proved to be a lie. He hoped against hope that he would find her up, waiting for him, wanting and needing him as much as he did her.

At the top of the stairs, Thad stopped and stood in confusion. He hadn't realized until that moment that he had no idea which bedroom was Darnell's. He had never been upstairs in her house before. There were six doorways lining the dimly lit hallway. Three doors were open, three closed. Dare he take the chance of walking into Bev Cameron's bedroom by mistake? He shuddered at the thought. He never would win her over to his side if that happened. Maybe it was best to turn around and go back now.

Swallowing his disappointment, he had turned to head back down the stairway when the muffled sound of music caught his attention. Tossing all former intentions aside, he followed the sound down the hallway. Stopping at the second closed door he listened to the melodious sound of Luther Vandross singing "So Amazing." Smiling, he turned the doorknob and entered with confidence.

The bedroom was empty, but that didn't stop him.

The music led him to the soft glow of light streaming from beneath the closed door of an adjoining room. Opening the door, he stepped into the light.

The bathroom he entered was huge, decorated in pastel yellow, with green marble vanities accented with brass accessories. The shower glass was etched in gold leaf; lounge chairs were placed in front of an entertainment center that dominated one wall. Plants hung from walls, ledges, and the cathedral ceiling. The fragrance of jasmine engulfed his senses as his eyes drifted to a huge, sunken oval tub of green marble, located in the center of the room.

Thad's mouth went dry, and his respiration spiraled. His groin instantly turned to steel. Darnell was standing beside the tub wearing a clinging silk robe, loosely tied and ready to be released. She didn't look surprised to see him as their eyes locked. Untying the robe, she let it slide slowly from her shoulders and slither to the floor.

She gave him a seductive smile. "As you can see, I don't take average baths, either."

Thad sat at the kitchen table with a cooling cup of coffee before him as he recalled the previous night's encounter with Darnell. Their lovemaking had been incredible. She had crooned love songs to him while they took each other to new heights of ecstasy. Never had he felt so completely for one human being. Sighing, he closed his eyes and savored the memory.

Sitting across from him, Ray tried to read the show-business trade paper, *Variety*, not unaware of the sighs of contentment emanating from across the table. Noisily, he snapped the paper as he turned the page.

Thad lifted a brow. "Was there something that you wanted, my man?"

"Yeah, to get down to business. That is, if you can pull your head out of the clouds for a minute. I don't see what you've got to be so happy about. Darnell's mother hates your guts, and we didn't get a lick of business done yesterday with you and Darnell making moon eyes at each other every time I looked up."

Thad grinned at his irritated tone. "Jealous?"

Ray waved a dismissive hand and reached for a cinnamon bun. Thad chuckled.

"Don't take it out on me because Bev Cameron rejected you."

"Rejected me?" Ray bristled. "What do you mean, *'rejected me'*? I've never been rejected by a woman in my life."

Thad grinned knowingly, his silence allowing his friend to retain some sense of dignity despite the obvious. Ray glared at him but modified his tone.

"She did say something about how I wasn't prepared to play love games with a grown women, or some such nonsense."

Thad whistled. "Low blow."

Ray scowled. "I will admit that the woman did interest me for a split second, but that was before I found out that her tongue was lethal."

"Like mother, like daughter, but when that tongue turns sweet—" Thad gave a wicked grin.

The sound of Bev's voice outside the kitchen interrupted their conversation. Ray groaned.

"Speak of the devil." His eyes shifted to the doorway as Bev entered the kitchen. Darnell was close behind. Both women were dressed in jogging suits.

Bev's eyes shifted from Thad to Ray, then back to Thad. "Isn't this a surprise. I didn't expect to see either of you up at this early hour." Her eyes swept the well-built frames of both men, each of whom was also dressed in sweats and wearing jogging shoes. "Don't tell me you jog?"

"Thad does." Darnell smiled at him warmly. "Good morning." Her voice was filled with memories.

"Good morning." So was his.

With narrowed eyes Bev glanced from one to the other suspiciously before heading for the coffee maker, where she poured herself a cup of coffee. Darnell joined the men at the table.

A smile tugged at the corners of Ray's mouth as he observed the look on Thad's face as he gazed at Darnell. He had never thought that he would see the day, but it looked as though his main man was in love. Ray shifted his gaze to the object of his friend's affection. She seemed to have eyes for no one but Thad. From the look of it, the feelings were reciprocal. He shot a glance at Bev, who was preoccupied with the coffee maker. It looked as if both Cameron women possessed the secret of how to enchant a man.

The telephone rang, bringing all of the room's occupants out of their individual musings. Ray watched Bev move across the kitchen gracefully to answer it. Yes, the woman was a distraction, but—. He sighed, then turned back to the entranced couple.

"Listen, you two, we've got to discuss the production of *Sensuous*, make arrangements for a screen test . . ."

"Screen test?" Darnell's attention turned to Ray. "I didn't know there was a screen test involved. When will it be scheduled?"

Ray took a sip of his coffee. "As soon as it can be arranged. Why?"

"I have a singing engagement in San Francisco next month. I'll be singing at a fundraiser. The President will be there."

Ray nodded. "The President? Of the United States?"

"Yes."

Thad winked at her. "I'm impressed."

"I hope by more than that," she said suggestively, warming at the fire that appeared in Thad's eyes.

"Darnell."

She jumped at the sound of her mother's voice. Her jovial mood disappeared instantly at the look on Bev's face. "What is it?" She looked from Bev to the telephone. Rising, she joined her mother.

"It's Lance."

"Lance?"

Bev nodded. She looked grim as she handed her daughter the telephone.

Thad stilled at the sound of Lance's name. So did Ray. The silence in the kitchen was deafening, as was the tension. All eyes were on Darnell.

Thad watched her closely as she answered the call, noting that her reaction to this one was much different than in the past. What did Lance want? Would she be going to South America sooner? He turned his attention to Bev as she took a seat at the table. She looked shaken. Thad could hold his curiosity no longer.

"What's this about, Bev?" His voice was even.

She took a sip from her coffee cup before answering. Her voice trembled.

"Lance was flown from South America to San Francisco last night. He's in the hospital in intensive care. He's dying."

CHAPTER 20

"It's been too long, Ray." Thad's voice was ragged with emotion. Dragging to the sofa, he fell down on it heavily, slouching among the pillows. It had been three weeks since he had left Darnell at the Monterey airport where she'd boarded a chartered plane to San Francisco to be with Lance. He hadn't heard from her since. He had left countless messages, but none had been returned. Mrs. Sharon had informed him that all of Darnell's time was spent in San Francisco at the hospital.

Growing more desperate as the weeks passed, Thad had driven to the city in the hope that he might catch her there. Wearing a disguise to keep from being recognized, he had gone to the hospital to find out what floor that Lance was on, but it was like trying to find out the combination to the safe at Fort Knox. No one would admit that he was even a patient there. He had driven back to Tiburon defeated.

Darnell's absence from his life affected everything he did. He hadn't had a good night's sleep in weeks. Food no longer appealed to him. He couldn't listen to the radio for fear that he would hear her amazing voice and fall apart. He was afraid to watch television. What if one of those entertainment shows announced her engagement to Lance, or worse, a marriage? He was an emotional wreck.

He knew that he was being irrational. Lance was very sick. He had hepatitis A. Thad had looked the disease up in a medical reference book. It was an infectious virus and was very serious. Ray reinforced that fact as he tried to reassure him.

"I know if any of my friends or family came down with something like that, there wouldn't be a day that I wouldn't be by their side, no matter how long it took." Ray's words were much too practical for Thad.

"But three weeks?" Thad shot up from his seat. "The woman has a cell phone. She could call! I've left messages everywhere." He stalked over to the window and looked out, seeing nothing.

Ray could hear his frustration. He had come to Tiburon out of concern for his friend. During their daily business conversations, he had noted a drastic change in him. He had to push him to read one of the countless scripts that he received daily. Thad had read a few of them, but he really didn't seem interested in business. He was short with him, edgy. He seemed lethargic. Picking up on his affect, Ray had flown to the Bay area from L.A. to see what was happening. What he saw shocked him.

His fastidious, impeccably dressed client and friend was unshaven and disheveled and so depressed that he was listless. Ray would have suspected the man had turned to drugs if he didn't know him better. Thad Stewart was one movie star on the Hollywood scene that everyone knew didn't indulge in alcohol or drugs. Having unfortunately indulged in both during his youth, Ray was proud that Thad had always had the fortitude to resist these vices. However, the power that this woman was wielding over Thad's emotions seemed more addictive than any drug Ray had ever taken. He made an attempt to help his friend approach the matter practically.

"Thad, three weeks, three days, three hours means nothing when someone you care for is ill. She's been with the man for ten years . . ."

"He's a *friend*, Ray, her best friend. That's all!" He tried to hide the resentment he felt and mask the uncertainty. His effort proved unsuccessful.

"Then what do you expect from her? He's been a part of her life for a long time. Do you want her to abandon him and come be with you while he's flat on his back?"

Thad's silence brought a quick reprimand. "I know you don't want that. You're a better man than that, and you know Darnell better than I do. Is that the kind of woman she is?"

Thad sighed. Ray was right. Darnell should stay by Lance's side as long as he needed her. Yet he needed her, too. He knew it was selfish, but he wanted to be with her so badly that it hurt.

Exasperated, he paced the living room. "I have to know what's happening, Ray. Why hasn't she called me? I've never loved a woman in my life the way I love this one. I have to know that I haven't lost her, that she hasn't changed her mind about us." His voice rose in anguish. "If I lose her, I don't know what I'll do."

Ray was silent for a moment, in awe of the power of love. He would never have thought it possible that the man would fall this hard. If it could happen to Thad, it could happen to him. That was a scary thought. He wasn't sure that he was ready for that. His voice softened in empathy. "It'll be all right, man. You'll see. Everything will be fine."

Thad gave a heavy sigh. "Funny, that's exactly what I told Darnell."

"Listen, why don't you fly back to L.A. with me? You've got the premiere of your movie coming up, but come down early. We can hang out, have some fun. It'll get your mind off your problems for a while."

"I just might do that. I'll have Donald make plane reservations." The ringing of the telephone interrupted their conversation. Thad grew excited. "Maybe that's Darnell." Eagerly he snatched the phone from its cradle. "Hello."

"Hi, neighbor."

"Oh, Regine." Thad checked his disappointment. She had called him several times in the past few weeks and had left quite a few messages. He hadn't returned any of her calls. Perhaps his dilemma was divine justice.

"I was driving around in your area, and I thought I'd stop by and see how you were enjoying your Bearden."

"It's doing fine." He tried vainly to be polite. It had been weeks since the painting had been delivered to his home, and her excuse for calling him sounded weak. He didn't like the idea of her calling him for any reason. Their business had ended long ago. "And what do you mean by 'hello neighbor'? I thought you lived in Oakland."

Regine's voice brightened. "No, actually I moved to Marin County months ago. I'm leasing a condo not far from Tiburon. I thought I told you that when you came to the gallery."

"No, I don't remember." Thad walked through the house aimlessly as he spoke.

"Anyway, I prefer Marin County to the East Bay. Things here are a lot more interesting."

"I see."

There was an awkward silence until Regine spoke. "Aren't you going to invite me over?"

Thad groaned inwardly. He was in no mood for Regine's game of pursuit. Taking his keys from his pocket, he motioned to Ray and mouthed the words, "Let's go."

As Thad followed Ray to the entranceway, he was as polite as he could be as he tried to complete the unwanted telephone call. "I'm sorry, Regine, but you caught me at a bad time. I can assure you that the painting arrived intact and that it's being enjoyed. Thanks for your call. Sorry, but I've got to go." He disconnected the call.

Placing the telephone receiver on the table in the entranceway, Thad called up the stairs to Donald. "We're out of here! I'll be back around six. Page me if . . ." He paused to swallow the sadness. "Page me if anyone calls." With that, he followed Ray out of the house.

Five minutes later, the front doorbell rang. Donald opened the door to find Regine Lexy standing in the doorway smiling at him. It was a smile that wasn't returned.

"May I help you?"

"Hello. Donald, isn't it?" Sugar would have melted in her mouth.

Donald nodded, but remained composed.

Regine forged ahead. "Please tell Thad that Ms. Lexy is here to see him."

"Sorry, Ms. Lexy, but Mr. Stewart isn't here."

Regine's manner changed immediately as her voice hardened. "What do you mean he isn't in? Where is he? I just talked to him from my cell phone less than five minutes ago."

"He had an appointment." Donald offered no further information. He remembered this woman well. She was demanding and condescending. He took pleasure in delivering the information that Thad wasn't there. He didn't like the woman.

Regine's jaws tightened, and her pleasant façade began to slip. "I see. Do you know when he'll return?"

"No, I don't."

She gave a frustrated sigh. It was obvious that she wasn't going to get any information from him. "When Thad returns, please let him know that I dropped by."

"I'll do that."

"Meanwhile, I'd like to use your bathroom. That is, if you don't mind." Her last words were said with sarcasm that she hoped he wouldn't miss. Why Thad put up with this man, she didn't know.

Donald started to point the way, but Regine pushed past him. Not surprised by her bodacious behavior, he started out the door. "I'm walking down to the mailbox to pick the mail up, Ms. Lexy. Please close the door behind you when you leave."

"Sure," Regine tossed over her shoulder, her angry strides indicating her displeasure with him.

As she disappeared into the bathroom, Donald hesitated for a moment, unsure as to whether to leave her alone in the house. Deciding that doing so would be fine, he closed the front door behind him and started down the stone pathway.

Inside the house, Regine gripped the sides of the marble pedestal sink until her knuckles ached. She was angry. It wasn't often that she degraded herself and chased a man, but Thad Stewart was worth it. She had fallen for him hard, and their breakup had been devastating for her. She had never understood the reason behind it and, despite the time that had passed since their parting, she still loved him. She wanted him back, and she wasn't about to give up.

Gaining control of her emotions, Regine squared her shoulders and left the bathroom. As she moved toward the living room, the telephone lying on a table in the entranceway rang. Regine continued toward the front door. The telephone rang again. She hesitated, eyed the telephone, and shrugged. Why not? Doubling back she picked up the receiver. "Stewart residence."

There was silence on the other end. Regine repeated the greeting.

"Stewart residence. May I help you?"

"Hello?" The voice on the other end seemed hesitant.

"This is the Stewart residence. May I *help* you?"

"Is this Thad Stewart's residence? "

"That's what I said. What do you want?"

"Is this Catina?"

"No, it's not." Regine had lost patience with this caller two questions ago.

"I'd like to speak with Thad Stewart, please." The voice was coolly polite.

Regine's brow furrowed. The voice sounded familiar. "Who is this?"

"Who is *this?*"

The voice held defiance, just enough for Regine to recognize who was on the other end of the line. "Thad's woman, that's who!"

Regine disconnected the call and gave a sinister smile. She knew the voice on the other end of the line. Yes indeed, she knew it well. It belonged to Darnell Cameron.

Since arriving at the hospital weeks ago Darnell's life had centered on medical jargon, visiting hours, hospital food, and catnaps. After contracting hepatitis in South America, Lance had been flown to a hospital there which was ill-equipped to handle his case. His parents had made arrangements to fly him back to the United States. It had been his mother who had called Darnell and informed her that Lance was ill.

When Darnell entered the hospital room to see him, she could barely recognize the handsome man that she knew. His once fit six-foot frame was emaciated. His light complexion had turned a dull yellowish color, as had the whites of his dark brown eyes. Darnell had been so shocked by his appearance that initially she had found it difficult to look at him.

His parents were near hysterics. Lance was their only child. Even Darnell's presence couldn't ease their fears. As physicians, they knew how much danger he was in. The virus had damaged his liver. He fought constant fevers and, at one point, delirium. Lance was literally fighting for his life.

Darnell and his parents kept a twenty-four-hour vigil. Mrs. Sharon kept her informed of all of her business and personal calls, including the ones from Thad. Whenever she sought to return his calls, another crisis with Lance would arise.

By the third week, Lance's condition had been upgraded. His fever was down, and he was lucid. Darnell felt confident enough about his prognosis that she left the hospital—the first time in weeks. She accomplished the feat by way of the freight elevator. So far, she had been lucky. The press was not aware of Lance's illness or of her presence at his side. The hospital had done all it could to maintain their privacy.

Having retreated to her high rise condominium with its breathtaking view of San Francisco, she knew that she should have been thinking of the man in the hospital who had been a part of her life for so long. Instead, all she could think about was the man who lived across the Golden Gate Bridge in Tiburon and how very much she wanted to be with him. She yearned for the touch of his hand, the taste of his kisses, the feel of him buried inside her. She was a woman in love, and as she dialed his number, her heart pounded with excitement in anticipation of hearing his voice. She was unprepared for the voice that she did hear—that of another woman.

She had been positive that she had dialed the wrong number, but the woman confirmed that she had dialed correctly. She didn't recognize the voice, but she would have to be deaf not to have heard the woman declare herself his girlfriend. And then she had been bold enough to hang up on her.

Suspicion and jealousy gripped her. Three short weeks had passed since she and Thad had made love. His fervent declarations of devotion were still ringing in her ears, and some *woman* was answering his telephone. Could it be that he had fooled her? Had everything he told her been a lie? She felt ill.

Staggering to the bathroom, Darnell barely made it to the toilet bowl before falling to her knees and vomiting. After rinsing her mouth, she tried to leave the bathroom but failed. Drained and exhausted, she slid to the cold tiles. Wrapping her arms around her legs, she buried her head and cried.

CHAPTER 21

The day had been a long one for Thad. After having lunch with Ray, Thad had taken Ray to the airport, promising that he would follow him to L.A. in the morning. Returning home, Thad had decided against his usual run along the beach. It seemed that he couldn't muster up the energy to do anything lately. The emptiness he felt at the absence of Darnell in his life was all-consuming.

After standing on his deck watching the sun disappear beyond the horizon, Thad drifted downstairs to the kitchen where Donald was putting the finishing touches on the evening meal.

Donald greeted his employer with a smile, receiving a slight nod of acknowledgment as Thad headed for the refrigerator and withdrew a bottle of water. Donald had watched silently over the past few weeks as the relationship between Thad and Darnell escalated. He didn't know the lady well, but he did know Thad, and he recognized the changes she had caused in him. He had never seen him so happy, but neither had he seen him as distraught as he had been in the past three weeks.

Ten years Thad's senior, he loved him like a brother. The man had helped provide him with self-dignity and a sense of worth. When no one else would give him a chance, Thad had done so, and for that he would always be grateful.

Donald had been arrested for passing bad checks. On his release from prison, he had found it impossible to find employment. As an ex-con, he had been rejected for every position for which he had applied. Defeated, he had all but given up hope when his mother told him about the position as housekeeper with the movie star Thad Stewart. She worked next door to him as Dr. Alan's housekeeper. She knew the actor and said that she would put a good word in for her son. Donald was skeptical. Why would someone like Thad Stewart trust him, let alone hire him to work in his household? He applied anyway. Thad interviewed him, then hired him at a salary that was beyond generous. He had been so happy that he had cried. When Donald tried to tell him the reason for his imprisonment, Thad had informed him that he had served his sentence. The past was the past. He was offering Donald a future.

There was nothing he wouldn't do for his employer. He owed all that he had to him, and today he was about to repay him in a small way.

Donald placed Thad's dinner on the table, then took a seat opposite him. "You know that Catina and Ms. Cameron got along pretty well when she was here. Once when they were talking, Ms. Cameron told Catina that she had a condo in San Francisco."

Thad looked up. "She does? Where in San Francisco?"

"I don't know, but Catina has the address. She's in the city today visiting her mother. She won't be back until tomorrow."

Thad shot out of his seat. "I can't wait until tomorrow." He grabbed the telephone and all but jammed it into Donald's hand. "Call her. See if she remembers it."

Donald dialed his mother-in-law's number. There was no answer. He called his wife's cell phone. Again, there was no answer. Thad looked devastated. Donald thought quickly. "Dr. Alan might have the address. Maybe Ms. Cameron gave him both addresses for her prescriptions or . . ."

The words hadn't left Donald's mouth before Thad was calling Alan. His adrenaline raced at the thought that he might be with Darnell soon.

Thad hadn't taken his usual run this evening. If he had done so, this would have been his last day on earth. This made Moody's entire trip to Tiburon an inconvenience, but he couldn't trust anyone else to do the job.

Initially, he had felt that Thad could be useful in tracking Darnell. She had been missing for weeks. Even his household staff had noticed her absence. He had overheard the gossip among them as they speculated as to her whereabouts.

It seemed that Mrs. Sharon wasn't talking about Darnell's whereabouts. Neither had she mentioned Darnell's relationship with Thad. None of the servants seemed to know about it. Mrs. Sharon had proved to be the kind of employee any employer would love to have—discreet.

So, it was up to him to figure out where Darnell was. For several days, he had kept watch in Tiburon, but there had been no sign of her being there with Thad. Moody was baffled. There were only two conclusions to be drawn. Either she had come to her senses and had dumped the loser, or she was vacationing somewhere other than Carmel. Whatever the case, she wasn't with Thad, and that was good because she wouldn't be around when he died. He still planned on killing him. The man had violated Darnell. He wasn't worthy of her, and just in case they were still seeing each other, he was going to put an end to it once and for all. The fact that the man had changed his routine today meant that it had to be another time. Damn! Of all the luck! That meant another trip to Tiburon, and too many appearances in the area could draw attention. That was the last thing he needed. Shadows didn't leave footprints.

It was nearly nine o'clock when Thad arrived at Darnell's San Francisco condo. The doorman and the guards all recognized him, so it wasn't difficult to convince them that he had a business meeting with Darnell. Thad was almost dizzy with excitement when it was confirmed that she was home. Her apartment was buzzed, but there was no answer. They let him go upstairs.

Nervously, he rang the doorbell. He didn't know what to expect on the other side of the door. Would she be glad to see him? Did they still have a future together?

He would know the answer by the time he left this evening.

There was no answer to the doorbell. He knocked. Still, there was no answer. Maybe she was asleep, or perhaps she had left the building without the guards and the doorman seeing her. He tried the doorknob. He was shocked when it turned easily and opened.

What was happening? She was in the apartment, and the door wasn't locked? He felt as if he was in one of his movies as he glanced at the doorjamb to see if there was any evidence of forced entry. There didn't seem to be. It was a good lock; a credit card couldn't be used to open it. Yet, it was open. Taking a defensive stance, he entered.

The apartment was dark and quiet. The curtains at the floor-to-ceiling windows fluttered in the breeze from the open door. He could see the lights of the city twinkling below. He stepped deeper into the apartment. As his eyes adjusted to the dimness, he noticed the Vanetta Honeywell painting that Darnell had purchased at Regine's gallery. It was hanging on the wall opposite the entranceway.

He called to her, alerting her to his presence. "Darnell!" There was no reply. Fear trickled up his spine. Something was wrong. His volume increased. "Darnell!" He proceeded down the hallway, alert to every sound. Listening closely, he heard a small whimper. It came from the cracked doorway to his right.

Cautiously, he approached the door. It was then that he saw her in the dimly lit bathroom. She was sitting with her back against the wall, curled up into a ball. Her head was buried between her legs.

Darnell's tears had been reduced to sniffles. She had heard someone enter but couldn't muster up the strength to be frightened. When her name was called, she knew who it was right away, but she hadn't answered. She couldn't. She was too tired. She felt as if she had no control over her mind or her body. So she sat there, wishing that everything and everyone would simply disappear.

Thad's heart constricted when he saw her. This wasn't his Darnell. It couldn't be Darnell curled up in a ball like a defeated child. He bent down to her. "Doe?"

Gently, he lifted her chin. Her eyes were red and swollen from crying. Misery etched her flawless face. He couldn't stand to see her this way.

Splaying his fingers through her hair, he rested his forehead against hers. "Oh, baby, what's wrong?"

She sat motionless as he pulled a hand towel from the rack, rinsed it in cold water and dabbed at her watery eyes.

"I've been so worried about you. Why didn't you call me? It's been weeks, baby. What is it? Has something happened to Lance?"

Darnell's head was pounding as she looked at Thad through slit eyelids. What was he doing here? What did he want? Let him go to his women. She didn't care anymore.

Closing her eyes, she shut him out. "Go away, Thad, just go away. I don't want you here."

She couldn't see his expression, but her words were meant to hurt him. Hopefully, they would get him to walk out the door. Instead, she felt herself being lifted. She didn't resist.

Managing to find Darnell's bedroom, Thad placed her on the bed and covered her with a down blanket. She seemed so fragile, but he knew better. The Darnell he knew was strong and feisty. She didn't like being thought of as needing anyone. Yet, everyone needed someone, and he planned on being that someone. He wasn't going to go away.

Sitting on the bed beside her, Thad caressed Darnell's cheek. "You know something, Doe Eyes, I'm getting tired of carrying you around."

Darnell's eyes flew open. "What?" Her tone echoed her displeasure. He had some nerve! Here she was stretched to the limit, as close to a nervous breakdown as she could get, trying to get over him and his skirt-chasing ways, while poor, sweet Lance was laid up in the hospital . . .

Thad saw the dull light in her brilliant dark eyes start to flicker. Just as he had intended, his words had caused a reaction. Her burn was slow at first as she pulled herself up by her elbows and glared at him. Then her nostrils started to flare. Thad knew that she would be coming to life very soon. He was right. It began to rain fire.

"You've got more gall than any man I know." She sat up straight. "Who asked you to carry me around?"

Her pointing finger hit Thad squarely in the chest as she poked him hard. "Here I was sick to my stomach, missing you . . ."

She missed him?

"My old boyfriend, my *best* friend is sick in the hospital . . ."

Old boyfriend?

"I'm trying to take care of him, get to a phone to call you . . ."

She wanted to call him. She wanted to hear his voice!

"And what do I find when I finally do get the chance to call you at home today . . ."

She had called him! She had called him today?

Darnell rose from the bed and stood over him, using her finger like a spear. "Some other woman answers the telephone."

Woman? What woman?

Darnell gave him some neck this time. No doubt about it! She did care.

"I've never loved a man the way that I love you . . ."

Love? Did she say love?

"And if you think that I'm going to sit by quietly and let you two-time me . . ."

She loved him! She loved him! She loved him!

"How in the hell did you find this apartment anyway? Did you have me followed? Did you follow me?" Darnell demanded, both hands firmly planted on her hips.

Thad hardly heard a word that she said as his heart soared out of his chest. She loved him, and nothing else on earth mattered. Pulling her to him he stifled any further words of protest by kissing her until they both were weak and throbbing with need.

216

Thad broke the kiss. His voice was fire. "Say it! Say it again. Say that you love me. You *do* love me. I know you do."

Darnell found it difficult to speak. Whatever protest she might have mounted before had vanished with the touch of his demanding lips against her own. "I . . . I . . . I . . ." she stuttered, unable to think, only feel.

"I . . . I . . . I . . . nothing," Thad mimicked, gathering her tightly in his arms. "You said that you were in love with me, so don't try to deny it. I'm a greedy man. I want to hear you say it again." He kissed her hair softly. "And again." He kissed her eyelids. "And again." He placed a kiss on her lips that was so tender it brought tears to her eyes.

Darnell moaned. Why did he have to be like this? Why did he have to have such a silver tongue, such a knowing way?

"Yes, I love you," she whispered hoarsely. "I am *in* love with you." She looked into his eyes so that the truth could be clearly seen. There would be no doubts, no second-guessing. "I love you, Thad Stewart."

Moisture gathered in his eyes, and he was barely able to contain his emotions. Darnell Cameron *was* in love with him. Of all the millions of men who adored her, who dreamed of being held in her arms, of making love to her, he was the lucky one. She loved *him*, and not because he was wealthy. So was she. She didn't love him because he was talented or famous. She neither wanted nor needed any of those things from him. She had it all. What she wanted and needed were the same things that he craved—trust, honesty, loyalty, companionship and love. These were all of the things that he was more than willing to give her for the rest of their lives.

His eyes devoured her hungrily. "Don't you know that there's no woman on earth that I've ever loved the way I love you?" His voice was husky with emotion as his mouth snaked down the soft flesh of her long, slender neck. "There's no woman on earth that I want to be with but you."

"Then who was the woman who answered the telephone when I called?"

"If it wasn't Catina, I don't know who it was, but I promise you that I'll find out. I swear to you, there is no other woman in my life and never could be. I love you too much."

He kissed her again, then with deft dexterity removed her blouse and unfastened her bra. For a moment, he gazed at the rounded perfection of her naked breasts before his mouth took greedy possession and he suckled. Greedily, his lips caressed the length of her body as, together, they discarded her clothing piece-by-piece.

With trembling hands Darnell traced the curve of his broad shoulders. She planted a kiss between the sharp planes of his muscular chest. Thad shuddered at her touch. When he allowed space between the two of them, she managed to unzip his slacks and strip them from his body, along with his briefs.

Standing naked before her, he reached into the pocket of his discarded pants and handed Darnell the foil package that he had withdrawn. Guiding her hands,

Thad's eyes fluttered closed and he inhaled sharply as she covered his throbbing shaft. Slipping it on carefully, she watched him with smug satisfaction as she brazenly caressed him. Thad swayed. With an impassioned moan, he sank slowly to his knees. "Darnell." One single word sealed his surrender.

Rising, he lowered them both to the bed and kissed her with an urgency that left no doubt about his desire. His torrid tongue left a blazing trail of fire down the length of her belly, lingering maddeningly at her navel. Then he moved slowly downward, where he rubbed his nose gently against the mound of thick, black curls before gently kissing each inner thigh.

Darnell's body tensed. The air around them crackled. Slowly, he entered her and she tightened around him as he moved skillfully within her. Every fiber of his being wanted to explode, but he prolonged the pleasure for them both. With purposeful intent, he maintained control until they both were lost in a frenzy of passion and the world as they knew it vanished.

CHAPTER 22

Still drugged by passion, Thad and Darnell savored one another as they lay snuggled together. Thad traced her kiss-swollen lips. "I'd better go. The doorman and the guards know I'm up here. If I stay much longer, we'll both be headlines before the morning edition hits the streets, but before I go, let me hear you say it one more time."

Darnell complied willingly. "I love you."

Thad showed his appreciation by reclaiming her lips once again, leaving her panting, pulsating, and craving more. This man could become addictive.

Shaken, Darnell scooted up in the bed and leaned against the headboard in an effort to escape the spell that Thad was casting. She shook her head in exasperation at the dimpled, self-satisfied grin that he flashed at her as he watched her retreat. She groaned. "Oh, Lord, I've created a monster!"

Thad laughed and sat up beside her. "Don't tell me that you've had enough."

Unfortunately, she hadn't, and that could prove to be a problem. Her mind traveled back to the woman who had answered his telephone earlier that day. She wouldn't degrade herself by asking who it was, but she wanted to make it perfectly clear that she would not tolerate infidelity.

"No, Thad, I don't know if I'll ever get enough of you. I do love you, but there's one thing you must understand. I don't plan on sharing any man who says that he loves me with another woman at any time."

Thad cocked his head in amusement as he observed Darnell. Her arms were folded across her chest and her mouth was tightened into a cute little pout. She was stubborn and demanding, bold and beautiful. The thought of loving anyone else was beyond his comprehension.

"Believe me, sweetheart, you have no reason to worry about another woman." He planted a kiss on the tip of her nose. "Nothing and no one is more important to me than you."

Darnell could see his sincerity. She wanted to trust him, hoped that she could trust him. There was no foundation for any kind of relationship between them without trust. Reaching out, she ran a finger down the length of his cheek.

"I believe you, but I still don't expect another woman to answer your telephone."

He kissed her fingertip and sparks splintered through her system like shards of shattered glass as she watched him reach for his cell phone.

"I don't know who that was, but I'm going to find out."

Dialing his home telephone number, Thad took only a few minutes to discover the truth. Regine! He recounted his conversation with his assistant to Darnell.

"She's on your case hot and heavy, isn't she?" Darnell couldn't blame the woman; Thad Stewart *was* a catch.

"But if she ever hangs up on me again, I'm going to be on her like white on rice."

"Good." He threw that deep dimple grin on her again. "Kick her butt."

"Oh, you'd love two women sparring over you like alley cats, wouldn't you?" Darnell pulled the pillow from behind his back and tried to hit him with it. Thad moved quickly, and she missed. Laughing uproariously, they tussled for the pillow and engaged in a mini pillow fight, rolling around on the bed until she ended up on top of him. Thad placed her head on his chest and stroked her hair soothingly.

"You don't ever have to worry about fighting for my love, Darnell. My heart belongs to you." He kissed her lightly. "Now why don't you tell me what was wrong with you earlier when I came in? You were on meltdown. Is it Lance? Has he gotten worse?"

Darnell sat up with a start. Lance! She had all but forgotten him. How could she have been so callous? He was in the hospital fighting for his life, and she was here making love with Thad. Unconsciously, she moved away from him. As much as she needed Thad's strength and support, at that moment she couldn't avoid feeling guilty.

"No, Lance is doing better, thank God, but it's been a long, hard road for him." She sighed. "I'm sorry that it took so long for me to call you. So much was happening."

"You scared me, baby. Not hearing from you was hell."

"It was hard getting away. I've been at the hospital night and day."

"I didn't know what to think."

Darnell took his hand and squeezed it. "I'm sorry I worried you. I was so frightened by his condition I didn't know what to do. He's so sick, and even though he's better, his health is still in jeopardy. His liver is damaged, and the doctors are saying that he'll need a liver transplant. I can't abandon him now, not while he's like this."

Thad's heart lurched fearfully. "What do you mean?"

Darnell could hear the apprehension in his voice. She knew that her next words wouldn't reassure him. She removed her hand from his. Rising, she grabbed her robe from the chair next to the bed and slipped into it. Then she turned to face Thad.

"Lance has been a part of my life since I was twenty-two years old. Like I told you, I love him." She watched Thad flinch at her words and steel himself for more. Sitting back down on the bed, she cupped his chin and looked into his eyes, "But, I am *in* love with you."

Darnell paused to let the impact of her words sink in before continuing. "So far, I've been lucky enough not to have the press involved in this, but that may not last long. So, as soon as Lance is well enough, he'll be recovering at a place that his parents rented. I don't know where we're going yet . . ."

"Where *we're* going?"

"I'm going with them."

"You're what?" Thad tried to remain calm.

She hurried on. "We'll be in seclusion for a while. I'll try and contact you . . ."

"Why are you going?" Fighting his conflicting emotions, Thad sprang from the bed. He wanted to sound understanding, but couldn't quite manage it. His voice rose in barely controlled anger. "His parents will be with him. Why do you need to be there?"

"It won't be for long, no more than a month."

"A month!" He looked stunned. "Are you kidding?"

Darnell began pacing the room. "Lance will get plenty of rest while we're there, and I have a benefit concert here in the city next month. I've got to choose my music, get my band together," Darnell babbled on nervously.

"You haven't answered my question, Darnell." Thad's tone was cold, no nonsense. He would no longer be put off by her avoidance. "Why do you need to be there?"

She sighed in resignation. "Because I have to be, Thad."

"You *have to be*? And I'm supposed to believe that? You *have to* die and you may *have to* pay taxes, but you don't *have to* go into seclusion with Lance. That's your choice, Darnell."

"You're right. I'm going because I want to go. I want to make sure that he's all right. He and I have been through a lot together, and I won't abandon him when he needs me the most. I love Lance's parents, and they love me. They think Lance and I are a couple . . . that we're headed for a future together. The truth is going to be hard on them when they find out that we won't."

"So you're going to tell him about us while you're in seclusion with him." It was a statement, not a question.

"If I get the opportunity, and depending on how his health develops."

"If you get the *opportunity*," Thad scoffed. He stilled Darnell's pacing figure and turned her to face him. "The truth of the matter is that Lance may never be well again, Doe, and God knows he'll never be well enough not to be hurt by what you have to say to him about us. Yet I sense that there's something else behind your hesitation in telling him. There's something you don't want to share with me. So why can't you trust me with the truth?"

Darnell closed her eyes, wishing that she hadn't made a promise years ago that had brought her to this moment. She had never planned on falling in love with anyone. In her heart of hearts, she had never thought that it would happen. Unrealistically, she had thought that love was something she could control. Now, here stood the man she loved demanding answers that she was not free to give. She opened her eyes, but remained silent.

Thad could see both her conflict and her resolve. He couldn't help her with either. "I'm a patient man, Doe, but how long am I supposed to wait? And what exactly is it that I'm waiting for? I love you, I need you and I want you to be with me. What could be more important than that?"

His words heightened Darnell's conflict and her feelings of guilt. "I'm only staying there a month, and I *will* tell Lance about us."

Thad pushed. "And when will you tell him? Week one? Week four?"

Darnell resisted, pulling away from him. "I don't know, and I can't deal with this right now."

Thad stood with his hands clenched tightly at his sides. "And you think that I can? You don't know how it feels, Darnell, knowing that the woman I love will be in seclusion with another man."

She faced him squarely. "The same way Lance will feel when I tell him that I made love with you."

Thad took a step back, his face clouded in confusion. "Why? Why should it matter to him if the two of you aren't in love? If he's your best friend, he should be happy that you've found someone."

Darnell shook her head slowly, clearly in distress. "Oh, Thad, there are things I just can't share with you. All I can ask is that you trust me. The man is sick, and I want him to get well. If my presence can help make that happen, then I'll be there."

It was Thad who felt guilty now. He hated the feeling as much as he hated feeling jealous. He didn't like being helpless in the face of love. This woman possessed him. She owned him, totally. Reaching out, he brought her to him.

"I can't stand the thought of losing you, baby. I just can't." He kissed her with the ferocity of a drowning man.

Darnell melted in his arms as she responded with the same aching need. They broke the kiss, and she whispered, "You won't lose me. I promise that you won't."

Reluctantly, Thad pulled away from her, still wrestling with uncertainty. He wasn't used to feeling helpless. He was used to being in control. So he took that control back and did the one thing that he knew that he shouldn't do with a woman like Darnell.

"I expect you to tell Lance about us as soon as you get where you're going."

Darnell drew back from him. An ultimatum? Was he giving her an ultimatum? Her jaws clenched. He should know better than to challenge a challenger. "Or what, Thad?" Time stood still as she waited for his response.

Thad inhaled deeply. "Or why continue this relationship?"

Thad stepped out into the crisp night air of San Francisco with a heavy heart. He knew that he had made a mistake with Darnell by issuing an ultimatum. What had he been thinking? He knew women well enough to have handled the situation differently, but he had let his heart rule his head.

Turning the collar up on his jacket, he headed around the corner toward the garage in which he had parked his car. With head down and feet dragging, all he could think of was Darnell. He walked unaware of his surrounding as he passed the alley located only yards from the garage, so the sudden jolt to his body caught him unaware. Surprised by the attack, his resistance was minimal at first as he was dragged into the dark alley with a chokehold. The assailant was slightly shorter than he was, but stockier and strong. Gagging, Thad grabbed his assailant's arm with both hands in an unsuccessful attempt to loosen his grip. He was pulled even farther into the darkness. He fought for air with every step. His mind raced with the realization that if he didn't do something quickly he would die. He choked and sputtered as he tried to tell his attacker that he could have his money, the gold watch he was wearing, the diamond in his ear, but speech was impossible. Yet he was determined not to go down in a filthy alley being robbed by some mugger. There had to be something that he could do before he lost consciousness.

Suddenly, Thad stopped struggling and went limp. The movement surprised his assailant, who was thrown off balance by his victim's full weight. He stumbled. Simultaneously, a shout came from the street adjoining the alley.

"Hey! What's going on?"

Startled by the shout and the sudden weight of a very large man, the assailant loosened his grip. Thad came to life and pushed away from his captor as he gasped for air, bracing against the wall for support. He could hear the sound of footsteps and shouts for the fleeing assailant to halt. Dazed, Thad dropped to his knees, taking deep breaths to inhale precious oxygen as he thanked God for allowing him to live another day.

His saviors turned out to be two policemen assigned to patrol the exclusive Nob Hill neighborhood. Thad felt like a cat with nine lives as he sat in the alley, grateful that he was alive to recount to the officer the evening's events. Unfortunately, his attacker had gotten away.

Realizing who he was, the officers cordoned off the alley to help maintain his privacy. Thad was thankful for that but refused to go to the hospital. Despite a sore neck, he had no other injuries. The only thing damaged was his pride. He informed the officers that he couldn't identify the mugger, that nothing had been taken in the attempted robbery and that he would rather the entire incident be forgotten. He didn't want, nor did he need, the publicity. The officers said that they would have to make a report anyway, but assured him that everything would be handled with discretion.

They attracted little attention as the policemen escorted Thad to his car in the garage. The officers got autographs before Thad drove home to Tiburon, grateful to have escaped his ordeal with only a bruised neck.

Later that evening, as he lay in his bed unable to sleep, the reality of what had happened really hit him. He could have died. This could have been his last day on earth. His last thoughts as he struggled for his life had been of Darnell. The very thought of not seeing her again had been unbearable. Tonight's incident had proven to him that tomorrow was not promised to anyone. He didn't plan on spending another day without the woman that he loved beside him. Forget the ultimatum. Whatever it took, they would work their problems out. He would not allow Lance, stubborn pride, or anything else to come between them.

It was two in the morning when he dialed her cell phone. She didn't answer. No surprise, she was probably asleep. He would call back tomorrow. Thank God there would be a tomorrow.

CHAPTER 23

Only hours after Thad left her condo, Darnell received a call from Lance's parents. Somehow, the media had discovered that he was hospitalized and he was being released that night. Hurrying back to be with him, she joined his parents and the nurse who would be attending him in a clandestine escape through abandoned tunnels to a waiting ambulance. By the time the media began to inundate the hospital for information, they were gone.

A plane whisked the party of five to Santa Barbara, where the Austins had leased a house from a family friend. It was a large Victorian located on a secluded ranch. An unmarked road led to the property that consisted of lush fruit trees and a private lake. The nearest neighbor was miles away. It was the perfect place for Lance to recuperate and for Darnell to think.

As she stepped out onto the veranda a week later, she looked out at the placid scene before her and wished that she felt as peaceful as her surroundings looked. But at least Lance was resting well. She glanced over at him as he lay sleeping on a chaise lounge. He had been reading a letter when he dozed off. It now lay abandoned on his chest.

Lance seemed to be improving each day. His appetite had returned, and he was starting to gain weight. He had lost the gaunt look that had plagued him in the hospital. She smiled down at his sleeping form. Even in illness, he was still one of the best looking men around.

Because of his light brown complexion, wavy dark hair, sharp nose, and thin lips, Lance was often mistaken as being the product of an interracial union, but he wasn't. He was the product of generations of intermarriage between light skinned African-Americans. When he had approached Darnell with romantic interest, she had been suspicious of his motives. She had a dark brown complexion and assumed that he would only be interested in women with straight, flowing hair and with skin like his. She had been proven wrong. Lance showed his love and concern for her in many ways.

As the relationship between them blossomed, she had discovered a brilliant mind behind his model good looks. Obsessed with following in his parents' footsteps, he ate, slept, and breathed medicine. If nothing else, their obsessions with their careers made the two of them compatible. They had become inseparable. And then, the automobile accident had occurred. Like the illness that he was now fighting, it nearly took his life.

Lance had recovered from his injuries a changed man. He became moody and reclusive. The closeness that they shared began to erode until he shared a secret with Darnell that would alter both their lives. His sharing proved cathartic. They patched up their relationship and remained the best of friends, always there supporting each other, always aware that their careers were first. Everything else was secondary.

Darnell sighed. What a waste. They had let so much of life pass them by. Neither of them could ever recapture those years. Since he'd fallen desperately ill with hepatitis, she had prayed daily that his life would be spared so that he could live a rich, fulfilled future. He was a good man and didn't deserve anything less.

As for her, she wasn't certain whether her future would include Thad. After issuing his ultimatum, he had left her condo in a huff. He had given her no choice. Either she told Lance about their relationship or it was over.

As she recalled that night, Darnell fought back the tears. He had left their future together up to her.

At one time, the glittering nightlife that came with the Hollywood scene was mother's milk to Thad. He was a master in social settings, a natural magnet, and this evening's event was no exception. Ray had invited Thad to accompany him to the opening night reception of an art exhibit at the Los Angeles Museum of Art. He had accepted the invitation, but he regretted it the minute he stepped into the museum. His presence had caused a stir, but the glitz and the glamour were lost on him. It no longer had any appeal. He moved through the crowded reception on mechanical legs, seeking escape from the attention he was receiving from women of all ages.

He tried to be gracious, but he was tired of smiling, tired of small talk, tired of pretending. He needed a break. Heading toward the restroom, he made a slight detour, slipping through a pair of patio doors, discarding the many telephone numbers that had been slipped into his pocket as he did so. Out of sight, he leaned against the patio rail, gazed out onto the peaceful grounds, and breathed a sigh of relief.

From a discreet vantage point, Regine Lexy had watched Thad all evening as he maneuvered through his crowd of admirers. Her eyes had followed his every move right up to the moment that he walked in the direction of the men's room and disappeared. He hadn't noticed her presence in the crowded room during the evening, and she had kept it that way, until now.

Moving through the gallery, she followed his path. The Museum of Art was like her second home. She had taken art lessons there and worked there as a tour guide. She knew every nook and cranny. So, when he did not reappear from the bathroom, she went looking for him in the secret places that she knew existed.

On the patio, Thad leaned against the railing, lost in thoughts about Darnell. He knew issuing an ultimatum had been foolish. He hadn't heard from her in over a week, not since the night that he left her at the condo.

All he had gained from that debacle was a mugging and deep regret. He wished that he had never made such a misguided move. Then perhaps they would still be in contact. He missed her terribly.

Closing his eyes, he visualized Darnell. A low moan escaped his lips as he fought his body's escalating need.

"Out here turning yourself on?"

Startled, Thad turned to see Regine standing behind him. A smile was poised on her moist lips.

"Where did you come from?" He didn't try to disguise his annoyance.

Regine moved to stand beside him. Leaning against the rail, she turned to face him. Thad's eyes swept her appreciatively. She was ravishing in a floor-length gown of pale blue. Its low-cut neckline and fitted waist emphasized her sculptured physique. He couldn't deny that Regine was a beautiful woman, but she was also a pariah. Thad's eyes slipped back to her face and narrowed as he remembered her part in keeping Darnell and him apart.

"Listen, I want you to know that I don't appreciate you coming to my house uninvited. As for your answering my telephone, you'll never get a chance to pull that little stunt again because you'll never grace my doorstep again as long as I'm alive. Donald remembers your coming over and when. So don't try to lie and say you didn't do it."

Regine couldn't help noting the controlled rage in his voice, but she hadn't missed his moment of male appraisal, either. She chose to ignore the former and address the latter. Leaning in closer to him, she gave him a clearer view of her bosom. "I came here from Sausalito for the opening. The artist is a friend of mine. What brings you here?"

"You heard what I said, Regine, so don't play games with me." Wearily, he ran a hand through his hair. He didn't need this. How did she find him, anyway?

"Yes, I heard you, and I'm sorry. I was in the neighborhood and you had been there when I called. How did I know that you wouldn't be home? When I answered the phone, I thought I was doing you a favor. Donald had stepped out, nobody was there . . ." Her voice would melt ice. Thad's look could freeze it. She tried another tactic.

"By the way, how is Darnell Cameron?" It was obvious that she had told him about the phone call. How effective had it been? "I remember she was with you at my gallery the day you bought the Bearden, but I didn't know that the two of you were close friends."

Thad looked at her steadily but remained silent. "I read in the newspaper that her boyfriend is sick. The rumor is that they'll be getting married soon since he faces such an uncertain future." Was there really something between them? She watched him closely.

Thad kept every emotion but anger in check. He wasn't going to give Regine the satisfaction of a reaction. "Those rags are always marrying somebody off. As I recall, they even had us walking down the aisle at one time, and that was after our first date."

"Yes, I remember." Regine tried not to sound wistful about what might have been. "But I didn't read it in one of those rags. I read it in the *Times*. They're usually pretty accurate."

He didn't flinch, giving no sign of being interested in her comment.

Regine shrugged. "Anyway, it's not important." She couldn't hide her smile as her heart beat double-time at Thad's seeming disinterest in Darnell's love life. Maybe he wasn't involved with the songstress. Maybe she still had a chance.

Pulling at Thad's arm, she started for the patio door. "Don't be mad at me for trying to help you out by answering your phone. Come on, forgive and forget. Don't hide out here by yourself like some old man. The band is playing, and I know what a fantastic dancer you are. Come on, dance with me. I'll protect you from all of those pants chasers in the room."

Thad wasn't amused by Regine's quips. All he wanted to do was go home. He would dance her toward the door, then make his escape. Without a word, he followed her to the dance floor with his mind racing a mile a minute. *Regine was lying! This was the first that he had heard about any impending marriage between Darnell and Lance! It had to be a lie! Darnell wouldn't leave him hanging like this. She wasn't that kind of woman.*

As they slipped onto the crowded dance floor, Thad in a trance and Regine reveling in the glory of being the one with whom he was dancing, a photographer appeared. When the music stopped, Regine, giddy from her dance with Thad, planted an inviting kiss on his lips. Neither one of them noticed as the photographer snapped the picture and disappeared back into the crowd.

The excitement in the old Victorian house had reached fever pitch earlier that morning. Word had arrived that a possible donor had been found for Lance. If the donor turned out to be compatible, this would mean that instead of facing years of waiting for a match for his liver, he might be facing only days.

The atmosphere in the household had lightened considerably, and as Darnell headed down the stairway for the veranda, she uttered a silent prayer of thanks. The time she had spent on the ranch had given her plenty of time to reflect on how precarious life could be. Nothing could be taken for granted. Yet, she had done so with Thad's love and now faced the possibility of losing him.

She had been angry at first about the ultimatum he had given her, but the more she thought about it, the more she knew that he was right. She had grown too comfortable in her procrastination, wanting to avoid the inevitable. Years ago, she had made a foolish promise to Lance about something that should have been dealt with long ago. Now it was time to deal with it and to tell him about her relationship with Thad. She planned to do so without further delay.

With that decision having been made she had called Thad to inform him. She wanted to—no, she *needed* to—talk to him, but she had been unable to reach him. He didn't answer her calls, so she had left messages on his cell phone and at his home in Tiburon. She had followed that up with a letter to him. In it, she told him how much she missed him and apologized for her indecisiveness, but that had been days ago, and she still had not heard from him. His silence hurt. Was their relationship really over?

Whatever happened between Thad and her, the conversation with Lance was inevitable. It was long overdue.

"God, Dar, you scared me!"

Lance's high-pitched exclamation startled Darnell as she found herself standing on the veranda looking down into his thin, pale face. The thick, satiny eyebrows were creased together in surprise. His deep-set brown eyes, accented by short curly lashes, peered at her in annoyance as he quickly folded the letter he had been reading and jammed it into his pants pocket.

"What were you doing spying on me?" His tone was accusatory.

"Spying?" Darnell was shocked by his accusation. She knew that the man didn't feel well, but she was growing tired of him taking it out on others around him. Since their arrival at the ranch, he had been quiet and withdrawn, and spoke in clipped, sharp tones to both Darnell and his parents. When questioned about his behavior, he reacted defensively. Everyone was walking on eggshells around him. "What are you talking about, Lance? I came out here to get a breath of fresh air. I didn't know you were even out here. And why would I spy on you anyway?"

Lance looked contrite as he noted Darnell's angry stance. He knew her well enough to know that he was pushing her with his attitude and she was about to let him know it. He relented. "You're right. I'm sorry."

Darnell didn't acknowledge his apology as she slammed back into the house, still perturbed by his behavior. Something was up with that man, and she had the distinct feeling that it was something beyond his health problems. A day later, her suspicions were confirmed.

Darnell was busy in her room gathering clothes for Mrs. Dawson, the seventy-five-year-old housekeeper who had been with the Austin family since Lance was a baby. She had come with them to the ranch, and she ruled this household with the same iron fist that she ruled the Austins' main household. In that house, Saturday was washday, and all clothes were to be delivered to her that morning or go dirty until the next week. Darnell wanted to make sure that she complied.

As Mrs. Dawson stood watching her tie her dirty clothes into the tidy bundle that she demanded from each person, the older woman absently searched through the pockets of a pair of pants she had gotten from Lance's room. She wanted to make sure that they were empty. They weren't. She withdrew several sheets of mint green stationary jammed haphazardly into the right pocket just as Darnell turned to hand her a bundle of clothes.

"Here we go, Mrs. Dawson. All tied together just like you like it." She noticed the stationary in Mrs. Dawson's hand. "What's that?"

"It looks like a letter or something Lance had in his pocket." Mrs. Dawson looked at the sheets of paper as if they had come from outer space and had invaded her home. "Now that boy knows I don't allow nothing to be in these pockets when I'm washing."

Darnell plucked the sheets of paper from the woman's hand in exchange for her bundle of clothes. "I'm sure he forgot, and it won't happen again. Here, I'll give them back to him if you'll take these."

The sheets of paper scattered to the floor as the exchange was made. Darnell bent to retrieve them as Mrs. Dawson sniffed indignantly and stalked out of the room, muttering her displeasure.

Darnell shook her head in amusement as she watched the door close behind her. Picking up the papers, she started toward the door and Lance's room to give the letter back to him when she happened to glance down at what she was holding. The words on the last sheet of paper caught her eye. *I love you madly, and I can't wait to have our baby.* Darnell stopped dead in her tracks.

CHAPTER 24

Lance watched the pulse at the base of Darnell's throat as it moved erratically. That had always been his way of measuring how angry she was with him. Right now, it was leaping like a Mexican jumping bean. Yet her outside manner appeared calm. He was surprised. When was the storm going to blow in?

In the many years that he had known her, Lance had found Darnell to be full of surprises. While he had pursued what he knew to be an honorable, solid, and profitable career, she had pursued a career he thought of as frivolous and self-indulgent. Despite his unspoken reservations, he had supported her choice, and she had surpassed all expectations. Darnell had signed a recording contract right out of college. The result had been that they both had benefited by her rising star.

Lance had discovered that his status as Darnell Cameron's " boyfriend" afforded him opportunities that he would not have imagined. He was invited to all of the *right* functions, met all of the *right* people and received coveted research grants with little effort, all because of his association with Darnell. Yet, during most of their decade together, they had been living a lie.

"Where did you meet her, Lance?" Her question brought him back to the subject at hand.

He swallowed, trying to remain calm. He didn't want to set her off. "When she worked on the research project with me at the hospital."

"And she was on the team that went to South America with you?"

He glanced down at the letter in her hand that told it all. "Yes, she was there."

"And you're in love with this woman?"

A shadow of confusion danced across his face. Was he in love with Ruth? He got a warm feeling when he was with her. He liked her easygoing manner and soft-spoken ways, and she was in his field, medical research. It was a subject about which they could sit and talk for hours. His relationship with Ruth was so much different than the one he had with Darnell. Was he in love?

"Yes, I think that I am."

Darnell looked at his downcast eyes, the stooped shoulders, and the painful expression of guilt on his face. She couldn't believe that she was having this conversation with Lance, of all people. "And she's in love with you?"

There was subtext in the question, and they both knew its source. He looked Darnell in the eye this time. "Yes, she is." His answer held no reservations.

Darnell sat looking at the man before her. For so long, they had been a part of each other's lives. She had been with him since she was twenty-two. Back then, she had hung onto his every word. She had been mesmerized by his good looks, awed by his brilliance. He seemed to have it all. A love relationship had not been for them, but a close friendship had been. It was a friendship forged by a secret he had shared with her— one that she had pledged not to reveal. It was for him to do so. She had been a young girl when she swore that allegiance. Things were different now. Life had changed drastically for them both. It was time for the pretense to end.

When she read the letter Mrs. Dawson had found, Darnell had been ready to kill. In a huff, she had stormed into Lance's bedroom and demanded an explanation. He had looked almost relieved when she tossed the evidence on the bed and stood over him with hands on her hips and lots of attitude. But she surprised herself when her bark turned out to be worse than her bite. As she stood there in all of her defiance, Darnell realized that she didn't feel that angry because Lance's actions had freed them both. However, some things still had to be explained.

"This letter seems to indicate—no, it states—that you and Ruth have been intimate."

Lance's gaze held hers steadily as he nodded. "We have been."

For a moment, Darnell hesitated, unsure how to word the next question. She and Lance had rarely discussed the subject. He sensed her dilemma. "I was able to consummate the relationship, Dar, and to the satisfaction of us both."

Darnell was unable to keep the shock off her face. "But you said—" She paused to gather her thoughts. "What are you doing, Lance? You told me after the accident that you were impotent. What is this about?"

Rising from his chair, Lance walked over to the window and braced his body against the windowsill as he spoke. "A while ago, I thought about my life and what I wanted out of it. I thought that if there was a chance, then maybe . . ."

"There is no *maybe* about it, Lance, either you are or you aren't!"

"I know, but my parents helped me . . ."

"Your parents?" Darnell walked over to stand face-to-face with Lance. "You said that you didn't want your parents to know. You said that you didn't want them to look at you differently. You cried and begged me not to tell anyone. You said that it would be awful if anyone knew but me! So when did you tell your parents?"

"Five years ago. They introduced me to the doctor who helped me."

Darnell was stunned as she struggled to understand the implications of what he had revealed. "You have the nerve to tell me that you've had some sort of operation, they've known about this, and nobody bothered to tell me for five years?"

Lance shrugged. "You were on tour a lot, and I guess I didn't think about it. I figured that my parents would say something to you."

Darnell shook her head in disbelief as she stared at the man she thought she knew so well. "Let me get this straight. We're best friends. You begged me not to tell anyone about your sexual problem until you were ready. So, here I am still under the impression that your parents think that we're a couple, and they let me think it, too."

"Well, you know how much they love you, and we *are* best friends."

Darnell held her hands up as if to ward off the information he was imparting. "Wait a minute, Lance, don't you see a problem with this?"

He looked at her in confusion and shook his head. "No, I don't. The only problem I see is that I broke our promise. I said that I would come to you and let you know when and if I found someone I cared for and who cares for me. Then I promised I'd let everyone know.

"But why didn't you tell me about all this earlier, Lance?"

"I'm sorry, but I'm telling you now. I found someone. Its been a year, and I didn't do . . ."

"A year!" Darnell took an intimidating step forward. "You and Ruth have been messing around with each other for a year?"

Lance shrank away from her. The calm was over, and the storm was rising. "Uh, I meant to say something but you were on tour again, and we didn't see much of each other, and didn't get to talk much on the telephone . . ."

"Oh, mister, you better make it better than that! You better put that brilliant mind of yours to work and explain to me why you didn't step up to the plate a long time ago. I told you from the beginning that being impotent wasn't something to be ashamed of. It was just something that happened, but you were so thoroughly convinced that everyone would think so much less of you and that your career would be affected, which was ridiculous . . ."

"At the time it seemed . . ."

"No! No more excuses. Oh, you were so certain that if I had a relationship with someone and it became sexual, word would get around that you were less than a man. What was it you said? 'The dude would know for sure that I wasn't handling my business.' As if sex is the only thing that makes a man. "

"Darnell, that was a long time ago . . ."

"It was yesterday for me!" Darnell had worked herself into a rage. She paused to take hold of her emotions. "Exactly what does this woman mean to you, Lance?"

"I want a family, Darnell. My parents want grand-children . . ."

"And she's pregnant?"

"I hope that I can get her pregnant."

"So you two will get married, and you *hope* she gets pregnant?"

Lance hesitated, then answered, "I told you, I want a family, and since the two of us weren't getting together—"

His words explained almost everything. Darnell sighed heavily. "Have you told this woman that you might not be able to have children?"

"No, but I might be able to. The doctors think there's hope, and so do my parents. Why burden Ruth?"

Darnell looked at him with a mixture of rage and pity. "I love you like a brother, Lance. I protected your secret at all costs. I never wanted anyone to think less of you, but right now *I* think less of you, and that saddens me. The woman deserves to know everything about you, and she deserves your love."

As she watched him struggle to answer her, Darnell began to look at Lance in a new light. He was a man in conflict, and there was nothing more that she could do to help him. He had to help himself.

She remembered their awkward attempts at making love in the early days of their relationship. No matter what she did, it seemed that she couldn't satisfy him. They couldn't seem to satisfy each other. Having both been virgins, they hadn't realized that they might be sexually incompatible. After his accident, when he revealed to her that he was impotent, it had seemed an answer to their dilemma. The same was proving true now. Despite the cornucopia of emotions that she was feeling about this entire situation, beneath the surface she felt as if a burden had been lifted. Things had been resolved, not the way that she thought they would be, but resolved nevertheless. She and Lance could turn the page and start the next chapters in their lives.

Alerted to the sound of a door opening downstairs, Moody moved to the doorway of Thad's bedroom as stealthily as a cat. He knew that he had disengaged the alarm, so he didn't expect it to go off; but whoever had entered did expect to hear it, and that could mean trouble. Remaining hidden, he peered down to the floor below. The muscle-bound man who worked for Thad was standing by the front door looking perplexed. Amused by the look on the big man's face, Moody leaned back so that he wouldn't be spotted. Fighting the muscular cretin hadn't been in his plan, but he was ready for him if it happened. He patted the gun tucked in its holster.

Below, a puzzled Donald stood looking at the silent alarm. He was certain that he had set it before he and Thad left for L.A. He had never forgotten to set it before. Prompted by instinct, he stood listening for a second for any sound that might alert him that he was not alone in the house. Crime had already touched this household when Thad was mugged a couple of weeks ago. All they needed now was a burglary. Cautiously, he moved further into the house, then from room to room downstairs. Nothing seemed out of place. His mother had been checking the house while they were gone. She must have disarmed it and forgotten to re-engage it. His guess was that he could put the disarmed alarm on the list of everything else that had gone wrong while he and his employer were away.

Walking into the living room, he shuffled the mail he was carrying, frowning in annoyance at his reason for having to return from southern California so early. It seemed that the answering service they had used for years at the Tiburon house had gone out of business without notifying its customers. Neither he nor Thad would ever know how many important calls had been missed. On top of that, Thad had lost his cell phone while in L.A. and had been frantic. After seeing that he was settled, Donald had taken care of the cell phone situation and then had flown back to the Bay area to see to matters in Tiburon.

As he struggled with the mass of mail that he had requested that the post office hold until his return, the telephone rang. He hurried to answer the ring, spilling several unopened envelopes along the way. Deciding that the ringing telephone was more urgent than spilled mail, Donald hastened to pick up the receiver. Breathlessly, he answered it.

"Stewart residence." As always, his manner was crisp and professional.

"Hey, Donald. How goes it?" It was Thad on the other end.

"The answering service thing was a real mess, but I got everything taken care of. Then when I came to the house, the alarm was off. No sign of anything being wrong. I think my mother forgot to reset it. How are things going there? Did you see Doctor Crenshaw like I suggested?"

"Donald, I was attacked weeks ago. If anything was wrong with me, it would have showed up way before now."

"You might think that everything's fine, but you were mugged, Thad, and you ought to get checked out."

"Like I said, I'm fine. Don't worry."

"But the headaches . . . the trouble sleeping."

On the other end, Thad nearly confessed to his friend and employee what was the real root of his physical problems. Instead, he said, "It's just stress. I'm okay."

"All right, if you say so." Donald was skeptical but changed the subject. "So you'll be back here Saturday, around noon?"

"Yes, I'll be there."

"Don't forget that Catina and I will be leaving on our little trip tonight."

He and Thad engaged in a few more minutes of small talk before saying their goodbyes. Disconnecting, Donald bent to retrieve the scattered mail. Satisfied that he had gathered it all, he headed into the back of the house, never noticing the envelope covered with yellow flowers that lay half-hidden under a table.

Reappearing in the entranceway, Donald started up the front stairs. His cell phone rang. It was Catina, eager for them to start on their mini-vacation. Anxious to please her and to get an early start, he bounced back down the stairs. Making certain that the alarm was engaged this time, Donald exited.

When he heard the front door close, Moody knew that it was safe to abandon his hiding place. He sauntered down the stairway, recounting to himself the part of the telephone conversation that he had heard from upstairs. So somebody had mugged Thad Stewart. Too bad he had walked away from the incident. Otherwise, his problem with the actor would have been solved.

Reaching the foyer, Moody once again disengaged the alarm as if he lived there. These fancy new alarms were no better than the old ones he used to bypass when he was a kid doing break-ins. They were just more costly. His eyes swept the living room. The man had expensive taste.

Moody was about to turn and leave the house when a spot of yellow peeking from under a table caught his eye. Curious, he bent and retrieved the colorful envelope. It was addressed to Thad. The writing looked like that of a woman. Without ceremony, he tore it open. He wanted to see what the slimeball was up to, and as he read the letter, his expression changed from one of curiosity to one of anger.

The letter spoke of shared love and passion. The words were powerful in their emotion. Finishing the letter, he crumpled it in his balled fist as the last words in the letter pierced his soul. It ended with a declaration— *I love you with all my heart* and was signed *Darnell.*

It wasn't a certainty that Bev would be home when Darnell called. It was later in Chicago than in California. Mother and daughter had exchanged houses. Darnell had flown from the Santa Barbara ranch to her mother's home in Chicago to avoid the press, while Bev was staying overnight in the Carmel house while attending to some business in the area. On the fifth ring, Bev's familiar voice answered the telephone.

"Hello, Mama. What are you up to?" Darnell tried to sound light, cheerful.

Bev wasn't fooled. "So you saw the picture of Mr. Hormones on the cover of the magazine?"

"Oh, Mama, please." What was the woman, a mind reader? "Let's not get into that. I called to see how you're doing."

"The same as I was doing yesterday when you called, so let's cut the crap, Darnell. I know the magazine has come to the house by now and you've seen Thad Stewart kissing that bimbo on the cover. You called to see what I would say about it, and you *know* what I have to say about him. So do you know who she is?"

Irritated, Darnell sighed. Her mother had never been one to be subtle. "I've met her before, but I'm sure there's an explanation. People in L.A. are always hugging and kissing each other. You never know when a photographer is around."

"Sure." Bev's tone was skeptical. "So what do you plan on doing about all of this?"

"All of what?" Darnell's voice was small, childlike, unlike the confident woman that she was. But at the moment she didn't feel confident. She felt like a helpless child. The feeling was unfamiliar.

Bev's heart constricted. Her daughter was hurting. "What are you going to do about Thad and about Lance?"

Darnell was silent as she thought about the questions. There was nothing to be done about Lance. The two of them had talked—really talked—admitting more truth than they had in years. Gradually, their discussion had turned to her relationship with Thad. Lance was accepting, and even encouraging, as both realized that so much time and so much of their lives had been wasted on foolish pretense. Although Darnell still had reservations about the direction that Lance had decided to take in his life with Ruth, she wished him well, as he did her. Lance and Ruth were now together at the ranch hideaway, ready to begin a new life together.

As for her relationship with Thad, what could she say to her mother? She was a woman in love. All she could do was trust him and believe in his love and loyalty to her. Having made that decision, she felt sure that there was an explanation for the picture on the magazine cover. If only he would contact her. Another three weeks had passed since their last encounter, three weeks without a word from him, despite her efforts to contact him. Faith in him was all she had at this point, faith and love—the most powerful foundations for any relationship. She could not waver in either. So, she reassured her mother that the picture had an explanation and willed herself to believe that her faith in Thad would be justified.

Bev was not convinced that Thad Stewart was as noble as Darnell claimed him to be. What her daughter had done in sticking by Lance during his illness was noble—not that he appreciated it. When Darnell called and informed her that he had found someone else, she could hardly believe it. She had been certain that Darnell's heart would always be safe with Lance and that their "friendship" would blossom. She had hoped that her daughter's attraction to Thad was just a fling. She was sure that Darnell would come to her senses eventually. Well, so much for that.

Men! She was sick and tired of them all. There had been only one man in her life that had ever mattered: her late husband, Colton. She had loved him with a passion. No man had ever been able to measure up to him. The men that she met these days were sorely lacking, and that included Thad's attorney, Ray Wilson. It turned out that he knew her younger sister, Dana, who was also an attorney. He had gotten her home telephone number from her and had called Bev in Chicago after their meeting in Carmel. He'd had the nerve to ask her out on a date. Of course she had refused. Insanity must run in Thad Stewart's entourage.

As Bev was about to leave the room, the telephone rang. She picked up the receiver. "Cameron residence."

"Hello, Mrs. Sharon?" The voice on the line was male, deep and sexy. She recognized it immediately.

"No, Thad, this is not Mrs. Sharon. This is Bev Cameron." Her tone was arctic. "May I help you?"

Thad groaned. Just great! Things seemed to be going from bad to worse. He *had* to speak to Darnell. He was going out of his mind. He had left messages for her everywhere he could think of, and she hadn't contacted him. The rumors of her engagement to Lance were rampant. The picture of him and Regine on the magazine cover was disastrous, and who should be the first one he spoke to when he called but Darnell's mother! He took a deep breath.

"Hello, Mrs. Cameron . . ."

"*Ms.* Cameron."

Thad sighed. She wasn't going to make this easy. "Ms. Cameron. I'm sorry, please accept my apology. I called because I'm anxious to speak to Darnell. Is there any way I can get a message to her? I've tried everything I know. I'm desperate."

Bev rolled her eyes. *I bet you are*, she thought. She said, "I'm sorry, too, Mr. Stewart, but Darnell is not available. You may have heard, or better yet, *read* why.

She's going into rehearsals to sing before the President of the United States. She can't be disturbed." That would fix him for hurting her daughter.

Thad clenched his teeth. He knew that he was being chastised for the picture on the magazine cover. It was doubtful that she would deliver any messages from him to Darnell. He tried anyway.

"I know that the picture on that magazine looks bad, Ms. Cameron, but . . ."

"Is there anything else, Mr. Stewart?"

"Yes, there is. I'd appreciate it if you could just ask her to contact me. It's very important."

"I'm sure it is."

If that was the best Thad could get from her, he would take it. He gave her his Los Angeles telephone number and his new cell phone number, full of doubts that Darnell would receive either. He would not beg Bev to follow through on his request. He did have some pride. Yet, the thought of never seeing Darnell again impaled his heart. His resolve weakened. Something stronger than pride was compelling his actions.

"When you see Darnell again, please tell her that I love her with everything in me."

On the other end, Thad's words were met with silence and then the dial tone. Reluctantly, he hung up. There was nothing more left to say.

CHAPTER 25

It was torture being in L.A., trying to function as a whole, thinking human being when he was neither. He walked and talked like a robot, a machine without a heart. He didn't have one. Darnell owned it.

As he sat in the limousine with Ray, headed toward the premiere of his latest picture, he was drained of all emotions except misery. He looked out of the window at the passing scenery, but everything was a blur. He didn't feel up to this event tonight, but it was a part of the obligations in this business he loved. His heart jerked. *Love*.

Thad closed his eyes.

He wondered what Darnell was doing right this moment. Was she with Lance? If so, he had no one to blame but himself if she had taken him up on his ultimatum. He was sure the picture with Regine hadn't helped matters.

Usually, he was on top of it when it came to the press. He had become an expert in charming them into dancing to his tune, but he hadn't seen *that* photographer. Nobody could control everything, especially spoiled, stubborn women like Regine. After that kiss, he had dragged her from the dance floor and given her a piece of his mind. He had made it clear that he didn't appreciate what she had done, either there or at his house. She had cried, trying to win his sympathy, but the tears had dried quickly when he didn't respond the way that she thought he would. She had accused him of tossing her affections aside for Darnell's. She dared him to deny it. He didn't, and told her in no uncertain terms that who he cared about or didn't was not her concern. He didn't need her approval. After having his say, he had stormed off and hadn't looked back. She was one woman that he never wanted to see or hear from again.

Thad sighed and opened his eyes. He could feel the tightness in his jaws, the tension building in his shoulders. What did it matter anyway? Darnell didn't want him anymore. She had chosen practicality over passion, but the least she could do was call and let him know that it was over. Thad slumped in his seat. The facts were clear. She had chosen Lance and not him. He might not ever see her again. He swallowed the lump in his throat. Hell! He would survive, and he would make sure that no other woman would ever hurt him like this again.

"We're here, man," Ray informed him.

Thad looked out of the limo window as it pulled up to their destination. The glare of bright lights and the roar of the crowd jolted him back to reality. He used to love these premieres—the crowd's energy and excitement, the anticipation of seeing the end product of so much hard work—but this evening was different. All he wanted to do right now was to go home.

The limo door opened, and the screams assailed Thad's ears as he stepped out into the night. The smile on his face was dazzling. It was showtime, and no one would ever notice the pain beneath the smile. He was a super-star, and his world was perfect.

"Moody, I'm telling you, man, this is serious." The urgency in Russ Ingram's voice verified his concern. "Wochev is trying to convince the rest of the cartels that the slip-up came from us."

"I don't see how. The thief wasn't in our camp." Moody restlessly walked the length of the oriental carpet that covered the floor of the downstairs office in the house he was renting. It was the first time that he had used the office. Russ had come to see him to discuss the latest development in the case of the missing shipment, a matter that Moody thought had been settled. It wasn't. His associate's presence on the peninsula signaled the importance of the information he was conveying.

"The way I figure it is that he knows that the cartels no longer respect his power, so he's desperate to save face and find a scapegoat. We're it. After all, the others were skeptical of this deal with the Colombians. They don't trust them, so when the shipment came up short, nobody was surprised. Wochev needs a distraction. He's walking on thin ice, so he's pulling our organization out on the ice to skate with him."

Settling in the leather wingback chair behind the desk, Moody processed Russ's evaluation of the situation carefully as he observed his protégé. In his mid-thirties, he was an ambitious young man. Unlike him, Russ hadn't come from a life of grinding poverty, but from a highly educated African-American family that had attained the American Dream. His father was a corporate executive, and his mother was a college professor. He had graduated with honors from Rutgers University with a degree in business management. His career could have taken any direction he wanted. The world was his. Instead, he had chosen a life of crime, a life of danger and intrigue where an early death was a real possibility. For what? Quick money? Excitement? Whatever the reason, Moody wondered if it was worth it. Whether it was or not, the younger man had earned a place of trust and respect in Moody's life.

He sighed. "What you're saying makes sense, Russ, but you see, we've got a paid operative in the Wochev camp." He smiled at his associate's surprised reaction at this bit of news. "I've been in this business long enough to know who I should trust and who I shouldn't."

"I see." Russ smiled.

"If the snitch falls down on the job, his life is on the line. If the tide turns too swiftly and we're in jeopardy, I should be the first to know, or he'll be a dead man."

The younger man continued to look at him thoughtfully. The lines of worry were still etched on his face. Much like him, Russ was a serious man who showed little emotion, and it was often difficult to know what he was thinking. Moody decided to change the subject.

"I'm glad that you're here, my man. Why don't you stay the night?"

"I've booked a hotel in Monterey for the night. I'm taking a flight into San Francisco tomorrow to see the town. It's been years since I've been to the Bay Area."

"No, cancel your hotel room. I insist that you stay here. Then you can keep me company when I drive to the city tomorrow," Moody informed him. "I have some business to take care of."

He certainly did. The muscled man had said that Thad Stewart was expected back in Tiburon on Saturday, around noon. By Saturday, around midnight, he would be dead.

Thad continued to operate by rote at the party after the premiere. He graciously accepted the many compliments bestowed on him for his latest cinematic effort. He got through the press interviews and posed for many pictures. As the evening wound down, he was finally able to take a seat at the VIP table and relax for a moment—which proved to be a second too long. Closing his eyes, he inhaled the sharp pain that inched across his heart as thoughts of Darnell resurfaced.

"Hey, man! What's happening? Are you okay?"

Thad opened his eyes to look into the face of Duncan Whittaker, another of Hollywood's young African-American superstars. Thad and Duncan had come into the motion picture business together. While Thad had done so through comedy, Duncan had broken into the business as a theatrically trained actor. The press had tried countless times to pit them against each other, but they refused to be used as pawns. They were not personal friends, but they did have mutual respect for each other and each other's work.

Thad stretched and gave Duncan a weary smile. "I'm a little tired, man. It's been quite a night."

Duncan looked around at the crowd of revelers. "Yeah, I know what you mean." His gaze returned to Thad. "Listen, I like the work you did on that screen. Nice. Real nice."

Thad nodded. "Thanks, man. I appreciate that, coming from you." Duncan was one hell of an actor, and the compliment meant a lot.

Settling in a chair beside him, Duncan decided to strike up a conversation. Thad wished that he wouldn't, but engaged in small talk with him anyway, responding to his chatter with a nod, a smile or an occasional comment. He tried to look interested, but the conversation didn't pique his curiosity until Duncan brought up the subject of a "songbird"—as he called her—as being his next romantic conquest. It seemed that he had been longing to get close to this particular woman for a long time, and it was only recently that she was free to be pursued.

"Free?" Thad looked at him with empathy. "Man, you better think twice about sniffing after some divorcee too soon. Not too many women are going to give up the alimony for love, especially in this town."

"Naw, man. It's not like that. This lady has never been married. She's just been hooked up with her man for a long time. There was even a rumor that she was engaged to him, but she's free now."

Thad tensed. *Hooked up to her man for a long time? Rumor of an engagement?* It sounded familiar. "Who is this woman? How do you know it wasn't just a rumor that she's free?"

Duncan leaned back in his chair and chuckled. "Do you really think I'm going to give you her name? I'm going to have enough competition as it is. I'm telling you, man, the line to mend her broken heart is going to be long, and I don't need the crowd. Her boyfriend just married somebody else. But I've got the inside track on this one—an invitation to a little event that's going to put me dead in the running for her attention." Then abruptly, Duncan stopped talking, as if aware that he had already said too much. He turned to address someone passing by.

Duncan had been right. He had said a little too much. Thad's brain went into overdrive as he fought for control of every muscle in his body. When he was a child of twelve, his father had taught him how to play poker. The major lesson that he had learned was how to bluff, and he had learned his lesson well. Measuring the timing of his words, he cocked his head at just the right angle, looked at Duncan with a trace of skepticism and said, "So, it's going to be you and Darnell Cameron, huh?"

Duncan's head whipped around so quickly it looked as if it might fly off his neck. His eyes were as large as saucers. "I didn't say a thing about Darnell Cameron!"

Bingo! The man was after Darnell! *His* Darnell! Thad fought to keep his anger in check. He wanted to slam his fist into the man's face.

Duncan sat eyeing Thad suspiciously. "I thought you were hooked up with that gallery owner I saw you with on the magazine cover." His voice was cautious, hopeful.

Thad gave him a noncommittal smile but didn't answer. Let him think what he wanted. He had business to attend to. Excusing himself, he went to find Ray.

Spotting Thad barreling across the room toward him at high speed, Ray knew the reason for the urgency— Lance Austin's marriage to another woman. A reliable source had just confirmed what had been a rumor as fact. It was obvious that Thad had heard the same news. Ray waved a hand above the crowd to get Thad's attention. The next thing Ray knew Thad was unceremoniously dragging him by the arm across the room. Finding a vacant spot, Thad pinned him against the wall and barked, "Lance Austin got married, and not to Darnell."

Ray grinned at the look of excitement on Thad's face. "I heard."

"I want you to get me into that San Francisco concert tomorrow, Ray. Can you do it before you go out of town?

"I'll make a call tonight, but something tells me you won't have a problem getting admitted."

Thad grinned. "You don't think so, huh?"

Ray slapped him on the back, glad that there might be a happy ending for his friend. "No, my man, you're as good as in already. This time, don't let anything stand in the way of making her yours."

The advice was appreciated, but unnecessary. He would let nothing stop him from being with Darnell.

CHAPTER 26

The household staff was abuzz with excitement at the presence of Mr. Ingram as an overnight guest. In the weeks since Mr. Waters had been in residence, there had been plenty of telephone calls, but not one single visitor to the house. The young man was personable, undemanding and as neat as a pin. At dinner that evening, he had thanked the cook for a delicious meal, and in the morning when the butler had offered to pack his clothing, he had declined. In the short time he was a guest, he had endeared himself to each of them.

As they stood watching Mr. Waters's car pull away from the house, the butler informed the others, "Those two men are gentlemen indeed. Mr. Ingram even refused my offer to drive him to the airport since Mr. Waters had already offered to do so."

"Where is he from?" The housekeeper was curious. It seemed that neither of the two men had inadvertently provided much information about themselves, which was the only way the staff usually learned anything about the people who passed through the house.

"I don't know," the butler answered. "But he told me this morning that he's flying back home today."

The housekeeper lifted a brow. "Oh, really? I thought I overheard Mr. Waters say that they were off to San

Francisco. He must be taking the plane from there. All I know is that he is more than welcome back here again. He was so pleasant."

They all agreed as the car pulled out of the driveway and onto the street. Russ Ingram was a very nice man.

The rehearsals had been going well. Darnell was now headed to the last one before the concert tonight. Earlier at breakfast, her mother had insisted that she drive her to this morning's rehearsal instead of them taking the limo. Darnell suspected that there was something other than generosity behind the offer. Bev had been restless since her arrival at Darnell's San Francisco condo, a good indication that she had something on her mind. Darnell's guess was that it was Lance.

He had called Darnell days ago to tell her about his marriage to Ruth and to expect the onslaught of publicity. Darnell had wished him all of the happiness in the world and meant every word, but as his friend, she still expressed her sadness and disappointment at his lack of honesty with his new bride. She gave him credit, however, for having been man enough to also call Bev and inform her. She had always treated him like a son, and their affection for each other was mutual. Her mother had been very upset by the call.

Darnell hadn't shared all of the details about Lance's situation with her. They were private, and unless Lance chose to reveal them, they would remain so. She understood her mother's anger and confusion about what had happened, but she had offered her little comfort. What was done was done. Mother and daughter hadn't discussed the evolving events in detail since the media broke the news and the initial phone calls between them, so as they drove along, Darnell leaned back in the automobile's plush interior, waiting.

At this point, whatever Bev had to say really didn't matter. She was numb anyway. Thad had not contacted her, despite her efforts to get in touch with him. Even the news of Lance's marriage hadn't warranted a telephone call or a message. Because he had remained silent, the message was clear: He no longer cared.

Closing her eyes, Darnell leaned her head against the headrest as she recalled their last encounter at her condo. She could feel her body react to the mere memory of that night. But that was then; this was now. He had issued an ultimatum, and she guessed that it hadn't been adhered to fast enough for him. His silence was testimony to that. Had the words of love and adoration that he uttered been lies? Had she allowed two men whom she loved to use her? She let the question fester. When she had time, she would allow herself to wallow in self-pity for a while. Then she would close the door on this bittersweet chapter of her life.

Bev took a sideward glance at her daughter. While she might look to be the picture of serenity to others, she knew better. Her child's face was pinched, and her body was tense. She had to give her credit. The woman had handled the situation with Lance in a mature manner.

She had accepted it with grace, but she was a little too accepting as far as Bev was concerned. Personally, she was still reeling from the stunning announcement of Lance's marriage. The man she loved like a son had betrayed her daughter. He had done the unforgivable. There was no longer anything good to be said about Dr. Lance Austin.

"I could kick that man's butt into Hades."

"Mama, let it go. It's over and done with."

Bev started, unaware that she had spoken aloud. Darnell opened her eyes and turned toward her mother.

"Lance did what he felt he had to do." She gave a heavy sigh. "I know what it is to love someone and have stumbling blocks in your way." She closed her eyes again.

Her daughter's words pierced Bev's heart as she realized that her child was suffering, and it wasn't because of Lance. She was in love with another man, and she loved him hard. Bev knew the feeling. It seemed that history was repeating itself. That's how she had loved Darnell's father, and it had nearly killed her.

She had been young when she met Colton Cameron, a high school senior. He was two years older, had no living relatives, and unlike her, had no plans on attending college. But he was working, and he was intent on having her as his. The pressure from her prominent family had been intense, but the love between Bev and Colton was stronger than the objections. Two days after her graduation, they eloped.

For twelve months, she had walked on clouds. She had never been so happy. Then came the thirteenth month, when she fell to earth and shattered into a million pieces.

Her husband had worked hard and had provided well. Whatever Bev wanted was hers. She had only to ask. As young as they were, they lived well. He had worked in the construction business, and it was booming. Struggle was not a part of their lives. He had been gone a lot, often days at a time. She was never quite sure where he was or what he was doing, but he had always came home to her. They were ecstatic about their impending parenthood and more in love than two people should be. Everything had been perfect—or so it seemed. Then, one day, he didn't come home.

She nearly went out of her mind. Prompted by her family's influence, the police search was exhaustive, and she held fast to the hope that he would return to her. It wasn't to be. They found his remains days later. He had been in a one-car accident that had decapitated him. The car had landed in the deepest river in town, where it sank. Her father had gone to claim his body—she couldn't do it. The shock of his death had hospitalized her and brought Darnell into the world early.

Bev buried her husband and her heart as well. She knew what hard love could do to you. That kind of love was enduring. It could remain your companion for the rest of your life.

The car was quiet for a long time. Darnell could almost hear her mother thinking, and she wondered what those thoughts were about. Finally, Bev broke the silence.

"You really love him, don't you?"

With great effort, Darnell tried to show no emotion. They both knew who her mother was talking about. She didn't want Bev to hear the pain in her voice, but her effort was unsuccessful as she sighed, "What does it matter, Mama?"

Bev drew a shaky breath and turned back to the road. "Because he called you last week when you were in Chicago and I was staying at your house in Carmel."

If her mother had hit her with a sledgehammer, the impact could not have been less powerful. The questions came fast and furious. "He called? Last week? And you're just now telling me this? What did he say? Did he leave a number? Where is he? How could you not tell me?"

Her mother tried to apologize, but all Darnell wanted to know was what he had said and how she could contact him. Bev gave her the numbers that Thad had left.

"Baby, I know that nothing I can say at this point is enough, but I am truly sorry. He tried to tell me about that picture on the magazine cover, but I wouldn't let him, and he asked me to deliver a message." She paused and looked at Darnell's stern profile. "He told me to tell you that he loved you with everything in him." Those tender words brought tears of relief to her daughter and tears of regret from Bev.

The next few hours between rehearsals Darnell spent desperately trying to reach Thad. She got one answering service after the other. She even tried to call Ray for assistance. If anyone could track Thad down, he could, but his message service stated that he was unavailable as well. It was only hours before the concert, and she had yet to speak to Thad, but she would walk out on the stage this evening sure of his love for her.

As Moody and Russ sped along the highway headed toward San Francisco, Moody had to admit that he was enjoying the younger man's company. Their topics of conversation ran the gamut from music to politics. The two men had a lot in common. He had no doubt that this was the young man that he wanted to succeed him. It had been his hope that when things worked out with Darnell as he planned, he could reduce his workload and Russ could handle more responsibility. He trusted him that much. The young man had everything going for him. All he needed was—

"How's that girlfriend of yours?" Moody recalled being introduced to a woman with a honey-colored complexion and matching hair at some affair. She was the only one he recalled seeing Russ with more than once. "What's her name?"

"Renee." Russ smiled. "And we're getting married."

"Congratulations!" Moody's response was genuine. "A strong leader needs a good woman by his side. It helps make him a better man."

Russ threw him a sideward glance. "I've been with you for years, and I haven't seen you with one you've taken seriously."

Moody grew pensive. "Women come, and women go, but if you find yourself a *good* one . . ." He paused as he thought about the love of his life. "All I can say is don't let her go, and don't let anyone come between you."

Russ heard the slight tremor in his voice. "I take it that's what happened to you?"

Moody didn't respond. He never talked about that aspect of his life. It was dead and buried. Anyway, what was there to say—that he was a man who had loved only one woman and that he would love her until the day he died? No other woman had ever come close to her, and he doubted that one ever would.

There was a moment of awkward silence in the car that made it clear that Moody had nothing else to say. Russ shifted uncomfortably, then cleared his throat.

"Do you mind if I change the radio station? I've got a taste for a little more variety."

Moody didn't object as Russ found an urban contemporary station and settled back in his seat. Soon, they were both enjoying the music that filled the car as they drove along. Each man was engrossed in his own world until an announcement on the radio made Moody take notice. Darnell Cameron would be performing in concert that evening in San Francisco before the President of the United States. The reporter recounted the recent marriage of her long-time boyfriend and speculated whether her performance would be affected by the recent event.

Moody discounted the latter. He knew all about Lance and his strengths and weaknesses. The latter prevailed, and he had never given him a second thought, but Darnell was in the city. He could see her, even if it only meant getting one precious glance. Unconsciously, his foot pressed down harder on the accelerator, and the car picked up speed.

Bev studied her daughter's profile as they were driven through the city to the theatre in which she would perform tonight. Sometimes, she had to pinch herself in order to make herself believe that this brilliant, confident, talented young woman was the little girl she had raised. She knew that Darnell was still angry with her because of her deception, but she also knew her well enough to know that she would get over it. Mother and daughter had been a team for much too long to let this come between them. She hadn't said much to her mother since this morning, and Bev hadn't pushed her, but it was time to break the ice.

"Am I going to be in the doghouse forever?"

Darnell wanted to stay angry longer, but she was feeling too good about the message that her mother had delivered from Thad and about tonight's concert.

"No, not forever." She tried to suppress a smile. "I'll let you out of it if you continue to let me live my life and don't interfere again. That's not like you, Mama. I don't understand how you could do that. What has Thad done to you that you're so against him?"

Bev sighed. "Nothing, really. Actually, he doesn't seem like a bad guy at all, except he had better be ready to explain that picture with that . . ."

"Mama." Darnell gave her a warning glare.

"All right. It's your life, and I raised you well. You've got good taste, and I trust you." Yawning, Bev stretched and shifted her body in the cavernous back seat as she made herself comfortable. "I hope things work out for you."

Darnell gave her a confident smile. "Oh, I have a feeling that everything will work out just fine."

Moody's plan was to drop Russ off at his hotel and then go by the theatre to see if he could catch a glimpse of Darnell, but Russ asked him to drop him off in front of a department store near the hotel in which he said that he would be staying. He had a purchase to make. Anxious to get to the theatre, Moody did so. Preoccupied, he drove away so quickly that he didn't remember until later that Russ's overnight bag was in his trunk. He would call him later and deliver it to him.

Moody's excitement escalated as he found a parking space within walking distance of the theatre in which Darnell would be performing. As he neared the facility on foot, he found the area blocked off, as he had suspected that it would be. Security was everywhere, from the police to the Secret Service. A small crowd had gathered behind the barriers to see if they could catch a glimpse of the President and the First Lady as they entered, as well as Darnell and the score of other celebrities who were to attend. From his position in the crowd, Moody knew that he wouldn't be able to see her. He told himself that since he had waited this long, he could wait a while longer, and he wouldn't have to wait in any crowd. After all, he was paying a small fortune to live across the street from her. When she returned home, he would step up his efforts to get to know her. It had been too long, and time was now at a premium.

He had turned to leave when a cheer went up from the crowd.

"It's Thad Stewart," someone said. He turned in time to see the face he had grown to hate peek from the open window of a limousine. Flashing a dimpled smile, he was waving.

Moody's jaws tightened. He should have known. Like a dog in heat, he was following her. The man couldn't leave well enough alone. This changed his plans to kill him today. This event was much too public. But the man's day was coming. Meanwhile, maybe he should try to see Darnell. With Thad around, there was no telling when she would be back in Carmel.

Angrily, he turned to walk back to his car. The crowd grew thinner, as did the security as he put distance between himself and the theatre. He was deep in thought when he stepped off the curb to cross the street. He didn't see the limo until it was almost too late. Swiftly, he jumped back on the curb, uttering an expletive just as the car came to a screeching halt. The back window came down, and the face of Darnell Cameron appeared as if summoned.

"Are you all right?" The familiar voice left Moody standing stunned and speechless. A voice on the other side of her made an inquiry.

"What happened? Why are we stopping?" The voice was husky, as if awakening from sleep.

Moody's heart threatened to explode. He found it hard to breathe as Darnell turned away from him momentarily to answer the question, then turned back to him.

"I'm so sorry. I'm sure the driver didn't see you. I know that he frightened you. Are you sure you're okay?"

Frozen in place, Moody nodded. All that he wanted to say to her, all of the plans he had made for when he met her face-to-face, were forgotten as he devoured her lovely face.

"Let me see. We didn't hurt him, did we?" He could hear the rustling behind Darnell. This wasn't how he wanted it to be. This wasn't how he had planned it. He stepped back further just as a second face appeared at the window and peered at him with curiosity. A mature version of her daughter's, the face was even lovelier than it had been that day on the beach.

Moody felt dizzy, but he willed himself to stand tall as he managed to mumble,

"I'm fine." Two pairs of large brown eyes examined him, reassuring themselves that what he said was true.

Darnell smiled, and he nearly lost it. "If you're sure you're okay—" She said something to the driver, then turned back to Moody. "Really, I'm sorry, and I'm glad that you're not hurt." Bev leaned back, the window went up slowly, and they drove away. He stood on the curb watching them until the limo disappeared.

Inside the car, Bev looked out of the tinted back window at the man standing on the corner. There was something about him.

"He's a cutie pie," she said appreciatively.

Darnell chuckled. "Watch it now, Ray might get jealous."

Bev's head whipped around to scowl at her daughter indignantly. She was fully awake now. "Ray? Girl, pleeeeze! You have *got* to be kidding!" She rolled her eyes so hard that they ached. Her daughter collapsed with laughter that lasted all the way to the theatre.

Moody couldn't remember how he got to his car. Still shaken, he leaned on the hood, trying to recover. It took him a while to become aware of the presence of someone behind him. Turning, he was surprised to see that it was Russ.

"Hey, man! Where did you come from?" Then he remembered the luggage. "Oh, yeah, your things. They're in the trunk." He started to move past him, then stopped. "Say, how did you find me? And how did you get here?"

Russ was unresponsive. His expression was blank. Out of the corner of his eye, to his right, Moody noticed a large, dark-skinned figure walking toward them. He turned slightly and saw a light-skinned man approaching them from the left. He didn't recognize either man. Then comprehension dawned. His eyes returned to Russ.

"*Et tu, Brute?*" The words from Shakespeare's *Julius Caesar* were the only thing he could think of at the moment. There was no doubt that they were appropriate for the occasion.

"I told you that it was serious," Russ said, looking him directly in the eye, "but you wouldn't listen." He motioned toward Moody's rental car. "Open the door and get in."

The two henchmen sat in the front seat. One drove. Relieving Moody of his weapon, Russ sat in the backseat beside him. Moody kept waiting for panic to come, but it didn't. It was strange, but he felt serene. It was as if instinctively he had known that this day would come. Actually, it was probably long overdue. There was nowhere to run this time, so he might as well sit back and relax. He turned to Russ.

"So, I take it that the house staff has been notified that I won't be returning."

"You decided to go back east with me. Someone will be sent for your belongings."

"I see. What about the rental car?"

"It'll be returned, and the bill will be paid with cash."

"So no one is expected to ever find me."

Russ turned from the window for the first time and looked at him. "No."

"How ironic." It was Moody's turn to look out of the window at the passing scenery. They were crossing the Golden Gate Bridge headed for Marin County. Retribution would soon occur, but he couldn't complain. How many men had he helped disappear over the years in his rise to the top?

Like Russ, he had betrayed his own mentor—a man who had treated him like a son. He had started working for him at the age of eighteen. The cover for his mentor's business was a thriving construction company, and his boss had taught him everything that he knew about the underworld. But as a young man, his ambition had been greater than his loyalty to his mentor. He had betrayed him for financial gain. When his duplicity was uncovered, not only was his life in jeopardy, but also the life of his pregnant wife. That was a price he was unwilling to pay. She knew nothing about his clandestine activities. Her life meant more to him than his own. If he was dead, then she would be safe. So an innocent stranger was sacrificed and sent to a watery grave as Colton Cameron.

A new man had emerged named Moody Lake. Plastic surgery made that possible. It wasn't difficult changing everything about himself. Yet his memories remained intact, and so did the love that had a hold on his heart. For a brief moment today, after seeing the objects of that love, he had felt alive again. He couldn't help appreciating that irony since this would be the last day of his life. But, it really didn't matter. He had been dead for thirty-two years anyway.

The driver turned on the radio, and the sound of music filled the car's interior. Leaning forward, Moody tapped the driver on the shoulder. He turned slightly, acknowledging him.

"Yeah?"

"I've got one final request, if you don't mind."

"What is it?" The inquiry came from Russ.

"Turn up the radio," Moody addressed the driver. He granted his request. Moody settled back in his seat as the singer's glorious voice enchanted the car's occupants.

Russ looked at Moody, who sat with his eyes closed and his head leaning back against the headrest. A look of pure rapture was on his face. He scoffed.

"Man, you act like Darnell Cameron is singing that song for you."

An ethereal smile teased Moody's lips as the image of Bev and his daughter smiling up at him floated through his memory. He nodded. "Yes, I like to think that she is. I love her. I guess you could say that I'm her biggest fan."

CHAPTER 27

Darnell stood bathed in a blue spotlight. Her form-fitting, hand-beaded gown glistened like diamonds. Her braids were pulled away from her face and gathered in a chignon at the nape of her neck. Words from the love song "So Amazing" tumbled from her lacquered lips like velvet.

She had dedicated the song to "someone who means the world to me," and had added mysteriously, "and he knows who he is."

Members of the black-tied gala mumbled among themselves. Hadn't she been dumped recently by her boyfriend? They had expected tortured songs of love lost, not of love found. Had someone mended her broken heart already? They glanced around the crowded ball-room. Could the lucky man be here? Every man in the room, available and unavailable, pretended.

In the back of the room, leaning casually against the wall, his arms folded across his chest, his eyes transfixed by the vision on the stage, one man didn't have to wonder or pretend. Thad knew that those words were meant for only him. It was a song that had been sung to him in a scent-filled bath in Carmel, and he was present to hear it again.

There was a chance for them. The tensions that had so dominated their relationship had dissipated, and friendship had replaced it. The obstacles that had been blocking their path no longer existed, but new ones would replace them testing their resolve. Their feelings for each other had been nurtured in an environment devoid of the pressures of media or fans. Public disclosure about their relationship would change all of that, but he had faith that the two of them could weather any storm, overcome any future obstacles, as long as they did it together.

Delayed in Los Angeles by unexpected business, he had arrived in San Francisco only two hours before the affair. Ray had been right when he said an invitation would not be a problem. One telephone call to the event organizers, plus a sizable donation to the cause, and Thad became an honored guest.

Arriving in the city with so little time, he had barely had time to shower, shave, and dress in his tuxedo before the limo arrived. At the theatre, he had gone through the customary routine with the Who's Who and the Wanna Be Who.

He'd smiled, posed and signed autographs, then found the spot in the back of the room where he now stood, glowing with pride, as he listened to Darnell's awesome talent.

He looked around the room at the faces captivated by her amazing voice and stage presence. Many of the faces he recognized. There were Hollywood superstars, political dignitaries of the highest level, and of course the President of the United States and the First Lady. Thad also spotted Duncan Whittaker. His presence was no surprise. Sitting in the VIP section reserved for the President, he saw Darnell's mother. Her love for and pride in her daughter was written clearly on her face. He knew how she felt. Returning his attention to the stage, everything else around him faded into oblivion. Darnell stood on stage bathed in a single spotlight—singing a song for him.

He had hoped to see her before the show. He had wanted to see the look on her face when she saw him, but luck hadn't been with him. Access backstage was limited to the president and a select few. Determined to be one of the latter, he had schemed to go backstage to her after the concert. A casual remark by the hostess assigned to him altered that plan, however.

Introducing herself as Brooke Presser, the young college student greeted him in the hotel lobby and escorted him to the limo. She was nineteen, a sophomore at Howard University, who was visibly nervous about meeting a movie star. Thad had put her at ease with his wit and charm until she was talking to him like an old friend. Flanked by guards to protect him from the overzealous, they had mingled at the reception given before the concert. She had fed him tidbits of information about different people at the affair. She obviously enjoyed her role as an ingenue gossip. Thad was amused.

At one point during the evening, Brooke had pointed out to Thad an influential young congressman whose face and name he recognized. He had seen him often on television. The man was active in the Black Congressional Caucus and an eloquent spokesperson for the rights of minorities and the underserved. In his late thirties, according to the media, the congressman had risen from extreme poverty and hardship to succeed in business and was now a man of some influence—a real power broker in Washington. He was wealthy and handsome and had been named on the same list as Thad as one of the country's most eligible bachelors. Darnell had spoken highly of him during their many discussions and conversations. She liked his politics, but it wasn't his politics that impressed Brooke.

"He's a major hunk!" she gushed girlishly. "And he's not married. All of the women in here are after him."

Thad chuckled. "Are you one of them?"

She looked at him, horrified. "Are you kidding? He's like, forty or something. He's too old for me. My mother would die!" Her voice lowered to a conspiratorial whisper. "I hear he's got eyes for our guest star, though." She didn't notice the muscles on Thad's face tense.

"And who would that be?"

"Darnell Cameron, of course!" She looked at Thad as if he had committed a crime. "You do know that she's singing tonight?" Thad nodded, but didn't respond.

"Anyway, he's a great fan of hers. I've heard he has every CD she's put out. He got her hotel room number from my mother."

Thad's eyes narrowed. He lowered them to his glass of punch to shield them from his enthralled hostess as she prattled on. "Did I tell you that my mother is the main hostess of this event?" She grinned proudly. "She's just got to meet you. She'll die."

His mounting anger under control, Thad threw her a disarming smile. "You were saying that he got Ms. Cameron's hotel room number?" The smile worked as Brooke all but melted before his eyes.

"Yes . . . yes . . ." She laughed nervously as all of her thought processes seemed to flee. Her friends would never believe that she had spent the evening with this man. She swallowed nervously, mesmerized by his dimpled smile. "My . . . my mother, she's such a sucker for him—the congressman, that is. He told her that he wanted to ask Ms. Cameron if he could take her to the private party he's throwing at his townhouse after the concert."

Thad raised a brow. "Oh, really? A *private* party."

Brooke nodded, too caught up in her tale to notice his reaction. "Oh yes! He sent flowers to her dressing room." Stopping to take a breath, Brooke looked perplexed. "But I don't know if she's going or not." She brightened. "But you're invited. All of the celebrities are invited."

A rush of fans interrupted them, and the concert began before he could question Brooke further. Spurred by her words, he had made a decision. There would be no private party for the esteemed congressman this evening. Neither would there be a private dressing room meeting for him and Darnell. Tonight was the night that the two of them would emerge publicly as a couple. No longer would there be any pretense. She had made demands of him to which he had willingly submitted. She had driven him to complete distraction. His love for her consumed him, but tonight she would dance to his tune.

The applause was deafening as Darnell finished her last song. She was always grateful when an audience showed how much it appreciated her efforts to entertain. God had bestowed on her a gift that she shared willingly. This audience's response was overwhelming. When they stood and cheered, it brought tears to eyes that subtly searched the audience of distinguished dignitaries, senators, congressmen, celebrities, and even the President of the United States, for the face of only one person. She didn't see him, but she had felt his presence from the stage.

Making her way back to her dressing room, Darnell could barely conceal her disappointment. Was she being foolish? Was he really here?

All access to the dressing room area had been banned by the Secret Service as the President and the First Lady made their appearance in Darnell's dressing room. After the First Family's departure, she hurriedly changed from her stage clothes to one of her favorite dresses, a sexy little yellow number. Her hostess, Mrs. Presser, then came to take her to the reception hall.

Her hostess was an energetic woman in her late forties who did everything with a sense of urgency. Led by a horde of security guards, she escorted Darnell from the theatre through an underground tunnel and a series of hallways until, eventually, they reached the reception. At their entrance, they were delayed by a horde of fans seeking autographs. Darnell obliged.

As she was signing, she thought that she caught a whiff of familiar cologne—his cologne. Her eyes flew up and swept the room discreetly. Nothing. She returned to the task at hand as she recalled the smell of him when they were last together, how his mouth had devoured her lips, how his hand had caressed her. The memory of the sensations that only Thad could arouse in her made her falter. Alerted, Mrs. Presser became concerned as Darnell swayed.

"Oh my goodness, are you all right, my dear?"

"Yes . . . yes, I—" Embarrassed, Darnell didn't know what to say. The lady would be the one to faint if she knew what was going through her mind.

Mrs. Presser started shooing the fans away. "No, no, no! She can't give any more autographs. You're crushing the poor woman. Give her room. Give her air. You!" She commandeered one of the security guards. "Get us over to our table, now!" She turned to Darnell. "Dear, we must get you something to eat."

Darnell smiled back at her weakly. How could she tell her that she didn't want food and she didn't want to be part of a social gathering? There was no gracious way to say that she would rather have skipped this part of the evening or to explain that all she really wanted at the moment was Thad Stewart and to be held in his arms. So she followed the security guards who did as directed and cleared a path as the small entourage moved further into the room.

Across the room, fans surrounded Thad, demanding autographs. He saw her enter the hall, a blur of yellow against a sea of moving bodies. She was no longer on stage, but in this room, only yards away from him. His eyes, his mind, his every sense had been aware of her as he moved forward. However, the commotion his presence in the room was causing became a problem. Before he realized it, he was trapped against a column, unable to move.

Thad looked up from signing an autograph to see Darnell and her party moving away from him. He thrust a pen and paper into the hands of an excited fan and broke free of the crowd. Ignoring the disappointed protests that followed him, he moved forward, rejecting all efforts to gain his attention. His eyes never left the splash of yellow, so near, but still too far to overtake. At this moment, he no longer cared about pleasing fans, or anyone else in this room. No telephone calls, no notes of love, nothing at all could replace his looking into those eyes and touching her.

As he drew closer, his determination to get to her became more acute. Standing in his line of vision, he saw the congressman who had been the subject of Brooke's earlier conversation standing opposite Darnell. With wineglass in hand, he laughed and chatted easily as his hand reached out to touch the woman whose attention he coveted—Darnell Cameron. Thad quickened his pace.

Darnell's energy was waning. She was tired. The concert had been nearly two hours long, and she had given her audience all that she had to give. She had smiled so much that her face felt tight, and the small talk in which she was engaged was becoming monotonous. Yet she remained gracious. This was as much a part of her job as singing. So when the handsome congressman, whose work she had admired over the years, stopped her to talk, she gave him her attention.

She had received flowers from him in her dressing room earlier, as she had from Duncan Whittaker. She took this opportunity to thank him and to inform him that she had been following his accomplishments in Congress and was well versed on the work he pursued. He seemed flattered and impressed. If she had not been so exhausted, she might have noticed the light of interest in his eyes, the slight tremor in his hand when he touched her, or the rapid rise and fall of his chest. She didn't notice. Her thoughts were elsewhere.

She tried to listen. She wanted to focus on what was being said, and eventually, when she did comprehend what he was asking, she declined the invitation he was extending to attend his after-set party. She gave fatigue as the legitimate reason. His expression of genuine concern for her health almost caused her to waver on her decision—almost.

It was the congressman who was the first to see Thad approaching. Initially, he had been so enthralled by the woman before him that he was unaware of anything else. Everything about her fascinated him—the sensuous movement of her lips, the exciting sweep of her lashes beneath those fabulous eyes. Like an adolescent schoolboy, he had harbored a crush on Darnell Cameron for years. He had tried in every way possible to meet her, but the opportunity had never seemed to present itself until tonight. Since her arrival, he had pulled no punches in getting to meet her. He had read of her involvement with some doctor, and also read about his recent marriage. It gave him hope. Like everyone else in the room, he had wanted the last love song she sang to be for him. He harbored the desire that one day it would be. Until then—

Glancing over her shoulder, he became curious as to why the women behind Darnell were whispering excitedly. Then he saw Thad Stewart approaching. He recognized him immediately. He also recognized Thad's purposeful stride and where his attention was focused. His eyes were trained on the woman in the yellow dress standing before him.

The dress Darnell wore was simple, a silk A-line slip dress that caressed every curve of her voluptuous body. It swayed seductively whenever she moved. The hemline stopped just above her shapely legs, which were covered in hose so sheer that her legs looked bare, except for the hint of gold glitter teasing the naked eye. Yellow high-heel pumps elevated her height. A sexy gold ankle bracelet rested comfortably on one ankle. She was breathtaking.

Darnell had taken her hair out of its chignon. It now cascaded over her shoulders in reckless abandon. A twist of yellow silk matching her dress held it back from her face. Every male in the room openly appreciated her beauty, and as Thad reached the cluster of people around her, the congressman saw the sweep of approval in his eyes as well.

He didn't blink as Thad's open palm pressed ever so gently against the small of Darnell's back, replacing his own. There was no change of expression on his face as he noticed the quick intake of breath from Darnell. All went unnoticed by the others in attendance around her. They were too excited by the sudden appearance of Thad Stewart.

Mrs. Presser was flustered with delight. She didn't notice the quickening of Darnell's breathing or the color that crept into her brown face. The congressman did.

"Oh, my goodness! Mr. Stewart! I was hoping that I'd get to meet you. My daughter, Brooke . . ." She looked around frantically for the young girl. "Well, she was supposed to be your hostess for the evening. I'm Elinor Presser."

As he stood with his hand against Darnell's back, time stopped for Thad. All he could feel was her closeness. The blood pumped through his body at accelerated speed, rushing from his heart to his head, leaving both throbbing with excitement. He had to work hard to control his lower body. He tossed a dimpled grin at Mrs. Presser that captivated her thoroughly. With his free hand he shook her hand.

"Mrs. Presser, your daughter has told me so much about you that I feel I know you. She was very complimentary, and she's also a very nice young lady."

The woman giggled like a schoolgirl. "Oh, thank you. Where is she anyway?"

Darnell didn't hear Thad. She couldn't hear a thing. She felt as if she were standing in a wind tunnel as garbled sounds rushed through her head. She kept her eyes on Mrs. Presser, not daring to look at Thad. But, her mind screamed out in ecstasy, *He's here! He's here!*

Thad's eyes shifted from Mrs. Presser momentarily as if searching the room for her daughter. His gaze took in Darnell's profile, drinking in the sight of her. His thumb made a semicircle on her back. With a flick of her tongue Darnell moistened her lips as heat infused her very core. The congressman drained his wineglass in one gulp.

"Oh, your daughter is around here someplace," Thad assured the woman as his gaze returned to her. "We were separated during the concert. I just wanted to come over and introduce myself."

Mrs. Presser blushed. "Oh, I'm so glad that you did, and I'd like for you to meet . . ." She turned to Darnell to introduce her to Thad. It was then that she noticed the placement of his hand. She became flustered at the intimacy of the gesture. "W . . . well, I see that you know . . ."

Deliberately pretending to misunderstand what Mrs. Presser was about to say, Thad thrust his hand out to the man nearest him, a senator, as he pressed Darnell closer to him. "It's not necessary to introduce this distinguished gentleman. I've seen him on television many times. Sir, I'm Thad Stewart."

With a practiced smile, Darnell watched as Thad worked his way around the group of men near her, shaking the hands of each while still managing to cling to her possessively. The devil. He was putting on the performance of his life.

The congressman was the last to receive a handshake from him. Their eyes locked briefly as the men firmly clasped hands. Thad's eyes and smile swept each one around him once again, then settled on Mrs. Presser. "Now, if you'll excuse us, gentlemen, Mrs. Presser." With that, Thad took Darnell's hand and led her toward the reception hall's dance floor.

Darnell's mind was reeling as she stumbled along, trying to keep pace with his long-legged stride. What was it about this man that had him embedded so deeply in her heart? She felt euphoric.

This was unreal. The connection between them was so strong that she had actually felt his presence from the stage. Her mind could hardly grasp the power of such emotions.

As the two superstars walked away, the congressman watched them with an air of resignation. There would be no further opportunities to get to know Darnell. Thad Stewart had made that clear. While his dazzling smile and pleasant manner had remained friendly and open, the congressman, a former child of the streets, had watched the man's eyes—the windows to the soul. The dimpled smile might have been reassuring, but the glint in Thad's eyes when the two men shook hands had been deadly. Darnell was his, and he was ready to challenge any man who dared get in his way.

The crowd in the reception hall seemed to part like the Red Sea as Thad and Darnell headed toward the dance floor, leaving a trail of electrical current behind in their wake. Out of the corner of his eye, Thad spotted an opened-mouthed Duncan Whittaker and nodded in passing. Reaching his destination, Thad claimed a spot and swung Darnell around smoothly to fit in his arms.

Breathless, Darnell started to speak, "Thad, I . . ."

She was startled into silence as he took her face in the palm of his hand and brought his lips to hers. Probing her mouth open with his tongue, he gave her a slow, deep, drugging kiss that brought moans of longing from deep within her.

Thad broke the kiss and crushed her to him. He buried his lips in the softness of her hair, inhaling deeply in an attempt to calm the trembling of his body. "I don't want to hear anything but three words."

Darnell's smile radiated sunshine. "I love you."

He rewarded her with a sweet kiss on her lips. "Say what?"

She kissed the curve of his neck, then whispered in his ear hotly, "I am in love with Thad Stewart, alias Art Waetsdaht, writer, producer, and soon to be co-star . . ."

"Co-star?"

"Yes, co-star of the movie *Sensuous.*"

Thad laughed and hugged her to him. "God, I've wanted to feel you, touch you, and kiss you like this for so long. It feels like we've been apart forever."

Darnell leaned into his embrace, trying in vain to remember where she was and her purpose for being here. She was lost in a fog. The only reality at the moment was the feel of his body against her body, the beat of his heart against her heart. He was right. They had been apart too long. "I missed you so much. More than you will ever know, and when we get married, let's make a vow to never be apart. "

Thad's smile was enormous. "Is that a proposal?"

"Yep."

The long, deep kiss he gave her was his unmistakable reply. It was the splatter of applause from the audience they had attracted on the dance floor that brought them out of their embrace. Peering sheepishly at the well-heeled crowd, Thad flashed his famous smile. With one arm still around Darnell, he gave a dramatic bow, taking her with him as he did so.

"Thank you. Thank you. Thank you."

The crowd loved it, laughing and clapping appreciatively as he swept a surprised Darnell around in a semicircle and announced, "And now we dance." With that, they began to move smoothly to the beat of the band.

"You go, girl!" someone shouted from the crowd.

"I guess I'll have to get used to this craziness," Darnell groaned.

Thad looked down into the face of the woman who had changed his life. "You don't have to do anything you don't want to do when you're with me, Doe Eyes. If you don't like the attention, I'll tone it down. For you, I'd do anything."

Darnell smiled up at him, touched by the comment. "It's a noble gesture, but then you wouldn't be you. And although I can hardly believe it, I love you the way you are." She kissed his cheek. Thad gave her a boyish grin.

"Do you want to know something?"

She returned his grin with one of her own. "What?"

"You're quite a woman, Darnell Cameron, and what a journey we're going to be taking together."

EPILOGUE

One Year Later

—PRESS RELEASE—

Hollywood is abuzz with the announcement of the secret wedding ceremony of two of the entertainment industry's biggest superstars. Actor, writer, and producer Thad Stewart and singer, actress, and producer Darnell Cameron were wed today at an undisclosed location. Family and close friends attended the ceremony. The wedding culminated a courtship that saw the couple sizzling on the big screen in the blockbuster movie *Sensuous*. The film, written by Stewart and produced by their joint production company, has garnered twelve Oscar nominations, including Best Actor, Best Actress and Best Picture. The multi-platinum soundtrack for *Sensuous*, written by Cameron, has generated five number-one singles and swept the Grammy Awards earlier this year, earning ten coveted statuettes, including Album of the Year.

Reportedly, the powerhouse couple was wed in a romantic affair held at sunset on the beach on an undisclosed island. The bride and groom were said to have both shed tears as she walked down the aisle to her future husband. Prior to her walk, in a surprise move, Stewart sang a stirring rendition of "A Song for You" to his bride-to-be. Her mother, Beverly Cameron, gave her daughter away. The bride's father is deceased.

THE END

ABOUT THE AUTHOR

Crystal V. Rhodes is an author and an award-winning playwright. Her first novel, *Sin*, received critical acclaim and her second novel, *Sweet Sacrifice*, was nominated for the Romance in Color Reviewer's Choice Award as Romance Suspense Book of the Year. Her third novel, *Grandmothers, Incorporated*, co-written with L. Barnett Evans, was selected Best Book of the Year by two online websites, and her fourth novel, *Sinful Intentions*, was received by the BlackRefer.com Annual Reviewer's Choice Award as Best Romance Novel. *The Written Word Magazine* has named Ms. Rhodes as one of the Ten Up and Coming Authors in the Midwest. As a playwright she and her work have been nominated for a Los Angeles Dramalogue Award, a Jefferson Award, and she has been the recipient of the Black Theatre Alliance Award for Best Original Writing for her play *Stoops*. Rhodes has a Masters degree in Sociology and has written for newspapers, magazines, radio and T.V. Visit her web site at *www.crystalrhodes.com*.

SINGING A SONG . . .

2009 Reprint Mass Market Titles

January

I'm Gonna Make You Love Me
Gwyneth Bolton
ISBN-13: 978-1-58571-294-6
$6.99

Shades of Desire
Monica White
ISBN-13: 978-1-58571-292-2
$6.99

February

A Love of Her Own
Cheris Hodges
ISBN-13: 978-1-58571-293-9
$6.99

Color of Trouble
Dyanne Davis
ISBN-13: 978-1-58571-294-6
$6.99

March

Twist of Fate
Beverly Clark
ISBN-13: 978-1-58571-295-3
$6.99

Chances
Pamela Leigh Starr
ISBN-13: 978-1-58571-296-0
$6.99

April

Sinful Intentions
Crystal Rhodes
ISBN-13: 978-1-585712-297-7
$6.99

Rock Star
Roslyn Hardy Holcomb
ISBN-13: 978-1-58571-298-4
$6.99

May

Paths of Fire
T.T. Henderson
ISBN-13: 978-1-58571-343-1
$6.99

Caught Up in the Rapture
Lisa Riley
ISBN-13: 978-1-58571-344-8
$6.99

June

Reckless Surrender
Rochelle Alers
ISBN-13: 978-1-58571-345-5
$6.99

No Ordinary Love
Angela Weaver
ISBN-13: 978-1-58571-346-2
$6.99

2009 Reprint Mass Market Titles (continued)

July

Intentional Mistakes
Michele Sudler
ISBN-13: 978-1-58571-347-9
$6.99

It's In His Kiss
Reon Carter
ISBN-13: 978-1-58571-348-6
$6.99

August

Unfinished Love Affair
Barbara Keaton
ISBN-13: 978-1-58571-349-3
$6.99

A Perfect Place to Pray
I.L Goodwin
ISBN-13: 978-1-58571-299-1
$6.99

September

Love in High Gear
Charlotte Roy
ISBN-13: 978-1-58571-355-4
$6.99

Ebony Eyes
Kei Swanson
ISBN-13: 978-1-58571-356-1
$6.99

October

Midnight Clear, Part I
Leslie Esdale/Carmen Green
ISBN-13: 978-1-58571-357-8
$6.99

Midnight Clear, Part II
Gwynne Forster/Monica
Jackson
ISBN-13: 978-1-58571-358-5
$6.99

November

Midnight Peril
Vicki Andrews
ISBN-13: 978-1-58571-359-2
$6.99

One Day At A Time
Bella McFarland
ISBN-13: 978-1-58571-360-8
$6.99

December

Just An Affair
Eugenia O'Neal
ISBN-13: 978-1-58571-361-5
$6.99

Shades of Brown
Denise Becker
ISBN-13: 978-1-58571-362-2
$6.99

2009 New Mass Market Titles

January

Singing A Song...
Crystal Rhodes
ISBN-13: 978-1-58571-283-0
$6.99

Look Both Ways
Joan Early
ISBN-13: 978-1-58571-284-7
$6.99

February

Six O'Clock
Katrina Spencer
ISBN-13: 978-1-58571-285-4
$6.99

Red Sky
Renee Alexis
ISBN-13: 978-1-58571-286-1
$6.99

March

Anything But Love
Celya Bowers
ISBN-13: 978-1-58571-287-8
$6.99

Tempting Faith
Crystal Hubbard
ISBN-13: 978-1-58571-288-5
$6.99

April

If I Were Your Woman
La Connie Taylor-Jones
ISBN-13: 978-1-58571-289-2
$6.99

Best Of Luck Elsewhere
Trisha Haddad
ISBN-13: 978-1-58571-290-8
$6.99

May

All I'll Ever Need
Mildred Riley
ISBN-13: 978-1-58571-335-6
$6.99

A Place Like Home
Alicia Wiggins
ISBN-13: 978-1-58571-336-3
$6.99

June

Best Foot Forward
Michele Sudler
ISBN-13: 978-1-58571-337-0
$6.99

It's In the Rhythm
Sammie Ward
ISBN-13: 978-1-58571-338-7
$6.99

2009 New Mass Market Titles (continued)

July

Checks and Balances
Elaine Sims
ISBN-13: 978-1-58571-339-4
$6.99

Save Me
Africa Fine
ISBN-13: 978-1-58571-340-0
$6.99

August

When Lightening Strikes
Michele Cameron
ISBN-13: 978-1-58571-369-1
$6.99

Blindsided
Tammy Williams
ISBN-13: 978-1-58571-342-4
$6.99

September

2 Good
Celya Bowers
ISBN-13: 978-1-58571-350-9
$6.99

Waiting for Mr. Darcy
Chamein Canton
ISBN-13: 978-1-58571-351-6
$6.99

October

Fireflies
Joan Early
ISBN-13: 978-1-58571-352-3
$6.99

Frost On My Window
Angela Weaver
ISBN-13: 978-1-58571-353-0
$6.99

November

Waiting in the Shadows
Michele Sudler
ISBN-13: 978-1-58571-364-6
$6.99

Fixin' Tyrone
Keith Walker
ISBN-13: 978-1-58571-365-3
$6.99

December

Dream Keeper
Gail McFarland
ISBN-13: 978-1-58571-366-0
$6.99

Another Memory
Pamela Ridley
ISBN-13: 978-1-58571-367-7
$6.99

Other Genesis Press, Inc. Titles

Other Genesis Press, Inc. Titles (continued)

Other Genesis Press, Inc. Titles (continued)

Other Genesis Press, Inc. Titles (continued)

Other Genesis Press, Inc. Titles (continued)

Meant to Be	Jeanne Sumerix	$8.95
Midnight Clear	Leslie Esdaile	$10.95
(Anthology)	Gwynne Forster	
	Carmen Green	
	Monica Jackson	
Midnight Magic	Gwynne Forster	$8.95
Midnight Peril	Vicki Andrews	$10.95
Misconceptions	Pamela Leigh Starr	$9.95
Moments of Clarity	Michele Cameron	$6.99
Montgomery's Children	Richard Perry	$14.95
Mr Fix-It	Crystal Hubbard	$6.99
My Buffalo Soldier	Barbara B. K. Reeves	$8.95
Naked Soul	Gwynne Forster	$8.95
Never Say Never	Michele Cameron	$6.99
Next to Last Chance	Louisa Dixon	$24.95
No Apologies	Seressia Glass	$8.95
No Commitment Required	Seressia Glass	$8.95
No Regrets	Mildred E. Riley	$8.95
Not His Type	Chamein Canton	$6.99
Nowhere to Run	Gay G. Gunn	$10.95
O Bed! O Breakfast!	Rob Kuehnle	$14.95
Object of His Desire	A. C. Arthur	$8.95
Office Policy	A. C. Arthur	$9.95
Once in a Blue Moon	Dorianne Cole	$9.95
One Day at a Time	Bella McFarland	$8.95
One in A Million	Barbara Keaton	$6.99
One of These Days	Michele Sudler	$9.95
Outside Chance	Louisa Dixon	$24.95
Passion	T.T. Henderson	$10.95
Passion's Blood	Cherif Fortin	$22.95
Passion's Furies	AlTonya Washington	$6.99
Passion's Journey	Wanda Y. Thomas	$8.95
Past Promises	Jahmel West	$8.95
Path of Fire	T.T. Henderson	$8.95
Path of Thorns	Annetta P. Lee	$9.95

Other Genesis Press, Inc. Titles (continued)

Other Genesis Press, Inc. Titles (continued)

Still Waters Run Deep	Leslie Esdaile	$8.95
Stolen Kisses	Dominiqua Douglas	$9.95
Stolen Memories	Michele Sudler	$6.99
Stories to Excite You	Anna Forrest/Divine	$14.95
Storm	Pamela Leigh Starr	$6.99
Subtle Secrets	Wanda Y. Thomas	$8.95
Suddenly You	Crystal Hubbard	$9.95
Sweet Repercussions	Kimberley White	$9.95
Sweet Sensations	Gwyneth Bolton	$9.95
Sweet Tomorrows	Kimberly White	$8.95
Taken by You	Dorothy Elizabeth Love	$9.95
Tattooed Tears	T. T. Henderson	$8.95
The Color Line	Lizzette Grayson Carter	$9.95
The Color of Trouble	Dyanne Davis	$8.95
The Disappearance of Allison Jones	Kayla Perrin	$5.95
The Fires Within	Beverly Clark	$9.95
The Foursome	Celya Bowers	$6.99
The Honey Dipper's Legacy	Pannell-Allen	$14.95
The Joker's Love Tune	Sidney Rickman	$15.95
The Little Pretender	Barbara Cartland	$10.95
The Love We Had	Natalie Dunbar	$8.95
The Man Who Could Fly	Bob & Milana Beamon	$18.95
The Missing Link	Charlyne Dickerson	$8.95
The Mission	Pamela Leigh Starr	$6.99
The More Things Change	Chamein Canton	$6.99
The Perfect Frame	Beverly Clark	$9.95
The Price of Love	Sinclair LeBeau	$8.95
The Smoking Life	Ilene Barth	$29.95
The Words of the Pitcher	Kei Swanson	$8.95
Things Forbidden	Maryam Diaab	$6.99
This Life Isn't Perfect Holla	Sandra Foy	$6.99
Three Doors Down	Michele Sudler	$6.99
Three Wishes	Seressia Glass	$8.95
Ties That Bind	Kathleen Suzanne	$8.95

Other Genesis Press, Inc. Titles (continued)

Tiger Woods	Libby Hughes	$5.95
Time is of the Essence	Angie Daniels	$9.95
Timeless Devotion	Bella McFarland	$9.95
Tomorrow's Promise	Leslie Esdaile	$8.95
Truly Inseparable	Wanda Y. Thomas	$8.95
Two Sides to Every Story	Dyanne Davis	$9.95
Unbreak My Heart	Dar Tomlinson	$8.95
Uncommon Prayer	Kenneth Swanson	$9.95
Unconditional Love	Alicia Wiggins	$8.95
Unconditional	A.C. Arthur	$9.95
Undying Love	Renee Alexis	$6.99
Until Death Do Us Part	Susan Paul	$8.95
Vows of Passion	Bella McFarland	$9.95
Wedding Gown	Dyanne Davis	$8.95
What's Under Benjamin's Bed	Sandra Schaffer	$8.95
When A Man Loves A Woman	La Connie Taylor-Jones	$6.99
When Dreams Float	Dorothy Elizabeth Love	$8.95
When I'm With You	LaConnie Taylor-Jones	$6.99
Where I Want To Be	Maryam Diaab	$6.99
Whispers in the Night	Dorothy Elizabeth Love	$8.95
Whispers in the Sand	LaFlorya Gauthier	$10.95
Who's That Lady?	Andrea Jackson	$9.95
Wild Ravens	Altonya Washington	$9.95
Yesterday Is Gone	Beverly Clark	$10.95
Yesterday's Dreams, Tomorrow's Promises	Reon Laudat	$8.95
Your Precious Love	Sinclair LeBeau	$8.95

Order Form

Mail to: Genesis Press, Inc.
P.O. Box 101
Columbus, MS 39703

Name _____
Address _____
City/State _____ Zip _____
Telephone _____

Ship to (if different from above)
Name _____
Address _____
City/State _____ Zip _____
Telephone _____

Credit Card Information
Credit Card # _____ ☐ Visa   ☐ Mastercard
Expiration Date (mm/yy) _____ ☐ AmEx   ☐ Discover

Qty.	Author	Title	Price	Total

Use this order form, or call 1-888-INDIGO-1

Total for books	_____
Shipping and handling: $5 first two books, $1 each additional book	_____
Total S & H	_____
Total amount enclosed	_____

Mississippi residents add 7% sales tax